Part-time Princess

(Ladies-in-Waiting, #1)

Pamela DuMond

To Nicole
To Pamela

Part-time Princess

(Ladies-in-Waiting, #1)

DEDICATION

Susan Marie Timmel DuMond

6/23/27 - 2/16/14

Always feisty, frequently opinionated and forever in my heart.

I love you always Mama. And I miss you so much.

ALSO BY THE AUTHOR

The Story of You and Me (Driven, #1)

The Messenger (Mortal Beloved, Book #1)

Cupcakes, Lies, and Dead Guys (A Romantic, Comedic
Annie Graceland Mystery, #1)

Cupcakes, Sales, and Cocktails (A Romantic, Comedic
Annie Graceland Mystery, #2)

Cupcakes, Pies, and Hot Guys (A Romantic, Comedic
Annie Graceland Mystery, #3)

Cupcakes, Paws, and Bad Santa Claus, (A Romantic,
Comedic Annie Graceland Mystery, #4)

The Annie Graceland Mystery Boxed Set (Books #1 - #4)

The Girlfriend's Guidebook to Staying Young

CHAPTER 1

I sat tall, posture perfect, practically regal on a cushy, leather seat in the First Class section of British Airlines Flight #1509 to London. My Chanel traveling outfit fit me like a dream: it was casual but screamed money. *More money than I earned during the last six months at my previous job.*

I tapped my matching Chanel bag and tote with the toe of my designer shoe and slid them a few inches until they were safely tucked under the seat in front of me. Even though I was inside a plane, I still wore my new designer sunglasses: when my new employer slid them on my face and instructed me to look into the mirror—they were so freaking cool! I've been called a lot of things in my life and trust me, cool wasn't one of them.

A female fight attendant leaned down toward me as passengers jostled past her on their way to the back of this fancy bus. "The flight's been delayed for a bit, Lady Billingsley. There are tornados in Oklahoma, Iowa and Kansas. We're waiting for a few passengers from connecting flights."

I glanced out the window: storm clouds bustled low in the skies overhead and a brisk wind ruffled the tarps on the baggage carts. "Bad weather," I said. "So typical this time of year in Chicago."

"Can I get you something to drink before takeoff? And, perhaps, a snack?"

I smiled and tried not to appear shocked as I looked at her nametag. "You are sweet, Kristine." The one time I'd flown before today the flight attendants practically ripped the water bottle from my sweaty hands prior to takeoff. But that was when I was in coach.

And that was when I was Lucille Marie Trabbicio—not Lady Elizabeth Billingsley.

"I'd love a..." What would Elizabeth pick if she were flying? She didn't seem to be the type to get trashed out of her mind, especially not on long trips. She wouldn't want to get dehydrated: there'd be too much damage to her skin, her make-up could smudge and possibly damage her outfit. She also wouldn't want to eat anything too salty as she might retain water. Bloating was a look that Elizabeth would not tolerate.

"A Pellegrino, please," I said. "Thank you. Is it okay—I mean might I send an urgent e-mail? It's for business."

"Of course." Kristine nodded. "Super quick! Captain says we'll be pulling back from the gate in a matter of minutes."

I nodded, reached in my purse for my state-of-the-art

iPhone and flipped it open. I logged into my new Gmail account that Mr. Philips had created for my part-time job. I typed a clandestine message to his and Elizabeth's BFF, Zara, using their secret code names.

Dear Lady and The Damp:

Slight delay in departing ORD. Will check in once I've landed in London and transferred planes. Excited!! Please wish E good luck on her important mystery mission. And hang in there with the bad back thing Damp. Maybe go see a good chiropractor.

Fondly,
Lucy

Then I remembered to use my code name, deleted ~~Lucy~~ and typed the word *Groucho.*

I fiddled with my phone until I found "Airplane Mode," and turned it on. I tucked my phone in my bag and pulled out a copy of *British Vogue.* Lady Zara encouraged me to page through the American, British and Italian versions of the fashion rag and familiarize myself with popular designers. I flipped through the magazine, glanced at the pricey clothes, expensive makeup and the pouty models. *Pucci. Gucci. Valentino. Oh my!*

I accepted the mineral water from the flight attendant and thanked her. I thought about my cushy signing bonus and couldn't help but smile. I'd paid my rent, as well as Uncle John's dues for the month at Vail Assisted Living. Score! I leaned back in my seat, closed my eyes and predicted that this new part-time job that I'd signed confidentiality clauses up the wazoo for would be a breeze.

I was already nailing it!

The flight to London would take around nine hours. Plenty of time for me to review the cast of characters in Lady Elizabeth Billingsley's life, as well as their names, titles and relationships with her. I had a two-hour layover at Heathrow before my connecting flight to Elizabeth's home in Fredonia—the small, crown jewel of a country tucked in the mountains between France, Switzerland and Italy.

When someone squeezed the top of my knee. "Well, well, if it isn't Lady Elizabeth Theresa Billingsley in the flesh. Isn't *this* a sweet surprise?" A guy asked as he settled into the aisle seat next to me. My gaze fixed on his muscular hand as he caressed my knee again and then ran his index finger up my inner thigh for a very-long heartbeat.

One of the reasons I scored this part-time job was because I swore to my new employers that I could roll with the punches and improvise during unexpected events. I planned on that happening when I landed in Sauerhausen, the capital of Fredonia—not on the nine-hour flight from Chicago to London.

You've got to be kidding me. The First Class section of British Airways had perverts? I smacked him, but only managed to slap my own knee because he had lightening quick reflexes; his hand had already vanished from my thigh.

"That might leave a bruise, princess. Which I'll happily kiss away," he said.

"Look, dickwipe," I hissed. "Who the hell do you think—" Oops. Reboot. I was now Lady Elizabeth Theresa Billingsley from post-card perfect Fredonia.

Not Lucille Trabbicio—a former cocktail waitress at MadDog bikers' bar on Chicago's Southside.

I cleared my throat and composed myself. "I apologize, sir. I do believe you accidentally bumped my knee and I over-reacted. "

"Oh, Lizzie. That was clearly no accident. 'Look, dickwipe?' Colorful language. I'm impressed. Apparently your time in the States has warmed your frosty demeanor. I can't believe my good fortune on running into you again." He settled into his seat. "How long has it been? Fifteen months?"

I blinked. This guy not only knew Elizabeth but also had a nickname for her. I combed my brain but I didn't recognize him from any of the pictures she or Zara showed me.

Mr. Cocky pushed his leather bag under the seat in front and belted himself in. Slouched back and ran his fingers through his jet-black hair. "Did you miss me love?"

I looked at his hand that had clutched my knee just moments earlier. It was large, had no ring on the important finger and now rested on top of his thigh—which was muscular, clad in jeans and ended in slightly scuffed leather boots.

Nice. Very, very nice. Whoa—hold the door... I shook my head. No, he was *not* nice. This knee-squeezer was an opportunist and obviously depraved. My gaze traveled up and took in his finely cut sports jacket layered over a V-neck T-shirt that exposed just the right amount of black chest hair. *Hmm.*

He leaned toward me as his index finger grazed the underside of my chin. "Has anything else warmed up Lizzie?" He tilted my face upward toward his full lips. "Do you remember all the fun and games we played? All the dirty, dirty things that you and I did?" He grinned. "And then—did again. I was done at round three, but you insisted on a fourth."

Holy crap did he just say what I thought he said?

I gazed up at his face into the bluest eyes I'd seen in my entire life. The highest cheekbones. The blackest hair that was cropped in a medium-length-style with one disheveled lock that fell onto his forehead.

Hello—this might have been the best-looking man I've met in my entire twenty-one year-old life. I inhaled sharply.

And quickly realized I was being a complete dork and gave my head a shake. *Get a grip, Lucy,* I admonished myself. Elizabeth, Zara or Mr. Philips would have shown me this guy's picture if he were at all important. This had to be a fluke. An accident. At the worst—a chance encounter. "I think you're mistaken." I decided to hedge my bets. Elizabeth might have hired a down-on-her-luck girl, but not a dumb one. "Do we know each other?"

"There you go with that dry sense of humor I always enjoy. Breathe, Lizzie. Take-offs and landings always frighten you. Do you want me to help you through it? *Just like I used to?*" He held out his hand and regarded me with a twinkle in his eyes.

Kristine the flight attendant stood at the front of the plane and spoke into the intercom. "Welcome to British Air Flight 1509 from Chicago O'Hare International Airport to Heathrow, London. In a few minutes we will be pulling back from the gate. Please take a moment to review the following safety information for this plane located in the seat pocket in front of you. While our captain and co-pilots are tip-top, we'll obviously be passing through bumpy weather as we depart the Windy City."

"Um." I wondered why my tongue suddenly felt awkward inside the confines of my mouth. "Um…" *Earth to Lucy. You are being paid a king's ransom. Do not screw up this job for a stunning pair of blue eyes, a little pitter-patter in your heart and a tingling in your nether-regions.*

"Excuse me, sir." A short, coiffed, helmet-headed Barbara Walters type peered down her nose at us. "I'm so sorry, but I think you're in my seat. 3B?" She peered at her ticket stub. "I do believe I am in 3B."

"Oh." He pulled his ticket stub from his pants pocket and checked it. "You're right, Ma'am. I'm in 4A." He unbuckled his seatbelt. "I must have been hypnotized by this young woman's beauty."

Phew! Lucky for me I wasn't going to be stuck next to Mr. Cocky for the next nine hours.

He leaned his head toward mine and whispered, "I know you're disappointed Lizzie. I'll make it up to you, I promise. There's always the Mile-High Club. I do believe you once said those very words to me. I'll never forget my initiation. Thank you. *Seriously, thank you.* That was a defining moment in my life."

I coughed, clamped my hand over my mouth and collapsed forward—my boobs slapping my thighs.

He grabbed his leather duffel off the floor and stood up. "Can I help you with your bags?" he asked the woman and moved into the aisle.

"You're not only handsome, but a gentleman. Thank you for your kind offer, sir, but I'm good. My name's Jane Dawson. I could swear I've seen you before. I'm bad with names, but I never forget a face." She plopped down into the seat next to me, looked up and winked at him. "It'll come to me."

He held out his hand to her. "You can call me Nick."

Jane smiled and shook his hand. "Nice to meet you, Nick. I'll figure out how I know you. I'm good at this!" She leaned down and pushed her carry-on under the seat in front of her.

I breathed a sigh of relief and then realized I was going to be seated next to *the Jane Dawson*—the famous news reporter whose career spanned decades. I clenched my hands together and gazed out the window as the plane backed away from the terminal.

"You look familiar too, miss." Jane said. "Albeit like you've seen a ghost or recently had food poisoning. First Class on British Air is practically like opening a copy of *People Magazine.* You never know whom you'll bump into here."

I smiled at her. "It's my pleasure to meet you, Ms. Dawson. You're an amazing reporter and your career is spectacular. My name is... Elizabeth." I leaned close to her and whispered. "Thank you for saving me from that man. I'd much prefer to sit next to you during this incredibly long flight."

"Luck of the draw, Elizabeth. I was in 3B after all. Are you nervous during takeoffs dear?"

"No. I've done this a million times." The plane taxied onto the runway and I gripped the armrests like a young gold-digger holding tight to an octogenarian billionaire's arm in a Vegas wedding chapel. The aircraft paused for a few moments as thunder boomed and lightning struck in the woods and neighborhoods in the near distance.

A piece of paper shaped like a tiny airplane flew over

my head and crashed onto my lap. I unfolded it and read:

My dearest Lizzie:

Liar, liar, pants on fire. Do we need to do something about that? I'm happy to help.

Always,
Nick

I scrunched the paper into a ball, flung it over my seat back toward him and heard a low chuckle. "I'll be just fine, Ms. Dawson. Nothing out of the ordinary or unusual about today." I smiled at her, inhaled deeply and held my breath.

Except that everything about today was out of the ordinary and unusual. Because this was the biggest day of my new part-time job. And I was indeed the poster-child for Ms. Liar, Liar, Pants-on-Fire.

I closed my eyes, leaned back, tried to ignore the hot guy kicking the back of my chair and remembered how I got here…

CHAPTER 2

"Yo, Lucy! What does a guy have to do to get a drink around here?" the Hulk Hogan look-alike grunted.

"Just need to ask me nice, Mr. Fitzpatrick." I shouldered a large, round tray holding a few dirty glasses and made a beeline to his four-top table on the right side of the bar. I cocktailed at MadDog—a beer-scented, hard rock 'n' roll playing, leather jacket-clad bikers' bar which until recently had been my favorite place in the whole world.

Mr. Fitzpatrick and his buddies were in their late sixties with bandanas tied over their long white hair. They were my favorite regular customers: rough around the edges, but incredibly sweet. I picked up a few more empties. "What can I get you?"

"Lucy, my angel," Mr. Fitzpatrick said. "I need three

Jack and Cokes and one fake lemonade with no sugar for Artie. He's on the wagon."

"Got it." I walked away, paused and swiveled. "Artie— you okay? Not another 'bout of the gastritis?"

"It's a blood sugar thing." Artie tapped the heels of his scuffed, black leather biker boots on the scratched, wooden floor. "My wife, Janelle keeps asking, 'Why don't you stop riding? When you going to stay home, watch *Jeopardy* and play with your grandkids?' Seriously Luce. I'm already retired. I spend twenty-two hours of almost every day at home. I hit the road with my buddies one afternoon each week and after that? I feel alive again. I don't think quitting our rides will affect my blood sugar."

"Those rides are good for you Artie," I said. "Fresh air. Oxygen in your lungs. Getting out in nature is healing."

"When are you going to ride with us Luce?" Artie asked. "We keep asking."

Never—I thought. I would never ride a motorcycle again.

"I appreciate the offer, but life is so busy these days with school," I said. "One sugar-free lemonade coming your way my friend." I weaved around the sober customers, the tipsy folks and all the in-betweens on my way back to the long, gleaming, dark wooden bar.

I hoisted my tray onto the counter and delivered my order to Buddy Paulson, the bartender, as well as the co-owner of MadDog. "Three Jack and Cokes, two Stoli and tonics, three Chivas on the rocks and one fake lemonade." I unloaded the dirty glasses onto a rubber mat.

My BFF, Alida Consuela Martinez, she of the tall legs and the dangerous curves, strode up in the same uniform I too had recently been forced to wear: a tight pleather mini, a deep V-neck Lycra top, fishnet stockings and black pleather, thigh pinching, high-heeled boots. She rested her tray on the bar next to mine. "I'm filing an official complaint, Buddy. I hate these new uniforms."

"I second Alida's motion." I tugged my mini lower onto my legs in a pathetic attempt to cover my private girlie parts. "These outfits make us look like sluts from Slutsville and I fear I'm getting a bunion. How come we can't wear our MadDog T-shirts and jeans?"

Buddy was thick around the waistline, covered in tats and sported a ruddy Irish complexion. Fifty years ago he could have been the poster child for a *Rebel Without a Cause*. Now he was a businessman who desperately wanted to keep his waning crowd of aging bikers happy while he catered to the bar's newcomers. "You both know why. I'm not in charge of this place anymore. Mark Whitford is."

"Whitford doesn't care that I have to change clothes in the bathroom because God forbid I go home wearing this, and my kid wakes up and sees hooker mommy," Alida said. "I'm putting meals on the table. I cannot deal with Child Protective Services."

"Alida, you gotta play nice with the new guys. It was sell a stake in the place or close the doors. I love MadDog. It wasn't an easy decision."

Buddy sold majority share of the bar to thirty-something businessman Mark Whitford. He came from family money and parlayed his trust fund into making a shit-load more dough in the stock market. Whitford got bored and then bought up his favorite interests like they were Tonka toys. His purchases included: a bowling alley, a Harley-Davidson dealership, a strip club, a Baptist church along with its charismatic leader and finally a biker bar—MadDog.

Which pained me.

While I'd only worked here since the day I turned twenty-one—nine months earlier, I'd hung out here for far longer. My dad used to frequent the joint with his buddies. And, before it was considered child-abuse to bring your kid to a bar, he'd bring me along on the nights Mom was working.

I hung out with the bikers, heard the stories about the rides and the Sturgis' outings. After my folks died in the motorcycle accident you'd think I'd want to get away from a biker bar. But the problem was, this place felt like family. And I didn't have a lot of that left.

So I started bugging Buddy to let me cocktail at MadDog. He hired me and my first shift was on my twenty-first birthday. At the end of the night Buddy opened a bottle of Korbel, the regulars sang "Happy Birthday", someone popped for cupcakes, Mylar balloons and I had my first *legal* drink.

You'd think I'd like the new clientele at the newly remodeled bar. They were, after all, closer to my age. But Whitford's crew was privileged and the majority of them were asshats. They always hung out at the biggest table in the middle of the joint. Whitford would make his nightly appearance and buy a round or two for the snotty boys. He'd play with his gold pinky ring like he was a short, chubby version of Marlon Brando in *The Godfather* as he sucked up all the cloying compliments about how he was "the man."

"Hey princess!" a twenty-something metro dude seated

at Whitford's table yelled. "Get your primo behind over here. I'm parched."

"Yeah, yeah, I'm on it." I loaded my tray with drinks. "You're sure this lemonade doesn't have sugar, right?" I asked. "Artie can't take the sugar right now."

"No sugar," Buddy said. "Hurry up. Stop spending all your time hanging with the old crew and wait on the new guys. They're our future. Be nice to them."

"They tip like shit."

"They're filling seats and buying booze," he said.

"They're assholes."

He shrugged. "The bar wouldn't be here and you wouldn't have a job if I hadn't taken Whitford up on his deal. Be nice to my new business partner and his friends. Please?"

"I'm not answering to Mark Whitford. He's got attitude to rival an elephant's behind. *You* hired me, boss. I'll answer to you."

Buddy cleared his throat.

"I'll take their table," Alida said. "I've already got the four-top next to them."

"Are you sure?" I asked.

"If they give me a problem I'll just smile and delicately curse in Spanish. They won't have a clue what I'm saying." She winked at me and walked off.

"Yeah but I will. You taught me all the good Spanish swear words," I said.

I dropped off the round to Mr. Fitzpatrick's crew. I picked up a half-empty pitcher and some water glasses that had barely been touched on a recently vacated table. I poured the water into the pitcher, stacked the glasses and was on my way back to the bar to stock up on pretzel mix when I heard Alida holler, "Beso mi culo, pendejo!"

I whip turned and saw her stomp away from Whitford's table, a big fat frown on her pretty face.

A young, sweaty, prepped-out drunk guy latched onto her wrist and yanked her toward him. "Do you not know who I am? I said this margarita tastes like someone pissed in it. You need to get me another one now. Border Bunny."

"I know exactly who you are," she said. "You're pinche idioto. I'll get your new drink as soon as you let me go."

I looked at Buddy. He hesitated behind the bar—weighing if he should race to the rescue or if Alida could handle this on her own.

"What the fuck, Buddy?" I said.

He held up one hand.

I flipped him my middle finger, turned and hustled in Alida's direction.

Whitford ambled out of MadDog's back office, eyed the scene playing out and stood there like a bag of manure.

"You own this place. Do something," I hissed.

He shrugged.

"I know what the word 'idioto' means," the drunk guy slurred.

Alida cried out as she struggled to get away from him—but his hand remained clamped on her wrist.

"Come on, dude," another metro guy at the power table said. "It's not her fault the drink's shitty. Let her go."

I pushed through the crowd toward them, my tray still on my shoulder, my anger building with every rushed step.

"Fine. Go." The drunk released Alida's arm. She

stumbled, dropped her tray, and glasses flew and broke. "You stupid wetback."

She burst into tears as she kneeled to pick up the mess of shards of glass on the floor.

"Go." I held out my hand and helped her to standing. "Grab some towels, a broom and a dustpan. I'll help."

"Thanks." She wiped a few tears away and walked off.

The asshat was already lounging in his chair. "Why do we even come here?" he whined. "We could be hanging on Rush Street."

"I've got that drink you wanted." I edged toward the table, smiled at him, and even though I still shouldered the tray, managed to toss my long brunette hair coquettishly.

"You see?" The drunk gestured to his friends. "You don't put up with lower class shit and you do the help a favor: you school them on how to cater to people like you and me. Help them learn their place in life." He smiled at me. "Thanks princess."

"No, thank you. We actually brought you a pitcher of margaritas to apologize for your inconvenience." I held it out to him, smiled…and then poured it on his head as he squealed.

"Sorry!" I said. "But you looked so thirsty. Like you needed to be a little wet-backed."

"Lucy!" Buddy yelled from across the bar.

"Lucy!" Mr. Fitzpatrick and his gang jumped up from their chairs and sprinted toward me.

"Oh no, Lucy!" Alida's hand flew to her mouth as she dropped the towels and the broom.

"Lucille Trabbicio," Mark Whitford strode toward me—his little piggy nostrils widening and narrowing faster than he ever turned his pinkie ring, "You are banned from MadDog forever. If I ever see you in here again, I will have you arrested for assault. And, oh yeah—you're fired!"

CHAPTER 3

Perhaps I should have thought twice about pouring a pitcher of watered down margaritas on some asshole's head because I was seriously out of money. I tossed and turned from all my worries that night I was fired, but vowed to find a job the next day.

I sat at my hand-me down, Formica kitchen table and paged through the job listings in *The Sun Times*—but there was next to nothing. I examined the jobs section in *The Tribune*. The pickings were slim as the actual pages in the newspaper.

Mid-day I desperately needed to clear my head, so even though the summer weather was heating up, I slipped my phone into an armband and picked my playlist with popular sixties and seventies from my iTunes ap. I grabbed a run at my local park, pumped some iron on the free workout machines and popped a few yoga moves as I listened to my fave music.

Back in my kitchen I turned on the small rotating fan in front of my sweaty face, opened up Daveslist on my computer, hit the part-time jobs section and trolled through the latest listings. Surely there would be a worthwhile job tucked away in here somewhere.

"Part-time Job: Driver Needed.
ME: Ran into some legal issues and need a driver to and from work. Mon.—Fri. Pick me up at eight a.m. at my house and drive me to work downtown. Pick me up at work at six p.m. and drive me home. YOU: Have a car and a cell phone with more-than-decent coverage. I will provide gas money. ME: Willing to pay two hundred a week. Can you be on call during the weekends from two a.m. to four a.m.?"

I don't think so…

"Part-time Job: Dog Walker Needed.
Sweet, rambunctious terrier needs animal-loving walker with strong arms! ME: I will supply yummy, organic treats for both you and Crusher as well as eco-friendly scoop bags. Lots of scoop bags. YOU: Proof of medical insurance and a signed waiver that you will negotiate with our insurance company in the highly unlikely scenario that you require medical attention due to circumstances that arise on the job. Pay: $15.00 a walk. Crusher's shots are up-to-date, the ringworm's completely under control and the doggie Valium has

really calmed him down!"

I'd love a dog some day but I'm not sure this was the job is for me.

"Part-time Job: DO YOU LIKE TO DATE?!
Do you want to meet exciting, powerful gentlemen, enjoy five-star meals and attend glamorous events? US: We are a totally above-board, legitimate service that sets up desirable women with sought-after men."

I do believe this translated to a Triple Slam meal at Denny's after which I'd be begged to perform oral sex on married, middle-aged men who were in town for a trade show.

Meh—I didn't think this job was up my alley.

The phone rang and I picked up. "Miss Lucille Trabbicio?"

"You got her," I examined my new acrylic nails. The glued-on crystals were sparkly and styling.

"My name is Mrs. Rosalie Santiago—"

"Hey Rosie! Why so formal?"

She sighed and whispered, "You gotta let me do this official-like."

"Um—okay?"

"My name is Mrs. Rosalie Santiago."

"Yes, Mrs. Santiago. Might I ask what this call is regarding?"

"I am calling from the billing department at The Vail Assisted Living Center in regards to your uncle, Mr. John

Trabbicio."

My breath caught in my throat and one hand flew to my chest. "Is he okay?" Uncle John was the 'artist' in our family: a painter, a scholar and a writer. He was always sensitive, but suffered a nervous breakdown a few months after his brother, my dad, died. He never quite found his way back to his or society's comfort zone.

"He is fine. We love your uncle. He's dapper and a gentleman with the ladies. He moderates our monthly Poetry Slam Night and plays a mean game of blackjack."

I smiled. "I know.",

"Which is why we would like to keep him here. Mr. John's account is past due. Management insists we transfer him to County Psych if we do not receive payment within five working days."

"Shit." I grabbed my checkbook from my purse, flipped it open and looked at my balance: twenty dollars and forty-two cents. "Could I put a little something down on his tab and pay you the rest in, say… two weeks?"

I looked back at the part-time job listing for the escort service. Maybe it wasn't Denny's. *Maybe it was Marie Callender's and I could get some pie before a guy suggested a different kind of job?*

"That is a splendid idea," Mrs. Santiago said. "Send us six hundred dollars today and then an additional two thousand by the thirty-first and his account will be current. For this month."

"I was thinking of, like, fifteen dollars today?" I wrung my hands. "Uncle John's been at your place for three years now. I've paid every month. This is really the first month I'm late."

"Actually, it's the thirteenth."

"Look, Rosalie—"

"Mrs. Santiago."

"Mrs. Santiago," I said. "Could you take fifteen now? I could probably get you another hundred in a couple of days. And handle the balance in two weeks. What do you think?" I asked super cheery, crossed my fingers on both hands, squeezed my eyes shut and held my breath.

"Oh, Lucy," Rosalie sighed. "You know I'm supposed to say no."

"I know," I said. "But Uncle John is so awesome. And you do such a great job with him. I've fallen on tough times recently."

"You mean tougher times," she said.

I exhaled. "Sorry."

She whispered, "Mercury's in Retrograde, a strange astrological time, where transactions and communications are constantly confused. Send me the fifteen dollars now and it will be temporarily entered as fifteen hundred. That will buy you a little time. But not much. *And you can't tell anyone that I—*"

I crossed myself. "Not a soul, Rosalie!"

"Mrs. Santiago."

"Mrs. Santiago," I said. "Thank you."

"Pedal to the metal, Lucille," she said. "Go find yourself a new job. I adore you and your uncle. Send us enough money so we can keep him in this over-priced, but top-notch facility."

"Thanks Rosalie. You're a peach. Will do."

I hung up the phone, sunk my head in my hands and felt a little light-headed. Stress and low blood sugar always did that to me. I opened my small, sweaty fridge, grabbed a carton of orange juice and poured myself a glass. Sat back at my tiny kitchen table, downed it and continued to troll Daveslist.

"Part-time Job: Wieners on Sticks seeks Sales Persons who love to bounce!
WE: Are an up and coming mall restaurant featuring the finest hot dogs and kielbasas. We are looking for a few ambitious sales persons who are happy to bounce on mini-trams while serving customers our delicious food.
YOU: Proof of medical insurance. Must pass stress cardiac test prior to accepting this job. An interest in fitness is preferred and if you are female—underwire bras are suggested."

I paged through at least twenty pages of listing when I ran across an ad that had been posted earlier in the week.

"Part-time Job:
Personal Assistant Needed. YOU: Twenty-something. (Not actress years—real years.) Blonde. (Or willing to become a blonde for this job's duration.) Medium height. Average weight. You are cute. Presentable. Can think on your feet. Willing to travel for job. You like older people—they do not creep you out. You are not a huge partier, but can sip champagne or enjoy a hearty lager. You are not addicted to drugs or alcohol. You have a high school

degree and preferably advanced degrees and/or are working toward that goal."

Hmm. I had a GED and was getting undergrad credits so I could apply to nursing school. I could knock back a few with the guys. Being a cocktail waitress at MadDog had definitely trained me to think on my feet. Older people? They had stories, experiences, and for the most part were so much more interesting than people my age. Unfortunately traveling made me really nervous. What did they mean by "Presentable?"

"JOB REQUIREMENTS: You *must* possess excellent people skills. You can improvise, aka 'roll with the punches.' (If you are an actress, you *cannot* be SAG and you can *never* list this job on your reel or resume.) You are 'sports friendly.' This means you have a rudimentary knowledge of a variety of sports."

Football: The Chicago Bears—check. Baseball: The Chicago White Sox—check. Hockey: The Chicago Blackhawks—check. Soccer: I'm the only person who doesn't care. Tennis: Love the guys' legs—check.

"It would be ideal if you spoke a foreign language but this not a requirement."

Hola my mejor amiga! Comò estàs? Quieres nachos y cervezas frías esta noche?

"THIS IS NOT A SEX-FOR-HIRE JOB! Prostitutes and escorts need not apply."

Perfect! I had no desire to attend a Learn-All-About-It Annex class where I sucked on a banana for three hours and strained my jaw.

"Everyone who does apply must submit to a stringent screening and thorough background check. Rest assured we are reputable with vast references. This Part-time Job position only lasts a few weeks this summer. It will require minimal effort and maximum pay if you are the woman we are looking for."

The job post was, to say the least, weird. *It was also intriguing.* I read the entire listing three more times and then printed it out. Yes, it was probably an 'I'm an imprisoned Princess in Nigeria, please send-me-money and you can inherit half of my captured billion dollar estate' scam. But, honestly, what did I have to lose? I sent an e-mail to the Part-time Job people, included my slapped-together resume and shut down my computer.

I called Uncle John. He told me about how he took the time to study the players in his shuffleboard group. Really learn their moves. And then beat them at their own game. *And for one night?* Uncle John Trabbicio was Prince of Shuffleboard at The Vail. He sounded so happy that I placed the phone down on the couch and applauded his win.

After we hung up I cracked open a fine bottle of three buck Chuck cabernet and poured myself a glass. I gazed at a framed photo that rested on my coffee table: a snapshot of my parents wearing big smiles as they sat on their Harley motorcycle. "I hope you're enjoying the rides in heaven." I raised my glass and toasted them.

I turned on the TV, and watched an episode of *I Love Lucy*. I half-suspected my parents named me after her because both she and I always had some *'splainin' to do'*. I flipped to the show about medieval royalty that I was addicted to. The one with the castles and dungeons, tribes and treachery, kings and queens, pretty dresses and creepy forest hovels. I imagined what everyone was doing back at the bar. And shut that thought down.

I wondered what it would be like if I could be a princess—of anything? Didn't even have to be full-time. Could totally be a part-time gig? I slugged the remainder of my glass of wine and nodded off.

And I dreamt of a stone castle with fog ringing its turrets. I wore a long white gown and raced, my breath ragged, across a steep drawbridge as uniformed men raised it. I leapt over the top and suddenly I was holding tight to a muscular man, my arms wrapped around his waist on the back of a motorcycle. We sped along mountainous roads that curved around mist-covered lakes and meadows with knee-deep wildflowers that poked out of melting snowdrifts.

We slowed, pulled to the side of the road and the man offered me his hand. I stepped off the bike and gazed up at him. He felt so warm and familiar—as if I had known him for an eternity. I didn't even know his name and yet I did know two things:

Number one: he had the bluest eyes and the blackest hair I'd ever seen in my life. Number two: I was completely, one hundred and fifty percent, in love with him.

CHAPTER 4

I woke up the next day and blinked my eyes open. The sun peeked around my curtains, attempting to melt my windows. Another glorious, Midwestern, summer day! Well—it would have been glorious except it was already ninety degrees with ninety percent humidity.

I stretched in my small lumpy bed, did wrist circles, then ankle circles and mentally reviewed my daily itinerary. Number one: Coffee. Number two: Check e-mails. Three: Call Uncle John. Four: Go to work. Hold on. Something was off with work…

When the whole freaking nightmare crashed into my brain. I was job-less, broke, owed money out the yin-yang and had no idea how I'd survive a week, let alone the month. I gave my head a shake, hopped out of bed, walked into the kitchen, made coffee and checked e-mails.

Hello.

I'd gotten a response from the part-time job people who wanted a smart blonde who knew sports, liked older people, could think on her feet and was cool with traveling. They admitted their interview request was last minute, but wanted to know if I could meet them today at noon in downtown Chicago. If I responded promptly and said "Yes," they'd e-mail me the specific address.

I hit the reply key so fast it broke the acrylic nail on my index finger. "Yes." I typed. "I would love to interview for your job today at noon. Thanks for considering me!!!" I added several smiley face emoticons to really drive the point home.

I shook my hands and paced. What should I wear to my job interview? Conservative? Sexy? Classy? *Concentrate Lucy. Concentrate.* This would totally depend on who was interviewing me and where that meeting would be held. I grabbed the printout and re-read the job description. These folks were incredibly specific and I surmised they might be a little uptight.

I had one pastel skirt and jacket suit from Cheswick's of Boston. There couldn't be a conservative interviewer on the planet that wouldn't appreciate Cheswick's. A blister erupted on my foot from the nasty high heels I'd been forced to wear at MadDog, so I paired my pretty outfit with pastel Keds. *Who didn't love Keds?*

I stood on the sidewalk on the curve of Lake Shore Drive peppered with swanky high-rise buildings as it rounded the bend of Oak Street Beach and headed north.

Oak Street Beach was a narrow patch of pricey sand

filled with tourists and posers and families. Lapping onto its shores was the grand mama herself—Lake Michigan—a body of water so large she was called Great. I held the printout in my hand and gazed up at the Drake Hotel.

The Drake was approximately twenty stories tall, majestic and reeked of old school fancy. This hotel had been around forever and was practically a Chicago institution. Marilyn Monroe and Joe DiMaggio had carved their newly wed names into the booth at the Cape Cod Room, the in-house seafood restaurant. Princess Diana stayed here on her only visit to Chicago.

Whoever the hell held a job interview in this place had to be interesting, let alone have the bucks to pay decent part-time wages. I crossed my fingers as I jogged across the intersection.

I examined the address on the printout. The interview wasn't just taking place in the Drake: it was being conducted in a Penthouse suite. Jeeza-Louisa. I shook my head, cracked my knuckles and wondered who in the hell advertised on Daveslist and still had the bucks to hold a job interview at this swanky joint?

Perhaps the part-time job people were millionaires? Or drug dealers? Maybe they were millionaire drug-dealers with a lucrative side business selling twenty-something women into sex-slavery? But that didn't make sense—didn't sex-slaver types usually deal in skinny girls with big boobs? I was far from being a twizzle-stick. Oh jeez, I was totally over-thinking this thing. I closed my eyes, gathered my courage, crossed myself and entered the hotel's front doors.

I knocked on the solid wood door to Penthouse #5. Took a

deep breath, ran my fingers through my waist-length hair and tucked a few errant wisps behind my ears. I fished through my purse, snagged my Maybelline Perfect-in-Pink Super Sparkly Lip-gloss, applied it and smacked my lips when the suite door flew open.

A late sixty-something, robust, crinkly-faced man with a full head of silver hair, wearing thick, black-rimmed glasses stood in the doorway and regarded me. "You must be Miss Lucille Marie Trabbicio." He extended his hand.

"Yes." I nodded, shook his hand and for some strange reason was tempted to curtsey. "But you can call me Lucy."

"I prefer Lucille. Do come in." He opened the door to the suite a tad wider. "My name is Mister Philip Philips."

"Mr. Philip Philips?" I blinked.

He sighed. "It's a family name. You may call me Mr. Philips. We've been on our tip-toes with excitement, eagerly anticipating your arrival." He pushed himself to his tiptoes for a millisecond and then dropped back down on his heels. He wore a sweater vest on top of his long-sleeve, crisp cotton shirt.

A sweater vest in the beginning of June, in Chicago—seriously?

"Wow. That's awesome. I'm so... honored to hear that." I entered the penthouse living room. There were sweeping northern views of the lake, the Gold Coast, DePaul University and Lake Shore Drive as it wound past beaches and parks. Hell, I could even see the pink towers of the famous Edgewater apartment complex miles up the Drive.

"I admit that I am a recent visitor to Chicago. It is a magnificent town," Mr. Philips said. "Stunning architecture. World-class culinary adventures. A robust art scene, as well as a music mecca." He pulled a monogrammed handkerchief with a large letter 'P' from his pocket and dabbed his forehead. "But the weather can be daunting." He folded his hankie and placed it back in his pocket. "Might I offer you a cooling drink, Lucille?"

"Water's perfect. Thanks. But you don't have to wait on me. I'll help myself." I walked a few feet around the mahogany-colored bar, knelt down and opened the mini-fridge. It was stocked with Evian, Pellegrino, two bottles of Cristal champagne and a clear, glass container that contained pea-green liquid. I peered up at him. "Can I get you something, Mr. Philips?"

He shook his head. I grabbed a Pellegrino, stood up, twisted the cap open, took a slug and fanned my sweaty cleavage. Phew, summer was arriving early in the Windy City.

Mr. Philips plucked a file off an immaculate desk. There were ten folders on the right side of the desk and probably over two hundred divided into five neat stacks on the left side. "Do have a seat." He gestured to a pretty loveseat next to the window. "I insist."

He seemed a little uptight. But heck, based on those sky-high stacks of files on the desk, he'd probably been through a ton of job applications and was likely exhausted. I plunked down, took a load off and took another drink of my bubbly water.

"We are in receipt of your Internet application. You signed the waiver for a background check, which we have performed," he said.

I swallowed and hoped the incident in MadDog hadn't shown up. Or that time I shoplifted the blue eye shadow on a dare from Walgreens when I was thirteen. That was supposed to have been expunged from my record. Or that thing when was I was eleven-years-old and Suzy Delaney started a rumor at my middle school that my mom had left us because she realized all the other middle-grade kids were cuter and smarter than I was. I wasn't the only kid Suzy Delaney mean-girled. But I was the only one who decked her.

"Your criminal record is clean which is a must for us—"

"I knew that," I said.

I totally didn't know that.

"Or you wouldn't be seated on that settee right now."

I glanced down. "You mean the love seat?"

He regarded me thoughtfully. "The settee."

"Right… the small couch? I mean… I assumed that… I would never apply for this position if I didn't feel that my qualifications matched the employer's expectations."

He nodded, opened my file and paged through it. "Lucille Marie Trabbicio. You were an A student in high school but dropped out at the tender age of seventeen before the end of your junior year. You earned your GED when you were nineteen. You're currently enrolled at Columbia Technical Academy in pursuit of your career as a licensed nurse practitioner. Is this correct?"

"Yes," I said.

Why did he pronounce every syllable of 'Lice end nerz prac tition er' like it was a disease instead of a healing profession?

"That sounds right," I said.

"Do you have *time* for a part-time summer job?"

Could I survive without a part-time job would be the better question?

"Absolutely, Mr. Philips. I'm not taking any pre-req nursing courses this summer as I decided to focus on..."

Aw frick. What the hell was I focusing on?

"Volunteering for Save the Environment organizations and the search for world peace. Yes, sir, I absolutely have the time and energy for a part-time summer job!"

"World peace?"

I nodded. "It's one of my most cherished dreams, sir."

Mr. Philips snapped my file shut. "I never assume, so I will ask you directly." He dropped it onto the desk where it landed half on, half off—teetering. "Why do you want *this* job Miss Trabbicio?"

I'd been on such a roller coaster the past couple of days, let alone the past four years, that I tried to think of something stellar to hit him with. "I'm broke," didn't sound great. "I don't want to be a prostitute," was a weak close second. "I could possibly qualify as a female mud wrestler, but I feared I'd spend a fortune at the Laundromat," trailed in third.

I played back the job description in my head. In all honesty, it was a little vague. So—I punted. "In answer to your question, Mr. Philips. I like older people and I'm more than capable of thinking on my feet. I know a little about football, baseball, basketball, hockey, shuffleboard, ping-pong, blackjack and riding motorcycles.

He sniffed.

"I'm a hard worker, determined. I persevere. I'm loyal as long as the people I trust are loyal and forthcoming with me. I turn the other cheek three times. Fool me once, shame on you. Fool me twice, shame on me. Fool me a third time, well, shame on the both of us. But the fourth time—I'm usually done."

"Ah-hah," he said.

"People have described me as... *(The word 'bitch' came to mind but I didn't think that was the best word to use here)* ...feisty."

He looked at me and raised one eyebrow and cleared his throat. "Excuse me for one moment," he said. "I feel a bit parched. I'd like that Pellegrino after all. Thank you."

I got up from the 'settee', walked behind the bar, pulled open the door to the mini-fridge, grabbed a Pellegrino and unscrewed the top. "Would you like that on the rocks and with a lime or a lemon? Or straight up?"

"On the rocks with a slice of lime, thank you."

I opened the ice container, plucked out a few cubes with tongs, dropped them into a glass and poured the water on top. Grabbed a lime from the fridge and chopped it quickly on a small butcher block on top of the bar. I dropped a wedge in the drink, stuck another on the glass rim and handed it to him.

"Thank you." He sipped.

"Perhaps, Mr. Philips, you could tell me why I *should* want this job," I said. "Because, no offense? Right now you all are shrouded in mystery. I don't really know what this job is, what you're paying, or what I need to do. And frankly, as much as I like to read mysteries and adore watching them on TV? I'm a practical girl. While I'm dying to find the perfect part-time summer job? I'm not sure I'm up for more mysteries in my life right now."

He blinked. "I see." He placed his drink on a coaster on a side-table. "Thank you for coming here today, Miss Trabbicio. I am so sorry but we will not be needing your services." He stood up, walked to the front door of the suite, opened it and gestured with one hand to the hallway. "I wish you nothing but the best of luck in your future."

My heart sunk. "But, *but...*"

"We are very practical people as well. I apologize for any inconvenience this might have caused you."

Another rejection. Another waste of time. I slunk toward the door.

"Wait a moment, Miss Trabbicio." He extracted a leather wallet from his pocket, snapped it open and held out a crisp one hundred-dollar bill. "I trust this will cover your travel expenses."

CHAPTER 5

I gazed hesitantly at that hundred-dollar bill. I felt like a hooker accepting a tip. But I had to keep my Uncle John at the Vail Assisted Living this month, next month and pay for my subway ride back to the south side.

I pulled the bill from his hand. "Thanks for the opportunity." I walked into the hallway and blinked back a few tears. I had a Tupperware container of mac and cheese in the fridge, which if the electric company didn't shut off my service, should last me a couple of days. Maybe Subway was hiring?

Mr. Philips's phone buzzed from the bar counter. He picked it up and put it to his ear. "Yes, Lady Elizabeth. I made a calculated decision based on…" He squinted at me. "Yes, I see your point…" he winced and held the phone away from his ear. "Of course I understand how stressful this has been for you… No, I did not realize you had been fitted for a mouth guard because you were bruxating and diagnosed with TMJ disorder."

I tried not to stare at Mr. Philips and his sweater vest as I punched the elevator button. Okay, truth be told, I slammed it five times because this was humiliating and I had to get the hell out of here. *Now.* I gazed up at the bank of elevator lights and realized they were stopping on Every. Single. Dang. Floor on their way up to the Penthouse.

Finally a light indicated there was a car just one story below me. I glared at its tiny beam, willed it to move, but it simply squatted there like it had all the time in the world. I hit the elevator button with my fist: *Bam! Bam! Bam!*

Ding! The Penthouse button light flashed. I took a deep breath. Escape was in sight. The doors slid open and I slipped into the tiny, pristine cubicle and pushed the Lobby button. I slumped against the side of the upholstered cage and dropped my head in my hands.

"Not so fast." A woman thrust her bejeweled hand between the doors, which slammed onto her wrist. "Ow! Holy freak! God bless Fredonia!" she said.

The doors rebounded open and I peered at a twenty-something, pretty, blonde woman who winced as she held her wrist with her other hand.

"Oh, crap!" I said. "I'm sorry. If you had hollered for me to hold the elevator, I would have done that. You okay?" I asked as the doors started to slide shut again. I stuck my foot between them and they bounced off my Keds.

"I believe so."

Mr. Philips and a coiffed, twenty-something brunette

chick stood close to the suite's doorway in the hall behind her and watched us.

I felt a new batch of tears welling and I didn't want to lose it in front of complete strangers. "I'm sorry, miss. I need to make tracks. Are you coming—"

She latched onto my arm and yanked me out of the elevator. I spun around and landed on my ass on the hallway's lush, tapestry carpeted floor.

What kind of girl would rip me out of an elevator at the Drake Hotel?

"Who are you?" I gazed up at her. "And what do you want from me?"

"I'm Lady Elizabeth Theresa Billingsley of Fredonia. I want to hire you to be my Personal Assistant for a part-time job. I'll pay you a king's ransom, I'll give you a signing bonus and I'll throw in a makeover and wardrobe expenses. Say yes. I insist."

Oh my God!

"Yes!"

She smiled and clapped her hands excitedly. "Swell-zies!"

The elevator made a low whooshing sound behind me as it departed and I wondered:

What the heck was Fredonia? And what kind of part-time job had I just signed up for?

Elizabeth leaned over and peered at me like I was a delectable but doomed mouse that a cat had cornered in the kitchen. "I've been looking for you for almost a month now." She held out one perfectly manicured hand. "Close your mouth. Stop gaping like a fish out of water and get up."

"All-righty." I took her hand and she hauled me to standing.

"Mr. Philips is *my* employee. *I'm* the one hiring you. You—whatever your name is—have captured my interest. I am incredibly sorry. I never forget a face, but I am terrible with names. What is your name again?"

"Lucille Marie Trabbicio."

"Right. I read your job application and I instructed Mr. Philips to invite you to interview," she said.

Elizabeth had glossy, styled blonde-highlighted hair, shiny white teeth, impossibly long eyelashes and immaculately groomed eyebrows. She looked like she could grace the screen in an animated Disney Movie. I squinted because her perfection blinded me or perhaps I'd poked an eye out during my fall.

"How motivated are you?" she asked.

"Very."

The brunette from the Penthouse's open door approached us. "Elizabeth—let me handle this."

Elizabeth shook her head. "I'm fine, Zara. What do you know about sports?" she asked.

"What kind of sports are you asking about?"

"Start with soccer."

"David Beckham's career was long but is basically over," I said. "American parents will take out a second mortgage on their house to finance their kid's way into soccer camps and clubs and tournaments. All for the dream."

She nodded. "Why did you drop out of high school?"

"My parents died unexpectedly," I said. "It threw me."

She paused and bowed her head for a moment. "I'm

sorry. I lost my mother when I was ten. It's not easy."

"No it's not."

"Elizabeth, this has to be taxing," Zara said. "I'll take it from here."

"You'll take it from here when I tell you to take it from here. Lucille—your Uncle John Trabbicio is in an institution for the mentally challenged. Does this affect your every-day-life?"

I shoved my hands on my hips. "Would it affect *your* every day life?"

"There's one in every family," Zara said. "My cousin practically cut off my dead grandmother's chubby, inflexible fingers to procure her rings seconds before we closed her casket. Elizabeth simply wants to know that you can get the job done."

I frowned. "Uncle John was with dad at the hospital after the motorcycle accident. He held his hand when he died. He lost it a few months later. I pay for him to live at Vail instead of County."

"I see," she said. "That's sad. It also means you're motivated. When can you start?"

"When do you want me to start?"

She eyed me up and down and crinkled her nose. "You're raw material, rough-around-the-edges. Mr. Philips, Zara and I need to train you and we need to do that quickly. Considering we have our work cut out for us, I think we should start immediately. You can start immediately, yes?"

"Um. Sure?"

"Fabulous. Zara—make the phone call please. I need to excuse myself for a moment." Elizabeth turned and raced back inside the Penthouse.

Zara slid her iPhone from her purse and hit one button. "I'd like to speak to D'Alba please. Tell him Zara Wentworth is calling on behalf of Lady Billingsley. No I will not leave a message. Yes, you can put me on hold but only for a moment. *He's expecting her call.*"

She glanced at her diamond-encrusted watch, then back at me and frowned. "Have you ever had your eyebrows waxed?"

"Absolutely not. I read those horror stories that describe—all too graphically might I add—what happens to body parts when you over-wax them. I *tweeze* my brows."

"You do know you're supposed to tweeze between your brows?"

I harrumphed.

"Can you work late tonight? She'll pay overtime."

"Yeah," I said.

"Yes," Zara said.

"Yeah, we confirmed that," I said.

"When speaking the affirmative we use the word, 'Yes.'"

"Okay," I said.

She shook her head. "You need to say, 'Yes.'"

"I already said 'Okay'. I can stay late tonight."

"For the love of God, say, 'Yes,'" Zara said.

"How many times do I have to say it?" I hollered and suddenly wondered if she was hearing impaired. A wave of guilt swept over me and I felt terrible. It was wrong and incredibly insensitive of me to yell at some young, overly-coiffed woman who was hearing impaired.

Zara ground her teeth and spoke into her phone. "Tell

D'Alba it's *Lady* Zara calling. This is in regards to the situation they discussed last week. The one where Elizabeth promised to pay him twice his going rate. Yes, dear. We will see him in twenty… what do you mean he can't see us for two hours?" She jabbed her thumb into her temple and grimaced. "Fine. We'll see him in two hours. Tell D'Alba I'm not as nice as Elizabeth. He'd better be giving us his A game or I'll be spilling-all on the royal circuit. And this time it will be about who really wore the tiara or what riding the polo ponies hard actually means." She hung up the phone and massaged her temples. "Good help is so hard to find."

"Yes," I said. "Yes it is."

This was totally my opportunity to impress upon Elizabeth's friend that I would not be simply good help—I would be great. I was not only hard-working but I was also a take-charge kind of girl who would go the extra mile.

"Why don't we work on something else before we meet with this D'Alba dude," I said. "I could get you all something to drink, and then we could organize Elizabeth's closets, or clean out her purse." I paced. "We could talk Mr. Philip Philips into wearing a shirt without a sweater vest?"

She arched one eyebrow. "Good luck with that one. Hmm. Not a bad idea, however. How long have you walked like a football player?"

"I know—good, huh?" I smiled. "That wasn't an easy gait to learn."

"I imagine not," she said.

"I had to toughen-it-up a bit after my parents died. Just 'cause I was single, young and unprotected, I didn't want guys thinking they could take advantage of me. I watched a bunch of Bears football games and imitated the linebackers until I had it down."

"Kudos on your determination. Unfortunately, you can't walk like a gorilla if you're to successfully assist Elizabeth."

"Gorilla?"

She punched a button on her phone. "Mr. Philips?"

"Yes, Zara," he said.

"We're conducting our first lesson with Elizabeth's new assistant. I require a larger room than this claustrophobic hotel suite. Ideas?"

"Absolutely. Let me make a few calls."

"Splendid. Bring the feather duster."

"What exactly does this part-time job entail?" I asked.

CHAPTER 6

It was a little after one p.m. The Drake's Grand Ballroom was filled with round tables draped in white-linen tablecloths surrounded by chairs in preparation for tonight's festive event. But the only people here were Zara, Elizabeth, Mr. Philips and myself. An aisle cut down the middle of the ballroom and several steps led to a stage.

Elizabeth sat on one side of the aisle, her feet up on a folding chair, a frown on her pretty face as she furiously texted on her iPhone. Zara sat next to her. Mr. Philips stood on the opposite side of the aisle with ramrod straight posture holding a pink feather duster protruding from a very long handle.

I slumped at the back of the ballroom and dabbed my sweaty brow with the hem of my Cheswick's shirt. I'd already marched, sashayed, strode and slinked down this walkway thirty times. Apparently once you learned how to walk like a linebacker, you'd always walk like a linebacker. Similar to cigarette smoking and crack cocaine, this was a tough habit to break.

"What are we waiting for, Miss Trabbicio? The second coming?" Mr. Philips crossed himself.

"Try it again, Lucille," Zara said.

"I don't know what you want," I said. "Maybe you could give me a little demo?"

Mr. Philips regarded Elizabeth who wiped a few tears from her eyes. Zara leaned over and rubbed her arm. He sighed, lumbered to the back of the ballroom and stood next to me. "Despite my aching back I will try my very best to interpret what Lady Zara has in mind."

"While you're obviously a man of many talents—I'm not sure prancing lady-like down aisles is one of them," I said.

"Lady Elizabeth has employed me for seven years now," he said. "You'd be surprised what I've endured—I meant—learned in seven years."

I raised an eyebrow and pointed to the center aisle. "Your red carpet awaits."

Mr. Philips composed himself. Sucked in his stomach, stood very tall and strolled down the aisle gracefully. "Imagine you are walking down an aisle at a royal court. There are important people, even a few celebrities gathered for a posh, news-worthy event in this formal room."

"How important?" I asked.

"Dukes, Duchesses, a couple Earls, someone from *Dancing with the Stars* and perhaps a member of Britain's Royal Family.

My eyes widened. "Like Prince Harry? I normally don't go for redheads, but he's hot—in a ginger kind of way."

Mr. Philips clutched his lower back. "You can imagine Prince Harry is in the audience if that helps you walk more lady-like. We're just beginning your training, but it's critical you learn these lessons. The people in your future audience are judgmental, gossipy and pretentious. They smile widely with their pearly-white capped teeth while they examine your every move, hoping and praying you will commit a giant faux pas that they can gossip about to all their friends."

"Why would they want to do that?" I asked.

"You dropped out of high school early, but do you remember the lunchroom?"

"Yeah," I said.

"Yes," Zara hollered.

"Yes." I sighed.

"These people are the high school bitchy girls—but on steroids," Mr. Philips said. "Your every move, your every little nuance needs to be as pristine as possible. Watch me closely." He minced down the aisle. "You sashay through public places like a moving airport walkway is under your pretty, delicate feet." He stared at my Keds and sighed.

"Size seven and a half," I said. "Delicate."

"Every step you take is elegant. You radiate wide-eyed innocence and virginal bliss. " He walked down the aisle and despite his bad back—for a few seconds—he moved so smoothly it appeared like he was skating.

"Zara—I need to step out for a bit. Will you...?" Elizabeth asked.

"Yes. Go. I've got this," she said.

"Try the walk again Lucille," Mr. Philips said. "Imagine you look ethereal. Middle-aged women weep when they see you." He pretended to cry. "Older women want to kiss your blushing cheeks and press you to their bosoms." He stooped over like a crone with a bad spine, winced and placed a hand on his lower back.

"Don't take this the wrong way, Mr. Philips," I said. "But you totally pull off the old-lady thing."

"Good to know. I fear my bad disc slipped again. I'm currently unable to stand up straight."

"Oh my God!" I said. "Lay on the floor. I'll walk on your back. I took a Learn All About It Annex course in Thai Massage. I'm pretty good."

"Thank you so very much, but my vest is designer and I fear it wouldn't survive. Back to the matter at hand. Girls your own age either want to be your BFF or rip your eyeballs out. But remember, you are the epitome of sweet and kind and to-the-manor-born. You are a dream girl. You are—a princess in training."

I closed my eyes and repeated to myself, "I am a princess-in-training." I pictured Prince Harry waiting for me at the other end of the aisle and kept walking. I imagined the fancy attired audience members rising to their feet as they beamed encouraging smiles and applauded.

"Much better. Now I want you to close your eyes, think of something you desire even more than Prince Harry and try that walk again." Mr. Philips said.

I closed my eyes, took a deep breath and thought of one of my favorite things in the entire word. I fluttered my eyes open and moved down the aisle as I smiled and nodded to my imaginary on-lookers.

"Oh my God," Zara exclaimed. "Mr. Philips. You are extraordinary. It's like she's been transformed. You're so close, Lucille. You're almost there."

So I pictured another Johnny's pizza—but this time it was super-deluxe and was piled high with mushrooms, sausages, homemade red sauce and goat-cheese.

"Yes!" Zara exclaimed. "You've nailed the walk."

"Splendid!" Mr. Philips collapsed into a seat on the side of the aisle as I practically floated past him. "I dare any gossipmonger to say one harsh word about your lady-like walking skills.

I cracked just a hint of a smile as I raised my hand and delicately waved to my pretend audience. "Why am I gliding? Why are people going to care about me? *What exactly does this job entail?*"

We sat in front of the large flat-screen TV in the suite's living room as Elizabeth punched a few buttons on the remote. "This is your primary focus as well as the main reason I am hiring you. His name is Cristoph Edward George Timmel the Third."

"That's a lot of names." I leaned forward and peered at the guy on the screen: he was a younger, more handsome version of Brad Pitt, a Ryan Gosling-esque darling. He could have been a model for an Italian men's cologne, designer underwear, or graced the cover of a romance novel. "He's smoking hot."

"Yes. He's also a hot property in the global search for every woman who wants to marry a prince," Zara said.

"He's a prince?"

"Yes. Cristoph is Prince of Fredonia. First in line to the throne," Elizabeth said.

"What's a Fredonia?" I asked.

"Fredonia's a small country in Europe—tucked between France, Italy and Switzerland in the Alps." Mr. Philips said.

"I've hired you for a lot of reasons, Lucy," Elizabeth said. "The first—I need you to travel to Fredonia and keep Cristoph interested in me for ten days or so until I can get back there. Because, due to circumstances that are not under my control, my trip has been delayed."

Zara sighed.

Mr. Philips coughed.

There it was—the elephant in the room—travelling. I hated travelling.

"Ah. Okay. Travelling to Fredonia is part of this job," I said. "Honestly, travelling makes me a little nervous. You know, leaving one's hometown can be daunting."

"That's an integral part of this job, Lucille," Mr. Philips said. "It was plainly listed on the ad you answered."

"I know, but not everything has to be a perfect fit. Like the ad said you wanted a blonde. I am clearly brunette."

"Willing to become blonde for the duration of this job," Zara recited.

"Fine. I'll travel. But how am I going to keep Cristoph interested in Elizabeth? You want me to tell him how great you are? You want me to report back to you if he's flirting with someone else? You want me to—"

"I want you to impersonate me."

I hacked, slapped one hand over my mouth as the other flew to my chest. How was this even possible?

Elizabeth was polished, perfect and coiffed to the nines.

I wasn't.

I looked at Zara and Mr. Philips. Surely they would burst into laughter. But they appeared very serious and held their collective breath.

"But he's going to know I'm not you."

"No he's not," Elizabeth said. "I haven't been back to Fredonia in fifteen months."

"But I don't look anything like you," I said.

She put her arm around me and we turned to face the gilded mirror on the wall. "Tell me about the girl you see in that reflection," she said.

"Well you're perfect and blonde and—"

"Tell me about you," Elizabeth said.

"I'm brunette, hard-working and kind of cute on a good day."

"Look at our cheekbones."

"We both have high cheekbones," I said.

"Look at our eyes."

"They look kind of similar in shape."

"Tell me about our lips."

"Your lipstick's perfect. I need a little more Maybelline."

"The shape of our lips," Elizabeth said.

"Full," I said. "Oh my God. We do kind-of look alike. I'm like your poor, unfortunate cousin."

"Not when we get done with you," Zara said.

"We've got the right girl." Elizabeth squeezed my shoulders. "Now we need to turn you into a lady."

CHAPTER 7

I wore a pair of Elizabeth's wrap-around sunglasses and her tasteful trench coat with its hood pulled up over my head. Mr. Philips hustled me down Oak Street in Chicago's Gold Coast neighborhood. We passed trendy boutiques, pricey restaurants, coiffed-to-the-tens shoppers, as well as sweaty, sunburnt tourists. I practiced my royal wave on a few of them until Mr. Philips caught several folks staring at us, grabbed my hand, curled my fingers into a fist and shut it down.

"Let go of me!" Sweat poured off my forehead, bubbled on my chest and trickled down my cleavage.

"Only if you promise not to call attention to yourself." He squeezed my hand even tighter.

"Fine! I promise!"

He dropped my hand.

"Why we couldn't take the limo to D'Alba's like Elizabeth and Zara did?" I asked.

"It's essential that the public *not* see you and Elizabeth together. *We do not* need a randomly snapped picture uploaded to Instagram to blow her cover. Besides, Elizabeth is paying you a tidy sum of money for serious reasons—one of which includes her privacy." He paused in front of the white-bricked facade of a tiny storefront. *D'Alba* was lettered in cursive on the bricks. "We're here."

"Who's D'Alba and clue me in on what we need to accomplish?"

"Please," Mr. Philips said.

"Please what?" I asked.

"Always say 'Please' when you ask someone for help or a favor." He pulled his handkerchief from his pocket and dabbed his sweaty brow. "Or if you have a preference. For example, 'Please don't smoke next to me.'"

"Got it," I said. "Please, Mr. Philips, could you pretty please take off your sweater vest when it's ninety-nine degrees outside?"

"More like, 'Please Lucille, could you please attempt to refrain from intrusive non-lady-like questions?' It's only a part-time job—remember? This won't last forever."

"Fine," I said.

"Oh, and by the way, D'Alba is a bit of a..." He looked up in the sky and frowned.

"Sweetheart?"

"No."

"Perfectionist?"

"Not exactly."

"Asshat?"

"Yes. But you cannot tell anyone that I divulged that information."

"Got it, Philips." I nodded.

He cradled my elbow with one hand and opened the door to the shop with his other. "Ladies first," he said.

I sashayed through the doorway in front of him and curtseyed to an older woman whose head was covered in small rollers under a hair-dryer. She squinted at me and looked perplexed.

"Don't call attention to yourself," Mr. Philips hissed.

"Do I know you?" the woman asked.

"I don't think so," I said.

"You look familiar. Did you just curtsey to me?"

"No Ma'am," Mr. Philips said. "She has a trick knee."

"Old powder puff football injury. Good luck with your perm!" I gave her a thumbs up.

"Do you not recall the privacy confidentiality agreement you signed three hours ago?" Mr. Philips asked.

"Of course," I said. "Was that on page forty-eight or eighty-four of the contract?"

Did anyone really read those "Click here to promise you have read the fine print" agreements?

"I have to practice this stuff if I'm going to pull off this gig. When am I going to get a chance to practice?"

"Soon. But not in public—yet. By the way, if D'Alba calls you a bitch—he means that as a compliment." He smoothed a hand over his silver hair.

"If D'Alba calls me a bitch I'll deck 'em."

"It's similar to how certain persons call their friends 'phat.' Another compliment."

"Where I come from calling someone fat is definitely

not a compliment."

"You stated in your resume you could roll with the punches." Mr. Philips said. "Improvise."

"There was nothing in your job description or on page forty-eight or eighty-four that stated people would call me a fat bitch."

We stood in front of a small granite-topped reception desk. Large framed photos of gorgeous models with immaculate styled hair hung on the walls. The receptionist sat behind the counter, glanced at us for a heartbeat and then gazed back at her computer screen. "I'm so sorry," she said. "We're booked for a month and I'm in the middle of important salon business."

I craned my head forward: she was playing Candy Crush on Facebook.

"But you're in luck. There's a Super Amazing Cuts right down the street, just two blocks away."

"Darling girl." Mr. Phillips leaned one forearm on the marble countertop, winced and propped up his lower back up with his other hand. "You are enormously helpful. I'll be sure to mention that to D'Alba during our private appointment with him. Check your book. *Groucho has arrived.*"

Her eyes snapped up at him then boomeranged back to her laptop. She double-clicked on her computer grid. "Groucho?" Her eyes widened. "Absolutely. We've been expecting you!" She catapulted off her ergonomically designed chair and beckoned. "Follow me."

She led us through the tricked out salon where women slumped in swiveling chairs with foil on their heads and dye on their roots as they checked their e-mails and flipped through gossip magazines.

Moments later I was seated in front of D'Alba's station facing a thousand mirrors while he snapped a vinyl cape around my neck. Hairbrushes and shiny tubes of hair products with his name emblazoned on them tilted in tall glass vases on the counter in front of us. Zara and Mr. Philips sat on folding chairs off to the side and sipped cool drinks in sweaty crystal tumblers.

"Where's Eliz—"

"She returned to the Drake. An urgent matter. She'll see you back at the Penthouse," Zara said.

D'Alba was a skinny dude in his forties, with overly gelled, slicked back hair. He wore thick, black glasses and sported a goatee. He ran his hands through my waist-length hair and breathed a little heavy. I looked in the mirror: he appeared to be enjoying this moment just a little too much.

"I was thinking, D'Alba," Zara said, "that you could cut and style Lucille's hair in soft waves that fall right at her shoulders: long enough for a casual, short ponytail for that fun look, as well as the perfect length to easily style into a chignon for more formal events. It has to be bouncy and frame her face when she wears it down for daily events. And weave in a few natural looking highlights. She needs to be blonder."

"That sounds just like Elizabeth's hair," D'Alba said.

"You're right!"

"Hah!" D'Alba laughed. "Second to 'The Rachel' it's the most copied hairdo in the world."

"Especially on the royal circuit," Mr. Philips said.

"No!" I reached behind my head and clutched my waist-length locks tightly with one hand. "I've been growing my hair since high school!"

"Lucille," Mr. Philips said. "You agreed to participate in a beauty make-over."

"I thought that meant a mani-pedi and perhaps an eyebrow wax because Zara made such a fuss over that. Long hair is my signature look."

"Lucy," Zara took my hand and squeezed it. "Have you never heard of Locks for Love?"

I shook my head.

"People with long, beautiful hair cut it off and donate it to a charity that benefits cancer-victims. You seem like sweet girl and I already know you're so helpful. I was thinking D'Alba could cut your gorgeous hair and you could help someone who was going through a rough patch. Besides," she leaned forward and whispered into my ear, "You need to look like Elizabeth."

I pulled her ear toward my mouth and whispered back, "Maybe Elizabeth grew her hair out during the last fifteen months she was in the States?"

Zara shook her head and stepped back. "Trust me on this one."

D'Alba fondled my hair. "You pretty phat bitch."

"Cancer victims?" I asked.

Zara, Mr. Philips, and D'Alba nodded.

"Do it before I change my mind." I shuddered. "But make him stop calling me that."

"It's a compliment," D'Alba said.

"Not where I come from!"

Two hours later I peered into the mirror as D'Alba rubbed mousse between his hands and dragged them through my hair. I had soft flowing layers, multi-colored highlights and hair that bounced.

"Wow!" Zara beamed like a kid on Christmas morning who discovered presents under the tree. "Now *that* is fabulous hair."

"It's so short," I said. "I don't even recognize myself. It's not me!" My eyes welled up for a second. But in all honesty, it really was fabulous. I don't think my tresses ever looked this good.

"Amazing," Mr. Philips lay on the floor with his legs and feet propped up on a chair. "Perhaps I was wrong about you, D'Alba. Perhaps, you are a gentleman, after all. And thank you for the Percocet."

"Oh Philips," D'Alba said. "You pretty phat bitch. I think this means you like me." He winked at him and snapped his fingers high in the air.

Mr. Philips face turned red as he attempted to rise from the floor.

A female assistant raced up to D'Alba's station. "Lovey," he said. "Escort Lucy to the back room for her next appointment."

"Yes, sir." She took my hand.

"Next appointment?" I trailed behind her, still wearing the smock as I peered over my shoulder at D'Alba, Zara and Mr. Philips.

"It'll be over in no time." Zara said.

"What'll be over in no time?"

Zara gave me a thumbs up and smiled.

Mr. Philips eyed me, winced and crossed himself as he knelt on the floor next to a chair and pushed himself to standing.

CHAPTER 8

The assistant opened a door to a small room with a tiny table with a sheet on it. A middle-aged brick of a woman with skin as shiny as Vaseline and perfectly groomed brows smiled at me. "My name ees Gertrude. Dese von't hurt a beet. Laze down here." She pointed to the table.

"Okay." I plopped on the table. "I mean, yes."

D'Alba's assistant raced out of the room.

"Take deep breath, hold it and don't move." Gertrude applied hot wax around my left eyebrow, stuck on some gauze on top, tamped it down with her finger and ripped it off.

I flinched.

"No bigzies, right?" she asked.

"No bigzies," I said.

She repeated the procedure on my right eyebrow and

then held a hand mirror in front of my face so I could inspect the results. Yowsa! I had brows that even Oprah would approve of.

I popped up off the table. "Thank you so much! I'll make sure Zara leaves you a tip. I never would have guessed in a thousand years that waxing would be this easy." I had one hand on the doorknob, when her meaty hand grasped my wrist.

"Back on zee table and drop pants pleez."

"I'm sorry?"

"I haz five customerz after youz. Hurry. No time for fun and games."

I laid back on the table and scooched my pants down my hips.

"Ach—virgin forest. So exciting." Gertrude applied wax to my nether-regions. "I am honored, Liebchien." She pressed the gauze down, a determined look on her face.

As she ripped it off I realized what the back room was all about and screamed like a chick in a slasher movie.

"You did gut! The exfoliating facial will be cake compared to zees," Gertrude said. "Go!"

My face was smothered in a gel concoction and I could only squint out of my left eye, as someone held my hand and led me to another stall in another back room. "Lie down here," a woman said. I did and blinked as a she peered at me through a large, round, lit magnifying glass aimed at my face. "Decent complexion for a thirty-year-old."

"I'm twenty-one."

"Oh. Sorry. I see blackheads around your T-spot

areas."

"I thought those were freckles."

"Nope. Blackheads. Don't you want to look pretty?"

"I thought I already looked kind-of pretty?"

"Perhaps to half-blind people. At D'Alba's we are dedicated to helping you look pretty to the world," she said. "You'll feel a tiny pinch." She leaned in and scraped a metal instrument across my nose.

"Ouch!"

I hobbled out D'Alba's front door onto the Oak Street sidewalk and glared at Mr. Philips. "Where's Zara?"

"She left to help Elizabeth. Except for your very shiny, red nose, Rudolph, you look beyond lovely." He popped a large straw hat on my face and slipped the over-sized, black Jackie-O sunglasses onto my face.

"I may not be who you envisioned hiring when you and Elizabeth placed this ad on Daveslist. I may not be perfect and coiffed and have every manner known to human kind. Or know who just won the Nobel Prize or who was indicted in the latest political scandal. But, Mr. Philip Philips—I, Lucy Marie Trabbicio, will be your star, your knight-tress in shining armor, your saving grace and the girl who never lets you down."

"We'll see about that," he said.

I pulled away from him and jabbed my finger in the air toward his face. "I'm your fucking one. Could you at least have been an honest soldier and told me what kind of battle I was walking into?" And my hand started to tremble.

He sighed. "I'm trying Lucille. This hasn't been an easy day for anyone. We've decided that you've learned enough for today." He stared at my hand.

"Let me tell you what's enough for today. What's enough for today was being yanked out of an elevator and landing on my ass on the floor of the Drake's Penthouse."

"Why is your hand shaking?"

"Because I haven't eaten since seven this morning, I'm hypoglycemic and if I go too long without food I get the shakes. *What's enough for today* is being made to parade down an aisle thirty-seven times while my gait is insulted with every step."

"Oh look there's a Sweetie Pies frozen yogurt shop. I heard this place has the best fro-yo in Chicago." Mr. Philips pushed the door open and gestured with one hand. "Ladies first. I'm dying for chocolate. Let's go inside and succumb to our guilty desires, yes?" He took my arm and shepherded me inside.

"I'd like a medium size of the white chocolate with the raspberries, please," he said to the woman behind the counter. "What would you like, Lucille?"

"*What's enough for today* is having all my hair on my entire body either cut or ripped off. And as much as I want to help cancer victims, I don't think they'll be wanting the remains of the hairs in my nether-regions, although at this point I'd gladly donate that to them as well." I glared down at the ingredients in the small metallic containers sunk into the counter top. "Jumbo size. Dark chocolate. Throw in some M&Ms and a dollop of cookie dough. Make that two dollops. It's been a tough day."

We were back on Oak Street walking toward the Drake as

we spooned yogurt from our cups.

"Do you want to terminate this job agreement right now?" Mr. Philips asked. "You can walk away with a two thousand dollar makeover. Say the word, Lucille, and I'll tear up your contract. You can call it quits and find another part-time job."

I thought about it. My hair was already gone. I still needed the money as well as a job. At least, in this gig, I didn't think I'd have to be a hooker. I shook my head. "No. I'm toughing this one out. You can't get rid of Lucy Trabbicio all that easily."

Mr. Philips coughed and I swear he covered a smile. "Good."

And just like that—the prep days for my part-time job flew by. Every morning I'd take the subway from Chicago's south side and make my way to the Drake Hotel approximately an hour away. Elizabeth, Zara and Mr. Philips had determined from my progress, or lack thereof, what the current day's teaching schedule would entail.

Manicure-Pedicure. Tina from We-Nail-It detached my acrylics, filed, buffed what remained of my real nails, pushed back the cuticles and gave me a sheer pink-hued polish. Very elegant. Very boring. Very royal.

Speech lessons: Apparently I had a 'Midwestern accent' and needed to homogenize that. A nice lady named Susan taught me how to correct my "lower back vowel merger." It wasn't as painful as the waxing.

And then there were:

Royal waves, handshakes, and curtseys.

How to sit like a Lady.

How to rise from sitting like a Lady.

How to eat like a Lady: Mr. Philips poured peas on a plate and insisted I spear them in an elegant fashion. When I elegantly told him off with my middle finger he made me watch the scene in *Pretty Woman* ten times where Hector Elizondo teaches Julia Roberts about fork placement.

How to dress like a Lady: Elizabeth and crew did not appreciate Cheswick's of Boston. I was a little curvier than Elizabeth but I could still wear most of her clothes. Her shoes however were a different matter. I wore a size 7 ½. She wore a nine. Suddenly the Drake suite was piled high in Zappos boxes filled with tasteful pumps, sandals and elegant shoes for evening wear.

"These are great," I tried on shoes made by some guy named Jimmy Choo. "Where are the workout shoes?"

"Elizabeth doesn't like to workout," Zara said.

"But I love working out," I said. "It's how I deal with stress."

"It's not that I don't 'like' working out. It just takes a lot of time and ruins my makeup and I'm not all that fond of sweating." Elizabeth held out some shoes. "Here, try on the Stuart Weitzman's. These are my favorites."

"Fine." I wrangled the pump onto my foot. "I'll bring my own Nikes."

But perhaps the most embarrassing part was the…

How to be Naked like a European Lady:

Because Europeans weren't all that nervous about public nudity. They got naked on beaches, in spas, stripped off their clothes in front of their royal dressers and assistants.

Mr. Philips reserved a private hot tub suite at the Drake's Spa that was upscale but still featured more modest

American customs. I squeezed my eyes shut and clamped my hands over them as Mr. Philips and Zara stripped down in front of me. "Please, Mr. Philips. Please I beg you," I said. "At least keep your sweater vest on. And possibly tug it a little lower on your body—like down over your hips."

I heard splashing.

"Ah," he said. "The jets are soothing for my lower back."

"Come on, Lucille," Zara said. "After all the stresses we've been under, the mineral waters feel incredible."

I opened my eyes, turned around and spotted them relaxing in the misty mineral hot tub. The scent of eucalyptus wafted through the air.

"Why can't I wear a bathing suit?" I asked.

"Do you have one on you?" Zara said.

I huffed. "Fine. Don't look." I stripped down to my underwear, flung my clothes onto a stand in the room's corner and descended into the waters.

"Puritan," Zara said.

"Be nice, Zara," Mr. Philips said. "After all this beautiful country was colonized by those brave, strong types of people."

"Yes, but they never got to enjoy the co-ed baths at Baden-Baden."

"The water feels great," I said. "This is a real de-stresser. I could totally get used to this." I rose up for a second to pull my hair back.

Zara stared at me, freaked. "Oh my God what are you wearing?" she asked. "We totally forgot to buy you decent underwear. Can you take care of that Philips?"

"Of course! I'll ink that note into my brain." He sunk

further into the tub. "Purchase fancy panties is now on my to-do list."

There were the endless memorization sessions in front of the large flat screen TV that included pictures and descriptions of Elizabeth's relatives and people I was supposed to know.

Elizabeth's dad, Lord David Henry Billingsley, was incredibly wealthy and looked a bit like George Clooney. When she was young, he was conservative, strict, overprotective and didn't give her enough freedom. She felt trapped. Now he'd mellowed, was more of a sweetheart and somewhat forgetful. He was to be called Papa—not Daddy.

His new fiancé was the gorgeous, fifty-something Duchess Carolina von Sauerhausen. She descended from the line of nobles that built the town of Sauerhausen, now the bustling metropolis and the capital of Fredonia.

They talked for a few minutes about Elizabeth's friends and flashed a few pictures on the screen: Lady So and So. Lady Blah diddy Blah.

Then they brought up the gossips and the ne'er-do-wells—apparently there were too many to mention. Be nice to everyone. Suspect everyone.

The list was endless: so many faces and names and titles. It was impossible to memorize all of them.

"There are a zillion people. How will I know who's my friend and who's out to get me?" I asked.

"You only need to remember the important people," Elizabeth said. "The rest you'll feel out. Get a sense of who they are. Then you'll have to wing it. You said on your application you were good at winging it."

"Yes, but this is an awful lot of winging," I said. "If we were at KFC, this would be three whole buckets of wings."

"Don't worry about that. Either Philips or I will be with you 24/7 or just a quick text away." Zara hit the remote and an image of a handsome older man with salt and pepper hair appeared on the flatscreen TV mounted on the wall. "This is the King of Fredonia—Frederick Wilhelm Gustave Timmel the Fourteenth. He speaks his mind, runs a tight ship with his country but is generally regarded to be a fair man."

"Got it." I said. Note to self: the guy who looked like a younger Sean Connery was the King. "Curtsey?"

"Definitely curtsey," Elizabeth said. "Next."

Zara clicked the remote. A photo of a pretty, blonde, middle-aged woman hugging three Labrador Retrievers popped up.

"She looks familiar," I said.

"Thirty years ago Cheree Dussair was a beautiful actress poised for stardom. But she dropped out of Hollywood to marry Frederick," Mr. Philips said.

"Queen Cheree adores her children and is obsessed with Labrador Retrievers," Elizabeth said.

"Curtsey?" I asked.

"Definitely curtsey," Zara said. "You can also earn her favor by doing or saying anything nice about a Lab."

"We could be here until next year looking at pictures," Elizabeth said. "Get to the good stuff."

Zara clicked the remote and an image of Prince Cristoph Edward George Timmel the Third—he of the wide shoulders and sexy smile appeared. My eyes widened and I dabbed a little drool from the corner of my mouth.

"Curtsey?" I asked.

"Under no circumstances curtsey. You need to be considered his equal. I've never curtseyed to him, shown him deference and I never will. I do need you to flirt with him, Lucille," Elizabeth said, "but when push comes to shove—"

"And trust me there will be 'shove,'" Zara said.

Elizabeth wagged her finger at me. "Which is another reason I hired you. You need work but you're not a working girl. So when he tries to get you in the sack—"

"Get out of town! A prince is going to try and get me in the sack?" I asked.

Mr. Philips nodded. "There will be sack-attempts."

"Oh my God!" I said.

"You can't give into him, Lucy. You won't give into him," Zara said. "You'll simply leave him wanting more."

I watched the screen as a video popped up of Cristoph played rugby with his mates while girls swooned on the sidelines: batting their eyes, tossing him articles of clothing, flashing skin.

"Cristoph's family and mine are in the process of sealing a business deal that they inked twenty years ago. Just keep him interested in me for ten days tops, while I finish up my pressing business and a few personal matters in the States," Elizabeth said.

"Um—okay," I said. "But I need to know. Are you all, have you all, like—have you and Prince Cristoph *done it*?"

Elizabeth rolled her eyes.

Mr. Philips and Zara inhaled sharply, stared wide-eyed at each other and held their breath.

Elizabeth shook her head. "No. We have not," she finger quoted, "'done it.' Although I do believe he's done it with just about every other girl that he's met."

Mr. Philips broke Zara's stare and looked at Elizabeth. "You need to tell her."

"I did," Elizabeth frowned. "Cristoph and I have never consummated our relationship, flirtation or sealed the deal on our family business agreement."

"Seriously, Elizabeth. I agree," Zara said. "I think you should tell her."

Elizabeth tossed her hair. "Fine. Yes, we've made out on several occasions and he's quite the kisser. Takes your breath away if I do remember correctly. But if I can resist—so can you."

I stared at Cristoph's wide, defined muscular shoulders. His dirty blonde hair and his sexy smirk. The sweetness on his face as he kissed that little girl's cheek. The kindness when he held that older lady's hand. The intensity in his eyes when he kicked a soccer ball.

Oh, just kill me now.

"I'll do it Elizabeth. I'll keep him interested in you and I promise I won't succumb," I said.

She sighed and placed one hand on her chest. "Perfect," she said. "Thank you."

"But I'm scared I can't pull this off. There's so much."

"I'm accompanying you, Lucille. I'll be there for you 24/7 should you get in over your head," Mr. Philips said.

"Everything will be just fi—" Elizabeth's face paled and she broke out into a sweat. She stood up—not so elegantly might I add—and raced out of the room. Zara ran after her.

CHAPTER 9

"What's wrong with her?" I asked.

"Nerves." Mr. Philips tapped the list. "Since Elizabeth will be incredibly busy, you'll be communicating primarily with Zara and me. Let's figure out our secret code names for communication once we depart base camp." He tapped his chin with his index finger and stared at the ceiling. "Your code name is Groucho."

"As in Marx?" I asked.

He nodded. "It seemed fitting. Now, you give it a try."

Ooh, I loved all this spy stuff.

I jumped to my feet. "I've got it!"

Mr. Philips frowned and shook his head.

I sat back down. Then rose gracefully. "I do believe I have your secret code names." I curtseyed.

He smiled, bowed at me, then winced and clamped

one hand to his lower back.

"You really should take me up on my Thai massage back-walking offer," I said.

"Proceed."

I kicked off my Keds.

"Not the massage—the code names."

"Oh," I said. "Well Zara is titled royalty—so I thought—*Lady*. What do you think?"

"Not that secretive," he said.

"Actually it is because there are a ton of Ladies. And it gets better," I said. "You, Mr. Philips, have a sweater vest addiction and perspire like a stuck pig in hot weather."

"Thank you for putting that so delicately."

"So for you? *The Damp*."

"Lady and the Damp?" He cracked a smile. "I think you're going to do better than we ever dreamed possible Lucille."

And just like that a week and a half flew by. I had one free day to wrap up my outstanding business, say goodbye and make excuses to my near and dear ones why I wouldn't be around for a couple of weeks. I could send the occasional e-mail but I wouldn't be giving hugs via Skype or Facebook—per my contract, I was to stay off both sites until my job ended.

My BFF, Alida, her son Mateo and I sat in the nosebleed section of U.S. Cellular Field's bleachers (please—it will always be Comiskey Park.) The White Sox were playing some team I didn't care about, but they were still the White Sox and I was a south side girl, which meant I loved them.

71

We stood up and sang along to "Take Me out to the Ballgame" during the 7th inning stretch.

"I just can't get over it, Lucy," Alida said. "You look like you and yet, you look completely different."

"It's the hair," I said. "I'm the same old Lucy. Nothing's changed except I have a little bit less in the hair and nail department."

"You still can't tell me the deets about your new job?"

"I signed a confidentiality agreement."

"I'm going to miss you," Alida said. "I already miss you at MadDog. That asshole Whitford hired some chick with big hair and long fake nails who wears bubblegum pink lip-gloss."

"That sounds like me."

"Well she's not you—she wears her skirt so high she's practically giving the goods away every time she bends over to drop off a drink. And the new customers are tipping her like crazy—way better than they tip me."

"You don't know what they're tipping her for," I said. "And I doubt you want to be in her line of work. Get over it. This job I'm starting is just a part-time gig. I'll be back home in no time. And if MadDog still sucks, we can look for new jobs together."

"I'll miss you!" She hugged me.

"I'll miss you too Señorita Sassy Pants." I hugged her back and my eyes welled with tears.

"What about me?" Mateo's long brown hair flopped over one eye as he tugged on my arm. "I'm going to miss you!"

I leaned down, brushed the hair back onto his forehead and squeezed him to me tight. "I'll miss you the most, dude. Take care of your mama for a few weeks while I'm gone. Yes?"

"Um..." He gazed out onto the field as the players took their positions.

So I tickled him. "Promise me, little man!"

"Yes!" He giggled and squirmed. "I promise, Lucy!"

A few hours later I squared off against Uncle John at Vail Assisted Living across a Ping-Pong table. I slapped the ball back at him and it skimmed the net. He leaned forward, scooped it up with his paddle and drop shot it over onto my side of the table. I leaned in for my shot but hit the net.

"And that my dear," he smiled, "is match. Your dear old uncle beat you three out of five."

"Hey I won two this time. I think that's a record. Are you happy here?" I asked and chugged from my water bottle. "I'm leaving town for a bit. And it's going to be super tough for me to leave if I know that you're not happy here."

"But you don't like to travel." He sipped from his water and eyed me.

"I know, but this is for my new job. And it won't be that long. Like two weeks—max."

"Promise me that you'll come back?"

"Of course I'll come back." I said.

"Your dad said the same thing. But then he and your mom were in the accident and they never did. Promise me. I want to hear you *promise me.*" His voice rose.

"I'll come back, Uncle John. *I promise.* I will never leave you." I hugged him tight as we both shed a few tears and both tried to hide it.

I wore Elizabeth's Chanel suit and sat composed, lady-like, in the cool air-conditioned back seat of the spit-polished, black town car that had picked me up at my tenement—I meant, apartment building.

"Thank you so much for picking me up today at my friend's place. How are you doing today?" I asked the uniformed chauffeur as my heart did flip-flops, my stomach churned acid and I tried very hard not to wring my hands, tap my feet or bite my fingernails.

"My pleasure Lady Billingsley. I am well. Thank you for asking."

"Splendid." I drummed my fingers on my knee. "Are we picking up Mr. Philips at the Drake?"

"I've been instructed to give you this." He handed me a white envelope with a wax seal on its back. I ripped it open, pulled out a card and read:

Dear Groucho,

I regret to inform you that I will not be accompanying you today on the first leg of your trip to Fredonia. My lower back pain flared last night and I am laid up at Northwestern Hospital's Spine Center for several days. Please don't fret. Everything will be fine. E-mail or text Lady or me if you have any questions. (FYI: Lady is quite busy attending to E and her secret mission.) However one of us will be winging our way to you and Fredonia shortly. We wouldn't have engaged your services if we didn't truly believe you were a smart girl who could roll with the punches.

Sincerely,
The Damp

I wrung my hands. I hadn't planned on pulling off this massive deception on my own. I'd counted on having Mr. Philips at my side and Zara on speed dial and text for emergencies. What if I couldn't do this by myself? What if I screwed everything up and ruined Elizabeth's big secret task? *I'd never forgive myself.*

The chauffeur drove past MadDog on the way to O'Hare Airport. I gazed out the tinted window and my mind drifted. I knew this was a journey of a lifetime, but I already missed my former job, my friends and my family. I wondered if they missed me.

Then realized that really didn't matter right now. I had a new job and I had promised—no, I'd actually sworn on my parents' graves—to give it my all.

CHAPTER 10

I reclined on my cushy, leather seat in the First Class section of British Airlines Flight #1509 to London and attempted to log into the LuLu inflight Internet service because I desperately needed to find out who this Nick character was—pronto.

But I couldn't access the LuLu site. Bad gateway, bad portal, bad vibes, whatever. I tried Lulu's helpful—*not*—chat service but still couldn't log on. Kristine, the flight attendant, tried to help, but we couldn't get there. Jane Dawson tried to help. It wasn't happening.

I peeked at Nick through the small separation between Jane and my seats. He was absorbed in his laptop, typing furiously.

"He's quite handsome. You two know each other?" Jane asked.

I boomeranged back into my chair. "No."

When I realized that Elizabeth probably *did* know Nick...

"By 'No,' I mean—kind of," I said. "We haven't seen each other in a very long time and you know how it is when you vaguely remember someone but blank on all the details?"

"Absolutely," Jane said. "I do believe that was called the sixties. But you're too young for that era. What's your excuse?"

"Oh. Um. Yes. We probably met at a polo match or a royal party. And there's just so much hubbub. Who can keep up?"

"That would totally make sense," Jane said. "Those soirées are packed with people. How can you possibly remember a third of the folks you're introduced to?"

Kristine made her way through the First Class cabin and jotted down our drink and dinner orders. "Did you get that Internet connection to finally work, Lady Billingsley?"

"No."

"That's just crazy. I'll try and help you again after the dinner service."

"Thank you," I smiled and nodded. "That would be terrific."

"Lady Billingsley?" Jane asked and arched an eyebrow on her expertly lifted forehead.

I waved my hand dismissively. "Half of Europeans have some kind of title. It's no big deal. It's not like I'm a Princess or anything."

"I'm keeping my eye on you. I have this gut instinct about people and I think you're going places," Jane said.

I laughed. "I'll let you know when I get there."

"Seriously. I get hunches, intuition, a sixth sense. I'm good with things like this." She dug in her purse and handed me her card. "Get ahold of me when whatever it happens." She wagged her index finger. "And if you don't and I find out about it—I will track you down, interview you and make you tell all!"

Over an hour later, my tummy still rumbled because I was too nervous and had only picked at my pecan-encrusted baked chicken with broccoli florets and new potatoes.

Kristine flitted around the First Class cabin clearing trays and refilling drinks. It was the perfect time for me to hit the ladies' room.

I scooched past Jane who was still eating, stood in the aisle and stretched my arms high overhead—it felt so good to move a little after all of today's stress. I made my way up the aisle when I sensed an interest, a gaze directed at me. I turned and caught Nick halfway out of his seat eyeing me with one arched eyebrow.

"No. Way," I hissed, pushed my way into the bathroom, slammed the door shut and fiddled with the horizontal slide-y lock three times before it engaged. I looked into the mirror and saw a red-faced, irritated reflection of Lady Elizabeth Billingsley. I didn't see a lot of Lucille Marie Trabbicio anymore and frankly—that kind of scared me.

I did my business, washed my hands, applied lip-gloss, smacked my lips together, and ran a hand through my blonde-streaked bouncy hair. I fumbled with the lock, pushed open the accordion door and stepped out.

Only to see Jane Dawson hunched over in the middle of the aisle while Nick straddled her from behind—his arms wrapped around her chest just underneath her boobs as he hoisted her up in the air—over and over again.

"Oh my God!" I exclaimed. "Let go of her you beast! Is there nothing you won't do to get a woman into the Mile High Club?"

Kristine and I shoved past each other as we hustled toward them.

"Leave the poor woman alone!" I said.

"Keep going!" Kristine yelled.

Jane Dawson's face was blue as she gurgled, hacked and spit out a chunk of pecan-encrusted chicken glombed onto a new potato. It flew through the air and landed on my foot. Actually on the toe of my designer pump. I feared for a second that Elizabeth and Zara would kill me. But then watched as Jane slumped back against Nick who caught her.

"Oh my God! Jane—are you okay?" I asked.

"Good job!" Kristine patted Nick on his shoulder, leaned in and examined Jane's face and throat. "Say something to us, Ms. Dawson. Anything."

Jane breathed heavily, her chest expanding and contracting. "You saved my life, young man. Thank you."

"It was nothing," Nick said.

I had experience in CPR. How did I not recognize this was a medical emergency and not sexual harassment?

"You're breathing freely Ms. Dawson. That's a very good sign." Kristine lifted the armrest between our two seats. "Can you help?" She asked Nick.

He nodded, scooped Jane up in his arms, moved in a

few feet and gently lowered her onto my seat.

Kristine popped open an overhead bin and we grabbed some pillows and a few blankets. She propped one under Jane's neck and her back, and one under her knees as her legs rested on her 3B seat.

I ripped the plastic bags off the blankets, shook them out and draped them across Jane.

"I'm fine, I'm fine," Jane said.

The other passengers in First Class were half out of their seats or craning to get an eyeful. One guy even whipped out his iPhone, which I snatched from his hand. "Show's over folks," I said. "Let's be respectful and give the woman some privacy."

"We know you're fine Ms. Dawson," Kristine said, "but I'd prefer that you rest here a bit. Do you have any medical conditions I need to know about?"

"High blood pressure and anxiety," Jane said.

"I'm going to alert the captain and get the blood pressure monitor. I'll be right back."

"But where will Elizabeth sit?" Jane rasped.

"Right next to me," Nick said. "There's an empty seat—right next to me." He pointed at the seat directly next to him.

Blech.

I frowned as my eyes swept the First Class cabin. It was indeed the only open seat remaining. I stepped around Nick toward the curtain that separated first from coach and peeked behind it. It was packed except for a few unoccupied center seats.

A baby screamed at the top of his lungs and up-chucked all over his mother. A guy with a greasy comb-over situated in the next aisle eyed me, winked and pointed to the empty seat next to him.

I sighed. "How many hours left in this flight?"

"Six hours and forty-five minutes if we're on time," Kristine said as she squeezed in next to Jane and took her blood pressure.

"Well then let's pray that time flies."

"And fly it will, my Lady." Nick took his seat next to the window and pointed to the aisle seat next to him. "You have nothing to worry about. I won't even talk to you. Not one question. Not one word. Not a sound."

I leaned closer to the aisle in seat 4B in case Mr. Cocky decided to grab me or grope me or trundle me off to the Mile High Club. But Nick was the perfect gentleman and no such thing happened. In fact nothing happened. Just like he said—he didn't even talk to me, let alone acknowledge my presence.

I'd sneak glances at him that he either didn't notice or ignored, as he was absorbed in his laptop, typing away. There was no way I could open my computer now, let alone get online, in case he saw anything that might compromise my job.

I paged through the European *Vogues* until my neck felt itchy and I feared I'd break out into hives if I laid eyes on one more anorexic, airbrushed model in a designer ad for a product I couldn't pronounce, let alone spell.

The in-flight movie selection was boring—no action adventure, no romantic comedies, nothing fun and hilarious like *The Heat* or *Bridesmaids*. Only earnest British stories, which had their appeal, or artsy European films that translated to nothing blowing up, no romantic banter, but featured a few scorching sex scenes. I didn't want to be watching that in case my seatmate decided to glance my way and take it as an invitation.

I glanced at my fancy watch fifty times but there was still a little under four hours flying time remaining. I desperately wished I could do yoga in the aisle or run laps up and down the plane's length. I also knew this would draw undo attention to myself and would not be considered lady-like.

Shit.

Who knew being lady-like would be so difficult?

I glanced again at the gorgeous male specimen named Nick, who now power-napped in the seat next to me, his long legs splayed out in front of him, his handsome head resting on the seat behind him. Was it my imagination or had his black facial hair grown a just a touch since we first met only hours earlier?

A sexy dark shadow travelled across his chin, crossed above his full upper lip and graced the lower part of his face. Dear God, he was so hot when he wasn't blathering on about something. No wonder Elizabeth had played slap and tickle with him.

I glanced at the door to the First Class bathroom facility and imagined us trapped in there. It would be tight. I would be warm. He would be 3/4 naked. We would be...

Get a grip Lucy!

I scrolled through the in-flight movies again:

Hitler's Last Days.

No.

Meet the Queen's Corgies.

No.

The Crocheter's Daughter.

And no.

When I had an idea. I tried to squash it. But it percolated, tempting me like a moth to a globe lamp on a moist, hot summer night. I told that thought to go away. But it jammed its fingers in its ears, stuck out its tongue at me and shook its head, 'No.'

I told that thought to take a hike.

It said, "Can't. We're on an airplane flying over the Atlantic."

I sighed. I simply couldn't resist.

So I did it.

CHAPTER 11

I tapped Nick's shoulder lightly, repeatedly, until he startled awake. "What?"

"Hey Nick," I said.

He grunted and rubbed his eyes. "What Lizzie?"

"I have an idea," I said.

He stretched his shoulders forward, then back and yawned. "That's awesome. However, I must remind you that I'm not talking to you."

"I know you said that earlier but I have this great idea for a game we could play together for the next four hours on this incredibly boring flight."

"Really?" One of his black eyebrows rose.

"No, no," I said. "It's not like that."

"Then I'm still not talking to you." He ran his fingers through his hair and stretched his legs.

"Hear me out. Let's pretend we don't know each other. Like—we're strangers who met for the very first time in First Class on a boring transatlantic flight."

His eyes lit up. "Tell me more."

"I get to ask you a question and you answer it. Then you get to ask me a question and I answer."

"Hmm," He rubbed his chin. "Are there prizes involved?"

I shrugged my shoulders and smiled.

"What are the rules of this game?"

"I think because we're 'strangers'," I fake finger quoted in the air, "we should start with PG questions and see where it goes from there. Yes? Okay. Great! I'll go first. Nick—what do you do for a living?"

"Hedge fund investments," he said. "I run my own company and handle investments for a few other clients as well."

"You must be very smart," I said.

"I am. But you already know that." He smiled.

"Oh sir." I batted my eyelashes. "How could I? We've only just met."

"Right. You're good," he said. "I hate to tell you but this is a major turn-on."

"That's not a question," I said.

"Um, right," he said. "What do *you* do for a living?"

I cleared my throat and fanned my face. "I'm on break from school. And I'm currently working part-time on a side project that's a little out of my comfort zone."

"What constitutes a little out of your comfort—"

"My turn," I said. "What brought you to the States?"

"Again, business. Trying to put out fires as well as

searching for opportunities. I love Fredonia but the long-term goal is expansion. My turn. Favorite movie?"

"Oh gosh," I said. "That's a draw between *While You Were Sleeping*, the first three *Bourne* movies with Matt Damon, not that other guy, *Terminator*—obviously the second one when Linda Hamilton kicks ass, and *Love Actually.*"

"That's six," he said.

"Count the three *Bournes* as one long, spectacular movie. Which brings it down to four. What are your four favorite movies?" I asked.

"Hmm. *It's a Wonderful Life.*"

"I loved Zuzu's petals," I angled to face him.

"My favorite part is when Jimmy Stewart jumped into the river to save Clarence," he said. "*Casablanca*. And *Die Hard*," he said. "The first one."

"As far as I'm concerned there are no others," I said. "You like the classics. I'm impressed!"

"And... *The Hangover*," he said.

"Meh! You had to throw a bromance in there. But I loved how in that movie things just kept going from bad to worse. Okay, okay!" I jumped a little in my seat and shot my hand up in the air. "My turn!"

"The movie question was your turn." Nick captured my hand in his much bigger one, pulled it down and held it. "Are you cheating this early in the game?"

"No!" I yanked it away and blushed. "Fine. Your turn."

"Best kiss ever? To make it PG-rated you must exclude me of course." He grinned.

"Oh." I bit my lip and thought and the answer popped

into my head—it just wasn't the answer I was expecting. "That would be the last time my mom kissed me—right before she died." My eyes welled.

"Oh, Lizzie, I'm so sorry. I think that qualifies as the best and worst kiss ever." He took my hand and squeezed it.

But this time I didn't push him away.

And just like that the hours flew by. I didn't even notice that we were late, delayed almost forty-five minutes. Our seats were in the upright position, our tray tables firmly locked. I pressed my toe against my tote and slid it back under the seat in front of me as we made our descent to London's Heathrow Airport.

"Best dessert?" Nick asked.

"Chocolate anything," I said. "The darker the better. You?"

"Chocolate and peanut butter all mixed up. But the peanut butter has to be crunchy," he said. "Favorite sport?"

"Hands down—football," I said.

"I think it's hilarious that the Americans call it soccer."

"Oh no. I don't mean soccer." I frowned. "I meant football. Like real football—you know the Chicago Bears, the Green Bay Packers—"

He reached out and grabbed my hand. "How long have you been in the States? Have you gone mad?"

"Um," I said. "Almost sixteen months?"

He laid the back of his palm against my forehead. "I think you're feverish. Possibly delusional? Who could like American football more than soccer? How could this strange twist of events happen to the girl I always admired? I might think differently of you here on out." He rolled his eyes.

And I giggled. "Might I remind you sir—we've only just met."

The plane shook a little as we descended through clouded skies. I held onto the armrest tightly. He put his hand on top of mine. "Breathe," he said.

I inhaled and exhaled slowly.

"That was perfect."

I nodded.

"Now try it again," he said.

I giggled. The next thing I knew we were on the ground. I said goodbye to Jane Dawson as they helped her off the plane first and plopped her in a wheelchair.

"And thank you, Nick," Jane said. "I will never forget your kindness."

"My pleasure ma'am," he said. "There's no greater honor than to rescue a true lady."

I looked up at Nick and shivers ran up and down my spine. He was totally growing on me. But my part-time job didn't include falling for a gorgeous man who happened to be someone Elizabeth used to be involved with. It totally didn't. Like no way. Not in a million years. Not if he delivered the best pizza ever. Nope. Wasn't happening. You could forget about it. Seriously.

Let's get this straight. Nick and I were both travelling on the next leg of my journey—the hopper flight to Fredonia's capitol city, Sauerhausen. And he had graciously offered to help me with my luggage. But I wasn't sure if Lady and the Damp wanted me to be seen with some smoking hot boy toy from Elizabeth's past.

So I thanked him politely for his time and his camaraderie but declined his offer to help me with my luggage. I would handle that on my own.

But by the time I cleared customs it was too late to check my—I mean—Elizabeth's bags through to Fredonia. I spotted a luggage cart vending machine, inserted the weird-looking bills and wrestled a trolley out of the contraption. I hoisted her bags onto it and pushed it forward only to watch in horror as two suitcases crashed to the floor and flipped over.

I lifted the cases off the ground and realized the bulky ones needed to go on the bottom. So I yanked the remaining suitcases off the cart, restacked them, wiped my sweaty brow and peered at my diamond-encrusted watch. Crap, I needed to get my ass in gear or I'd miss my connector to Fredonia.

"Based on your leisurely pace, I take it you're planning on staying over in London tonight," Nick said as he walked next to me pulling his one tiny suitcase.

"No." I pushed the cart forward. "I'm going to make that flight." But the wheels wobbled and it veered to the right as if it had a mind of its own. It clipped the heels of a dapper, elderly man pulling two suitcases and nearly took him out. "Sorry! So sorry!" I said.

He wobbled but Nick raced to his side, grabbed his arm and stopped him from falling. "I think this means she likes you," he said.

"Oh!" the geezer said. "You can bump into me anytime, love. That's the most excitement I've had since TSA did a full-body search on me last month. Wait until I tell the Missus." He toddled off.

Nick pushed and prodded a few of my suitcases so they lined up more evenly. "Let me push this thing," he said.

"Thanks. I will totally take you up on that offer."

"Fredonia Airways is in Terminal Two," he said and placed his suitcase on top of the pile. "Which is about fifteen minutes away from here—and that's if we sprint." He checked his watch. "Flight 711 to Sauerhausen starts boarding in five minutes. I know you hate to exercise, Lizzie, but you need to pick up those pretty toes and run if you want to make this flight."

He started jogging. "And as much as I'd love to spend another night alone with you in London?" He looked through the airport's windows at the gathering storm clouds. "This is the last flight out before the storm hits. We could be grounded for...um... days. Hmm..."

"I'm on it!" I threw my tote over one shoulder, my purse over the other and jogged. I sped past a couple of slow-moving tourists. "We can make it!" I swiveled my head—but Nick wasn't even near me.

He stood motion-less ten yards back in the wide airport aisle filled with passengers who were coming and going. His head was tilted to the side, a curious look on his face.

"What are you waiting for?" I threw my hands up in the air. "Christmas?"

"Lizzie. Would it kill us to relax in London for a couple of days? We could get a suite at the Savoy. Take in some theatre. Visit a museum. Meet up with my friend Harry and his blokes. Get massages at a spa. Try out a new restaurant. Visit some galleries."

I strode toward him exasperated. "I'm the one who's supposed to race to catch a plane but instead I'm losing yards and valuable time because I'm running in the opposite direction—back to you. Hurry it up or just hand me that cart. Because I'm making that flight and I'm boarding that plane to Fredonia if it's the last thing I do."

"Okay." He shoved back a grin, picked up the pace and jogged toward me pushing the cart filled with suitcases. "But I don't want to hear any complaints when you realize we could have been all cozy and happy if we stayed in London for a few extra days."

"No complaints. Glad to see your legs work as much as your mouth does." I said. "I can't even imagine what caused you to freeze like a Popsicle."

"Your breasts," he said. "Your very beautiful breasts."

Five guys turned and stared at my chest. I slapped my hands over my boobs as my tote and purse slid down my arms. "Shut up!" I hissed. "Stop it!"

CHAPTER 12

"Stop what? I don't think I've ever seen you run. Your breasts are totally bouncy in that outfit. And I mean this in a good way. Why did I never notice this before? Have you had a late growth spurt? Gone up a size? Maybe once we get back to Fredonia we could go on runs together ..."

I ground my teeth, forced myself not to look at him, flung my bags back over my shoulders and resumed jogging.

"There are other forms of cardio workouts you know," he said. "Should I remind you of that time our paths crossed in Paris?" He looked off into the distance and smiled. "Somehow I know what Bogy really meant when he said, *'We'll always have Paris.'*"

I was breathless, sweaty and nearly disheveled by the time I boarded Fredonia Airlines Flight 711 from London to Sauerhausen. The jet was small—approximately twelve seats—and the only other passengers was a posh, silver-haired couple that sat next to each other at the rear of the cabin.

The lone male flight attendant was nattily attired in Fredonia's royal colors: purple, white and gray. (I learned that word "nattily" from Mr. Philip Philips when I told him his sweater vest looked precious.)

We arrived just moments before they were closing the door to the jet way. I looked at my boarding pass in the short aisle, glanced up at the markings overhead, located and took my seat. Nick started to sit next to me.

I was sleep-deprived, jet-lagged, running on stress and simply needed to relax. The last thing I needed was to exchange sexually laden or cagey conversations with Mr. Gorgeous Cocky. So I slugged his shoulder. "Check your ticket, Nick. This isn't your seat."

His eyes widened. "Physical violence, Lizzie? That's so not like you? Or perhaps you've read the *50 Shades* series since the last time our paths crossed." He hovered somewhere between standing and sitting and pulled his ticket from his pocket.

"I have not read… okay, fine, I read the first one. Look, Nick. You're in 4D. I'm in 2A," I said. "Do. Not. Sit. Next to me."

"Except for Grandma and Grandpa back there, we're the only people on board. No one's going to bump me out of the seat next to you."

"I'm going to bump you out of the seat next to me."

"You're kidding me?"

"I'm not kidding you. I need to get a little shut-eye. I've been awake since... forever. I've going to see Dad—I mean—Papa and meet his new fiancé shortly after we land. I just need to chill and/or nap for an hour. Please? Please?"

"But our naps were always fun." He waggled his eyebrows.

I was going to kill Elizabeth—who I should have code-named 'Layed'—the next time I talked to her. Why didn't she tell me in advance about Nick?

"That's *exactly* the kind-of-fun I don't need right now," I said. "I totally appreciate all your manly help getting me to the plane on time and assisting me with my bags and the um..." Oh what to call his sexual innuendos? "...compliments. But, I beg you. Just leave me alone for a tiny bit. If I don't relax for like a half hour, I predict that I'll have a meltdown. Okay? I mean—yes?"

"Oh." He arched one eyebrow and stood up. "Got it. Yes, I'm all too familiar with your meltdowns, Elizabeth. Your last Chernobyl was why we haven't seen each other in sixteen months. Not a problem." He turned and walked down the very short aisle. Took a seat on the opposite side of the plane, several rows back from me.

Oh God, this was it. Soon I'd be in Fredonia pretending to be Elizabeth for all her friends and family, not just one guy. I could feel my blood pressure rise. Could I do this on my own? What had I gotten myself into?

The flight attendant stood at the front of the aircraft, clicked his heels and saluted. "Welcome to Fredonia Airlines Flight 711 from London to Sauerhausen, Fredonia. My name is Karl and I'll be pleased to serve you during this flight. Our flying time is estimated to be one hour and thirty minutes. Please store your personal items under the seat in front of you or in the generous storage bins overhead. Place your trays in the upright position and fasten your seat belts low and tight across your laps. Please power off all electronic devices at this time. There is one exit door on this plane…"

Which I stared at, fantasized about breaking through it and running across the tarmac.

"Once the captain has given the all-clear sign, we will be serving complimentary soft drinks and snackies. Alcoholic beverages and organic Fredonia sausages can also be purchased at this time with your credit card. We invite you to sit back, relax and feel free with Fredonia Air."

I peered out the tiny window at all I would ever see of London: Heathrow Airport. The sky darkened as monstrous, storm clouds bore down on us at an alarming rate. But there were terrible storms when we left O'Hare, and except for a few bumps in the first half hour—we had smooth sailing.

I predicted we'd fly through the European skies smoothly and soon we'd be touching down—soft like the skin on a baby's bottom—in Sauerhausen. Once we landed, according to Mr. Philips's instructions, there would be a car and driver waiting for me. And no, I was not going to share that with Nick. Mr. I'm-Too-Sexy-for-His-Everything could fend for himself.

We pushed back from the gate, taxied and, after a few brief minutes in line on the runway, took off. I white-knuckled the armrests as the plane bumped and jostled a bit while we ascended through the clouds.

And then we were above them. Sun shone through my small window as the tiny plane's engine whirred loudly. I couldn't really see anything of the large metropolis below because the cloud cover below was thick, like a comforting, fuzzy, gray blanket.

"You are now free to move about the cabin," Karl said on the intercom. Why he needed to use the intercom on a jet that had twelve seats was a mystery. "I will be coming through the plane at this time and taking your beverage and snack orders."

I glanced back at Nick: his handsome head was leaned back against the seat and he appeared to be power napping. Dear God, the man was totally out of my league. Obviously Elizabeth had a few secrets she hadn't shared with me. Why hadn't she told me about Nick when they obviously had a past?

I pulled out my laptop, fired it up and clicked on my secret code-encrypted "Free Donna" file. I needed to find out more about Nick. Even though I never accessed the Internet, maybe there was something in the file that I had missed. When the plane shook abruptly from side to side.

I rested one hand against my laptop and peered out the window. Those dark clouds were well below us. All I saw was sunshine and happiness.

"The captain has informed me that we will be winging our way through a wee bit of choppy air." Karl spoke into the intercom. "There's the possibility of minor turbulence. Please fasten your seatbelts and remain in your seats until the captain gives us further notice. Unfortunately, this will delay the beverage and food service."

Yeah, whatever—not a problem. I was totally getting used to this flying thing, especially in minor turbulence. I pulled my seatbelt tight across my legs. When the plane plummeted and my laptop levitated six inches into the air. I grabbed it, slammed its lid shut and clutched it to my chest.

"Air pocket!" Karl hollered, "Hang on!" He threw himself into the nearest seat and strapped himself in.

"We're all going to die! We're all going to die!" The grandmother screamed from the rear of the jet.

"Holy crap!" I'd marched a hundred miles to perfect a walk, practiced the royal wave until I developed tendonitis in my right wrist. I'd memorized faces and dates and names, had my skin insulted and survived an overly close encounter with an Eastern European waxer.

Apparently all for nothing, because I was on a tiny jet diving toward my early death. Below me, piercing, rocky, snow-covered mountaintops drew closer outside my window. "Ack!" I screamed.

I clutched my fancy laptop as I sobbed, hyperventilated and tried to remember how to cross myself. "Dear Jesus. I know it's been a while since we've had a private moment. But—I'm still your biggest fan!"

Nick bounced into the seat next to me and reached for my hand. "Everything's going to be okay."

"Leave me alone!" I yanked my hand away. "I respectfully request, God, technically-I mean-pray, that I do not die here and now on this pitiful plane—" and just like that the plane leveled out but the bumping continued.

"Pitiful my arse!" Karl swiveled his head toward me like Linda Blair in *The Exorcist*. "We just had the seats reupholstered."

We hit another air pocket and dropped another couple hundred feet. "Help me Jesus! I don't want to die in a tiny, old, POS plane that disintegrates over the Swiss Alps!" I gritted my teeth as the small jet shook like a Shamrock Shake.

"The French Alps." Nick secured his seatbelt low and tight across his impressive lap.

Oh for God's sake, Lucy. A Come-to-Jesus moment should not include ogling a hot man's package in the middle of a plane crash during the last moments of your young, pathetic life.

"We're going to die!" I said.

"Yes we are." He took my hand and squeezed it as the plane quivered and rattled as every ancient nut and bolt on the contraption shuddered to hold it together. Our shoulders bounced off each other. "But not today. It's just a little bit of turbulence. We've been through worse."

We hit another air pocket and plummeted hundreds of feet. "Shit!" I rasped for breath and peered out the window and watched, horrified, as frosty white, razor sharp mountainous peaks drew closer to our plane as well as my Chanel outfit. "Forgive me God," I hacked, "for I have sinned. It's been fourteen years since my last confession."

Nick yanked the armrest that separated us backward and wrapped his arms around me. "That's a great idea," he said. "Pretend I'm a priest. I'm Father Nick O'Malley. Close your pretty eyes, confess all your sins to me and get them off your shapely chest. It'll distract you." He lowered his voice dramatically. "Fourteen years, you say, Lizzie. You haven't confessed since you were ten years old? That's an awful lot of sinning."

"Nooo—" The airbags popped out of the overhead containers and dropped toward our heads and I shrieked again. "I haven't confessed since I was seven!" I grabbed a mask, placed it over my mouth and hyperventilated. Then remembered I was supposed to help others first, ripped the bag from my face and jammed it on top of Nick's mouth.

He gulped and his eyes bulged. He tore the contraption off his mouth and placed it firmly back over mine.

We hit more wind and the plane jittered back and forth like a cockroach racing across my kitchen floor. I clung to Nick, my hands dug into his biceps that flexed hard under my grip.

"But, love, that would mean you're still twenty-one. And we both know you're twenty-four."

I tore off the mask. "I'm only twenty-one! I'm too young to die!"

I realized that probably the majority of folks who were dying also believed they were too young to die. And I also realized, a little too late, that Elizabeth was indeed twenty-four.

CHAPTER 13

"Oops, sorry, I suck at math," I said. "I'm supposed to help what's left of my family and people, like Artie, who are really having a hard time. I'm supposed to be the tough one. The person folks can rely on. And then some day, God's going to smile down on me and I'm going to get my Happily-Ever-After."

"Tell me more." Nick hugged me tight against him and kissed my cheek.

The stubble on his chin tickled, then ground against my face, as shivers zapped over my body and my mouth suddenly grew jealous of my cheek.

Get a grip, Lucy. Maybe, just maybe, you could hook up with Nick for just one night. Only if I had nothing what so ever to lose. And frankly—that was totally not right now.

"I predict that you're going to get your Happily-Ever-

After Lizzie. Because you are smart, have worked hard for it and, basically, this is relatively minor turbulence." He pulled me closer to him.

"I can't die yet! Some day, I'm supposed to fall in love with a great guy and walk down the aisle and get married and maybe even have a kid or two. And then we get to change dirty diapers and cry when we send our girl to her first day of school. And my husband hides next the to school window and peeks inside to make sure she's doing okay. And, and…" I looked out the window, "and—holy crap it's snowing outside!"

"I know."

"It's July 1st!"

"I know."

"It's not supposed to snow in the summer."

"It does in the Alps. Remember?"

"We're in the middle of a freaking snow storm?" I asked.

He squeezed my hand. "We survived more than a couple in the past. I predict we'll make it through a few more."

"Hold me?"

He wrapped his strong arms even tighter around me as I buried my face in his chest and trembled. "Whatever happens, Nick? I just want you to know that right here and now, I think you're a great guy. Thank you for this."

"You just told me 'Thank you?'" He asked. "For real?"

"Yeah," I said. "I mean—yes. For real."

"That's a first," he said. And if it was possible—he hugged me even tighter.

I lay buried in his arms, my face pressed against his

wide chest. The plane shook, the rocky air belted us back and forth, up and down. The plane bucked as I clung to him.

"Close your eyes love. Everything's going to be all right. Everything's going to be fine. You are safe. You are protected. It's not our time yet." He held me so tight and whispered sweet, reassuring things into my ear...

Around five years or possibly a half hour later, the nightmare turbulence on Flight 711 ended. Nick held my hand while I white-knuckled his as the jet's wheels bumped down on the Sauerhausen runway. The wind buffeted us side to side, while the landing gear screeched as the plane bounced on the runway.

"Made it Lizzie," he said. "I told you we'd make it."

"Whoo-hoo!" I exclaimed.

The pilot pulled the plane to an abrupt halt. I looked out my window—it faced the snow-capped mountains. "There really is snow in July in Fredonia?"

"Yup," Nick said. "The mountaintops get snow all year round. A well-known fact about Fredonia. What? You bumped your head and got amnesia when you were in the States?"

"No." I looked down at my hands—they were shaking. Obviously the stress. My stomach rumbled, I felt a little faint, was hypoglycemic and needed a sugar fix.

I heard strange sounds: screeching, honking and blaring. "No. What in the hell is that noise? It sounds like my high school marching band."

"I didn't know All Saints had a marching band?"

"It was small."

"Ah." Nick ran his fingers through his black hair and squinted out the window in the direction of the music and frowned. "I think that's the welcome wagon."

Karl stood at the front of the plane and took the mic. "I bet you're thinking, *'Phew. We are so glad we didn't die.'* But we at Fredonia Air always planned to get you safely to Sauerhausen. However, I'm tasked with delivering the unpleasant news that the doo-hickey that connects to the what-ya-ma-call-it has separated."

"Not *the* doo-hickey?" I asked.

"Crap," Nick said. "Not *the* what-ya-ma-call-it?"

"Are we going to be all right?" I inhaled sharply.

"Does this mean we can't leave the plane," Nick asked. "Because seriously, after flight from hell and no sausages—I could totally go for a single malt Scotch and some pretzels right about now."

My stomach rumbled loudly and I felt woozier. "Pretzels would be awesome," I said. "Or even better some fruit? Or possibly chocolate?"

"No, no," Karl said. "The doo-hicky problem simply means our jet way gear can't connect to the gate. You can, however, exit the plane via our staircase. We've already alerted the tower. Once you step foot on the tarmac, a limo will be arriving in no time to whisk you away to your destination. Thank you for flying Fredonia Airlines!" He saluted Nick sharply. "Might I say, sir, it's been an honor serving you."

Nick saluted him back. "Thank you! You are a patriot. You ready, Lizzie? Not going to puke on your pretty shoes are you?"

"Why'd he salute you?" I asked.

"Because I'm a Fredonia Airways Platinum Level Frequent Flier."

"Ah." I took a deep breath. "I can't wait to see my beloved Fredonia. It's only been sixteen months, but it feels like forever." I reached down to retrieve my bags, but he'd already grabbed them for me. "You don't have to—"

"Not a problem." He nodded to the thin aisle between the seats in front of us "Ladies first."

A timely reminder that I needed to act like a lady.

Pull it together, Lucy.

I rose like I was regal, to the manor born and walked down the aisle in front of him. I held my head high and kept my shoulders back. "Thank you, Nick." The mountain winds continued to batter the small aircraft and I held out my arms, hands extended, and bounced off a few seatbacks as the plane wobbled from side to side.

"No, thank you! I've got a much nicer view of your ass from back here. I don't remember your bottom being that round, Lizzie. Have you started working out this past year? Lunges? Squats? You used to hate to exercise. Seriously, I do believe we could work out together during our time back in Fredonia. I'd be happy to spot you."

I ground my teeth.

I frowned, clutched the railing and cautiously descended the jet's steep, narrow staircase leaving Fredonia Air Flight Seven-from-Double Toothpicks hell. I stepped onto the concourse's solid ground and contemplated for a long second about kissing it. But kneeling on greasy pavement might screw up Elizabeth's suit and quite possibly invite more "ass" commentary from Nick.

The winds whipped around me and blew my expensive hair off my face as I got my first official look at Fredonia. This was what I'd been paid for. This is what I was here to do. Impersonate a Lady. Keep Prince Cristoph interested—but at bay—until Elizabeth was able to complete her super urgent mission and return to Fredonia.

The origin of the previous musical stylings became apparent when a small marching band rounded a compact, pristine, two-story building that was Sauerhausen's only terminal. The festively attired crew headed toward me with a bandmaster dressed suspiciously like the Energizer Bunny in the lead. "Um?" I asked.

"Looks like we're getting the *official* welcome wagon." Nick stepped off the plane's stairs and stood beside me on the tarmac, shielding his eyes with his hand as he stared at the band.

"Do they do this for everybody?" I shook my head. "Always?"

A horse-drawn carriage appeared behind the marching band. The buggy was old-fashioned, painted purple, white and gray and accented with gilded gold. The two horses that pulled it were gleaming white as the mountain snow and, in sharp-contrast to the marching band, they high-stepped in perfect coordination.

An older man in a black suit and a top hat held their reins and sat tall on the carriage's driver's seat. Behind this dog and pony show, six news vans with satellite dishes on their roofs followed at a snail's pace—a respectful distance away.

"What's going on? Where's the limo?" I asked.

"This is the limo," Nick said.

The marching band played a song that was a blast from my parent's past. "Oh my God," I said. "They're playing "I Think I Love You" by The Partridge Family."

"Who?" Nick asked.

The procession approached us until it was about fifteen yards away. When the bandmaster lifted his hands into the air in a dramatic moment, paused and brought them crashing down. The band stopped playing on a dime.

I blinked.

The carriage door creaked open and a tall, mid-twenty-something guy wearing a finely cut black suit and tie hopped out. He dragged his fingers through his thick mane of blonde hair, turned toward me, grinned and then bowed. "Lady Elizabeth Theresa Billingsley. Welcome home!"

Holy crap! This was the guy Elizabeth and Zara had told me about. The guy I was supposed to be nice to because her family's survival depended on it: Prince Cristoph Edward George Timmel the Third. Not only was he was the heir to the Fredonia throne—he was a hell of a lot hotter than his pictures.

I performed the partial, bent-knee, curtsey-thing Zara taught me, when I remembered Elizabeth had told me to *never* curtsey to Prince Cristoph. He needed to see her as his equal. "Oh thank you your Royal…" no-no—Elizabeth told me I should call him by his first name. "Cristoph! What a lovely—" I pointed to the band, "—greeting. Like—super thoughtful of you."

He strode across the tarmac toward us. "Anything for you, my dearest Elizabeth. Hey, Nick," he frowned. "You're an unexpected surprise, dude. I thought you were in the States on business." The guys gingerly bear hugged for a second. *A very quick second.* "You and Elizabeth shared a plane back?"

"Two planes. All the way from Chicago, can you believe it?" I asked.

Cristoph frowned. "You're late. Did you… detour?"

"No." Nick cleared his throat. "Tornados in the States pushed us back a bit. Then a snowstorm in the Alps. Weather, Cristoph. Simply, weather."

"I trust you haven't been trying to steal Elizabeth away from me?" Cristoph circled Nick, eyeing him suspiciously.

I peered at my shoes and remembered Nick's strong, muscular arms holding me tight during the bumpiest ride of my life. How he crooned into my ear. Let me dig my nails into his arm. *Hell, he even encouraged it.*

Nick cleared his throat. "Cristoph—you're heir to the throne. Elizabeth would never be interested in me."

"Aah." He nodded, rubbed his chin and then laughed. "You're right." He turned, pointed to the bandmaster and held his hand high up in the air for a few moments… and then brought it crashing down.

The band launched back into "I Think I Love You".

The doors to the news crews vans popped open. Camera persons, five female and one male reporter dressed in business suits poured out and encircled us. They spoke in hushed tones into their mics while their behind-the-scenes people swiveled and focused their cameras on this whole circus.

I felt like a bug under a magnifying glass in the bright sun. I hadn't eaten in hours and the last of the adrenaline from the near plane-crash vacated my body, leaving me with a solid case of hypoglycemia and mild shakes.

"Elizabeth Theresa Billingsley?" Cristoph smiled at me. "I need to ask you something." He whipped out a large bouquet of red roses and handed them to me.

My hands trembled as I took the flowers. "Thank you. That is so sweet," I said. "And I need to ask you something too."

CHAPTER 14

I felt hot—but not in a good way—and fanned my face.
"Do you have anything sweet I could snack on? Something
with a little sugar? A piece of fruit. Some chocolate?" In the
near distance, a blonde female reporter's bouffant hair
looked suspiciously like cotton candy and I willed myself
not to bolt in her direction.

The reporters smelled weakness or blood and boldly
tightened their circle around us. Their cameras *clicked and
snapped, popped and whirred.*

Cristoph frowned. "I'm so sorry, Elizabeth. I'm not in
charge of the menu for today. I think Mother has that
covered."

"Aah. Yes. Mother." Fredonia's queen was the
beautiful, blonde, former actress, Cheree Dussair.

"Does anyone have a granola bar?" I asked. "Like,

seriously—all you lovely people out there—" I dropped the flowers on the tarmac and dug through my Chanel bag groping for my wallet. "I'd pay ten euros for one granola bar. In the States it would cost ninety nine cents at a White Hen Pantry." My hand quivered as I held out a bill. "I beg you!"

Reporters, photographers and band members dug though their purses and pants pockets and in seconds five wrapped bars flew through the air toward me. One hit Cristoph on his head and he winced. Nick caught another. Two bounced off the airplane and dropped onto the tarmac.

I leaped up, reached like a Chicago Bears wide receiver on game day and in a Herculean moment caught a bar. I turned away from the cameras, hunched over, ripped open the foil and shoved the cinnamon-raisin snackie in my mouth.

Nick turned with me. "What's wrong?" he whispered.

"I get incredibly light-headed when my blood sugar drops. If it's super bad, I have a history of fainting." I munched and already felt the sugar oozing into my system. "But you can't tell anyone—it's a secret."

"Okay. I'm sure the paparazzi haven't noticed a thing. Are you planning on fainting now or in the near future?"

"Not anytime soon." My hands trembled as I jammed the remains of the bar into my mouth. "The fainting thing only happens if my blood sugar is so low and I am completely exhausted, stressed, shocked or a combination thereof." I swallowed the last bits, crumpled the foil in my hand and crammed it in my purse. "This totally did the trick. No worries. But thanks for asking."

I turned toward the reporters and the band and delivered my royal wave. "Thank you kind people of Fredonia! It's so good to be home!" I looked at Cristoph. "I apologize for that interruption." I gestured at his crew behind him: the band members, the paparazzi and the guy on top of the carriage holding the reins.

Nick elbowed me discretely.

"What?" I hissed.

"Your lower lip. Left-hand corner."

"What now? Do you want to suck on it?" I hissed. "Do you want to meet up with it at the Mile High Club? Leave. Me. Alone."

"You've got a glob of granola with a raisin on your upper lip. Looks like a witch's wart."

I swiped my hand over my mouth, captured the crumb and flicked it behind me.

"Are you all right Elizabeth?" Cristoph asked.

"Yes! Carry on," I said. "All is well. Disaster's averted. And by that I mean the turbulent airplane flight."

"Aah. Yes. Good to hear. So I'd like to get on with the program if I may."

"Absolutely," I said. "What's on the program? I've been flying all day and I'm pretty exhausted. I could totally go for a quick bite to eat and then grab a nap."

Cristoph stood in front of me, smiled and took both my hands in his tan muscular hands. And squeezed them. "Lady Elizabeth Theresa Billingsley?"

"Aw crap," Nick mumbled.

"Um, yes?"

"I, Prince Cristoph of Fredonia, have been in love with you since we met on the playground eighteen years ago."

111

"Get out of town. For real?" I asked.

"For real," he said. "You stomped around clutching your favorite doll and you were pouting something fierce."

"I can't believe you remember that?" I regarded Cristoph seriously for the first time. He was stunningly beautiful with sharp cheekbones and dirty blonde hair that kept traipsing across his forehead. "That's incredibly sweet you remember."

He nodded and smiled. "I remember everything about you Elizabeth."

"Do you remember that you yanked her doll from her chubby hands, tore off Betty Wetty's arms and legs and then tossed them over the schoolyard fence?" Nick asked.

"I have never had chubby hands!"

"And then you called her a baby when she cried," Nick said. "Do you remember that?"

Cristoph frowned.

"Do you remember Elizabeth chasing you around the playground screaming at the top of her lungs while all the girls your own age called you The Doll Butcher?" Nick asked.

Cristoph grimaced. "That's all in the past. What matters is the present. What matters is now." He got down on one knee on the tarmac in front of me and pulled a black velvet box from his pants pocket.

I inhaled sharply and clutched my chest with one hand.

"I always knew it was you Elizabeth. But today's the day that I formally ask." He popped open the box and revealed an engagement ring the size of the bunion on my Great Aunt Hazel's toe. Except this bunion sparkled. "Will you marry me, Elizabeth?"

"Um…" What remained of the adrenaline in my body left in a big whoosh.

The tuba player tooted his horn and I jumped. "Say yes!" the big guy yelled.

"Hmm?" A blast of mountain air swooped onto the tarmac and blew the cotton-candy reporter's hair straight up like a Tootsie Pop. I swayed.

The uniformed trumpet players shot each other a look and blasted their trumpets in unison. "Say yes!" the head trumpeter grinned.

My eyes widened. "Uh?"

The cymbalist clashed his cymbals and the drummers drummed. "Say yes! Say yes!" they chanted.

In spite of the chilly mountain winds, I felt hot and fanned my face. I glared at Nick but he wouldn't meet my look.

Cristoph reached over and took my trembling hand. "Say yes, Elizabeth. You've been my princess since your first day of kindergarten. Now I'm asking you to marry me, be my wife and become Princess of Fredonia. What do you say?"

The camerapersons stomped their feet as they filmed this whole shebang. The female reporters chanted, "Yes! Yes! Yes!"

I gazed at the brilliant, sparkling bunion and then at the gorgeous guy kneeling in front of me. I wondered for a millisecond why Lady and the Damp didn't forewarn me about this possibility—when I realized a prince was proposing to me.

But not really to me.

My entire body broke out into a sweat followed by a wicked dose of the shivers. "Cristoph..." I clutched my stomach, "my answer is..." I swayed, as everything grew dim and gray around me. "My answer is..."

And everything shot to black.

I woke up to two, pretty, twenty-something female faces hovering over me, both wearing a healthy dose of concern. One girl chewed her lip and frowned. The second wrung her hands.

"God bless Fredonia, she's awake!" A cute redhead with cropped, glossy hair exclaimed. "Elizabeth. Can you hear me? It's Joan Brady."

"Who's Elizabeth?" I asked. "Of course I can hear you." I glanced around at the small, white, sterile room with a uniformed guard stationed next to the door. "Where the heck am I?" When it dawned on me who Elizabeth was—my employer—and I better ix-nay these kinds of answers from here on out.

"She has amnesia!" A blonde woman hissed and chewed her lower lip. "Oh fudge, I haven't talked to her in a year except on Facebook and now she has amnesia? How am I going to explain all this to her?" She cracked her knuckles and then her neck.

"Maybe you need to be thinking about Elizabeth right now and not yourself, Cheryl," Joan said.

"I am not simply thinking about myself. I go through Facebook posts twice daily and click 'Like' on everyone's posts. Except for the scary ones that involve bungee jumping or if one of my friends recently added the 'I'm in a relationship but it's complicated' status. Those frighten me because that's just secret code for they're dating a transvestite, or someone who's married, or both. And I just don't see it turning out all that well, but God forbid you try telling them that because they just get pissed off and stop following your feed," Cheryl said. "Or worse? *They un-friend you.*"

"Hello," I waved my arms in big semi-circles in front of them. "It's me: Elizabeth Theresita Bill Me Too-much-I'm Done," I said. "I do *not* have amnesia. Who are you ladies? I'm concerned that this place looks like a James Bond villain's lair circa the 1960s. Are we trapped here? Do we need an escape plan? Trust me, I'm good with shit like this. Why is the guy guarding that door wearing an enormous cod-piece?" I rubbed the back of my head and felt a lump the size of a goose egg and winced. *"What happened to me?"*

Cheryl and Joan rolled their eyes and clucked their tongues. Joan pulled a small silver flask from her purse, unscrewed the top, took a sip and handed it to Cheryl. "Single malt. Prince Harry's private reserve. The good stuff."

Cheryl accepted it, placed the flask to her mouth and downed a shot and grimaced. "Most excellent. Thanks." She held it out to me.

"Thanks." I accepted it, knocked back a shot and handed it to Joan.

"Elizabeth—look into my eyes and concentrate. My name is Lady Cheryl Cavitt Carlson. Our great grandfathers were first cousins and served together during the Great War."

I blinked. "World War I? For real?"

"Not *that* Great War," Cheryl said. "The Great War of

1965 when the Fredonia bakers declared war on the fisherman. To protect themselves from the hardened loaves of bread and stale rolls that, when properly aimed, could take out a man more efficiently than a volley of bullets, the fisherman fashioned armor from petrified fish scales. That codpiece—" She pointed to the guard's groin, "—is a revered, time-honored, traditional outfit for a Palace Guard of the Inner Circle. The nuns taught us that in grade school at All Saints. Remember?"

"Huh?" I asked.

Joan took my hand. "Elizabeth. You blacked out on the tarmac and hit your head."

"We were waiting for you in my family's limo next to the runway and watched the whole thing happen," Cheryl said. "You fell over like a fat redwood after a lumberjack took a chainsaw to your trunk. We followed your ambulance to the hospital."

"I'm not fat." I frowned.

"No, but you've picked up a few curves in the States. Tell all—did you get your boobs done?" Joan asked.

"No!" I held my hand to the lump on my noggin. "I don't feel so good."

"I read that if you talk about what you remember immediately following a head injury, your memories might come back." Cheryl grabbed an ice bag from a stainless steel medical stand and held it firmly against my head. "What do you remember?"

"Airplane turbulence, no freaking food—not even one piece of fruit on the entire flight—a loud marching band, hot guys—a blonde and a brunette—and a ring the size of the bunion on my Great Aunt Hazel's toe." I crossed myself. "May she rest in peace."

"That's totally Cristoph's style," Cheryl said.

"He's big on the over-the-top bling." Joan pulled her buzzing phone from her purse and tapped the screen. "Your father's fiancée texted… your dad's on his way here. I didn't know you had an Aunt Hazel? Which side of the family is she on?"

Oopskies. "A distant relative on Papa's side." I suddenly remembered the sweetness of Elizabeth's Dad's face. "No!" I pushed myself to sitting on the hospital cot. "Call Papa immediately and tell him not to come here. I'm going home. I'll meet him there."

"Done." Joan keyed a message into her phone and hit send.

"But what about Cristoph's question?" Cheryl asked.

"What about it?" I asked.

What was it would have been the more appropriate prompt as I could barely remember Cristoph let alone his question. I plopped my feet onto the floor. The guard leaped across the room, knelt down and slid industrial hospital slippers on my tootsies. "Thank you, officer." I tried to meet his eyes but could only stare at his metallic groin.

He grunted, lunged back to the door and cracked a smile.

"It's not like you haven't been expecting this," Cheryl said.

"Expecting what?" I trudged across the room in my threadbare hospital gown. A chilly breeze traveled up my spine and drew goosebumps. I realized my ass was more-than peeking out the vertical split in the gown's rear. I twisted one hand behind my back and attempted to hold the two pieces together.

Joan and Cheryl regarded each other, torn.

"Elizabeth, sweetie." Cheryl said. "You have to remember. It's only like the biggest question of your life?"

"Head trauma," Joan tapped her index finger on the side of her head. "Maybe I shouldn't be giving her alcohol right now. I fear we'll be dealing with this debacle for a while longer."

"I'd like to pose a bigger question," I said. "Why did I arrive here in Free Donna?"

"Fredonia," Cheryl and Joan said.

"Question. Why did I arrive here with two guys who are conspicuously absent from this hospital room? Slick and Mischief? Right?"

Joan rolled her eyes and twirled her finger next to her head.

"*Nick and Cristoph*," Cheryl said.

"Right. You ladies are here. Where are the guys?"

"They're in the hospital's waiting room. They're waiting for us to give them the thumbs up to see you," Cheryl said.

"They're waiting for *your approval—why?* Are you the Mafia? The Vatican? The CIA?"

When the hospital door flew open and slammed into the guard, who grunted. A full-figured thirty-something woman wearing a red and black flamenco dancer's outfit, complete with a red cowgirl hat adorned with feathered plumes, strode into the room and headed toward me. "No bitch. We're your Ladies-in-Waiting."

My breath caught in my throat, my eyes widened and I

pressed my palm over my paper-thin gown to my chest. "Who are you? What do you want?"

"I am Lady Esmeralda Ilona Castile Hapsburg the Fourth." She pointed at me with one black-gloved hand. "And I want you Elizabeth."

CHAPTER 15

"No, no. You totally don't want me—I might have brain damage." I pointed to Joan. "Take the redhead. She's super cute, seems smart and you could probably sell her on the black market for her weight in shekels."

"No way girlfriend." Esmeralda grabbed me, pulled me to her large bosoms and squeezed me so tight I couldn't breathe and I squeaked. She whispered, "I missed you so much. Don't tell the other bitches-I-mean-ladies. They'll detect I'm weak and go for the jugular. Shh." She pulled away from me.

"Okay?" I squinted at her.

Esmeralda clacked her heels together three times, raised her arms overhead, tossed her long mane of auburn hair back and clicked castanets high in the air. "The 'guys' are waiting for us—*your Ladies-in-Waiting*—to give them the heads up, the okay, the all-righty-then, the get-the-job-done, before *we allow them* to see you."

She eyed the guard collapsed against the wall, lifted her skirts seductively over her knees, posed a little Marilyn Monroe-esque. "Cancel your plans for tonight, soldier." She winked and blew him a kiss. "Because I've got far better ideas for you. God, I love me a man in a uniform."

"My '*Ladies-in-Waiting?*'" I asked. "Why do I have Ladies-in-Waiting?"

"Oh Mr. Palace Guard," Esmeralda held out a lace handkerchief and dropped it onto the floor between them. "Show me chivalry."

He crawled to her handkerchief, picked it up, his hand shaking, and held it high in the air. "Yes, my Lady."

She leaned down, grabbed his shoulders, yanked him toward her and kissed him hard on the lips.

"Oh for God's sake," Joan said.

"Get a room, Esmeralda," Cheryl said. "And do not think you can pull that 'I'm half Spanish and love runs through my veins' excuse for the umpteenth time. We know your Latin Lover explanation is but a poor thesaurus choice for hussy."

Esmeralda sucked the handsome guard's mouth so far into hers I thought it might pop out the back of her head. When she slapped him resoundly on the ass and then pulled away. "And that, Ladies, is chivalry! We've put up with your shtick forever, Elizabeth, because we knew that some day it would come down to this. Someday you would need us. And each of your Ladies-in-Waiting has a kind of a super-power."

"Super-power?" I asked.

"You're totally exaggerating yet again." Joan said.

"Am I?" Esmeralda raised an eyebrow and held onto the skirts of her dress. "No matter what the occasion, I, Esmeralda Ilona Castile Hapsburg the Fourth can dance." She twirled in the middle of the small hospital room, picked up speed and spun like a dervish. She took out the guard who flew across the room, hit the wall and dropped to the floor like a flattened bug on a windshield.

Joan and Cheryl crouched behind my hospital gurney and winced.

"Esmeralda!" Joan said. "Stop being a fucking show-off. We need to get Elizabeth home to her family so she can make a decision on her very important question."

"Of course," Esmeralda scrawled her phone number on a hospital napkin, leaned toward the guard and tucked it down the front of his codpiece. "Who says chivalry is dead?" She held her hand to her ear like an old-fashioned phone and mouthed "Call me."

I had changed into designer sweats and a T-shirt as I watched the TV coverage from my 'family's' luxury penthouse on the top of the Alpine Towers in downtown Sauerhausen. City lights clustered around the streets twenty-five stories below and twinkled around the elite shopping and restaurant districts.

Six flat-screen TVs mounted on the wide living room wall aired the coverage from the six news channels that were on sight for the Royal Fredonia Almost-Engagement Debacle *(That's what the media had dubbed it—not I.)*

Each news feed showed me on the tarmac, the wind whipping through my hair. Nick stood next to me as

Cristoph dropped to one knee, held out the velvet jewelry box, popped it open and asked me to marry him.

Lucky for me, each channel also featured video of me as I wobbled, my legs giving way beneath me, as I collapsed into a heap while Nick and Cristoph dove toward me to see if I was breathing.

Five local networks placed a fuzzy banner across the explicit view up my conservative designer skirt that had hiked all the way up to the tippy-top of my thighs that lay flopped wide-open. The sixth chose to display my new, pretty underwear. I thanked my lucky stars that Zara had insisted I'd get the full Brazilian and not its less-aggressive second cousin—the half Argentinean.

I watched the relentless, looping coverage while reclining on a velvet chaise lounge and noshing double dark chocolate ice cream from a crystal bowl. "This is like the best ice cream ever." I regarded the older, handsome, silver-haired man seated next to me who happened to be Elizabeth's father—Lord David Henry Billingsley. Their family money was legendary, passed down from generation to generation. They were widely regarded as the Medicis of Fredonia: wealthy, benevolent, conniving, supportive of the arts, back-stabbing, and well once again, extraordinarily wealthy.

He patted my hand. "Organic milk from free-range cows who are grass-fed in the pastures surrounding our mountain chateau."

"Right." I flashed to the photo of the picturesque country villa that Zara had shown me. "Totally yum. I'm glad you stayed home, Papa. The hospital was crowded." I remembered Mr. Philips told me Elizabeth's father was a little dotty, but very sweet.

He wiped a tear from the corner of his eye. "I feel terrible. I haven't been there for you."

"That's not true Papa." I took his hand and squeezed it.

"Except for that one quick trip to the States, honey, I haven't seen you in almost a year. And then I watch you collapsing on national television? It scared me."

"I'm fine. I'm just really tired and the flight over the Alps was bad, I mean turbulent. My blood sugar dropped and I passed out. It's nothing serious, I promise."

Why hadn't Elizabeth seen her Papa in almost a year? I wish I still had my mom and dad. Someone who would hold my hand while I ate ice cream. Someone who would miss me if I died, or care if I passed out.

A pretty, fifty-something woman with long, layered, jet-black hair walked toward us and smiled. "Elizabeth. You have color in your cheeks. Thank God, you seem to be recovering quickly."

Duchess Carolina von Sauerhausen was Daddy's—I mean *Elizabeth's Papa's*—new fiancé. She was beautiful and had greeted me kindly when the Ladies dropped me off at the condo's front door.

"Carolina, this is the best chocolate ice cream I've ever had," I said.

She tilted her head. "That's so sweet. You've totally missed Fredonia's second most important export. Our organic chocolate."

I stared at the bowl and contemplated licking it. But decided that might not be lady-like. "I'll say."

Carolina placed her well-manicured hand on Daddy's shoulder. "It's time for your nap, David," she said.

"But I'm spending time with my only daughter."

"Your only daughter will be here when you wake up. Besides, the doctors said that a little rest every day is necessary for your health. It will help you live years longer."

Daddy gazed up at her and blinked. "Jean?"

"No, my darling. Jean was your first love. I'm Carolina. I'm your fourth love." She caressed his arm. He smiled, got up and followed her like a smitten puppy.

Then stopped in his tracks, turned and stared at me. "It's been a very long day, Elizabeth. I'm going to take a nap and then we can determine what to do. Yes?"

"Yes, Papa," I said.

Carolina smiled. "I'll be back."

I nodded and gave her a thumbs up.

I got up, stretched and looked out the windows. The view from the condo's floor to ceiling windows was dark: thick gray clouds bumped up against each other in the night sky. I doubted I'd see Papa again before morning. And because I'd passed out before I gave Prince Cristoph an answer to his marriage proposal—apparently the entire population of Fredonia was holding tight to their lederhosen because they didn't know if I was injured and lying in a hospital room, dead on a mortuary slab or if I just said no.

At least that's what one news anchor speculated. That I'd turned Cristoph—aka The Playboy Prince—down because he'd slept with half of Fredonia's royal court as well as several adjoining countries and a principality—or five.

Another reporter insisted I was in seclusion, surrounded by my nearest and dearest, while I contemplated my answer. A third channel featured relentless close-ups of my stomach while their female anchor pointedly suggested that I sported a baby bump.

I had three slices of Johnnie's Chicago deep-dish pizza the night before I left. Cut a girl a break.

I finished the rest of my ice cream and checked out the view from my family's digs. Great views of the capital city of Sauerhausen: old buildings mixed with new. A pretty castle sat on a hill in the distance. I squinted. It looked like it had a moat around it. Seriously—castles still have moats?

I was past tired, but perhaps my adrenaline had kicked in. I pushed myself off the couch, held the bowl close to my chest and wandered down a hallway.

I found my way into the kitchen. It was large, immaculate and filled with shiny, state-of-the art appliances. Oil paintings of fruit lined the walls. I rinsed the dish in one of three stainless steel sinks, opened the cabinets beneath them and searched for detergent. I foraged through twelve drawers and cupboards until a woman barked, "Elizabeth! Vat are you doings in my kitchen?"

I swiveled and saw a short, older woman who looked like the salt half of a salt and peppershaker set. I recognized her from my tutoring sessions with Lady and the Damp. She was Helga: chief cook and bottle washer for the Billingsley family since Elizabeth was seventeen-years-old. "I'm looking for soap—"

"Hah-hah! Youz alwayz crackers me up, Elizabeth." She leaped on me, encircled me with her arms and smothered me in a bear hug. If a bear could be four foot eight inches tall.

"Oof!" I gingerly hugged her back.

She laughed and released me. "You need ze rest. I vill

vash. Vat az you stinking?"

I lifted one arm and sniffed my armpit: I was indeed a little stinky. "Sorry about that."

"Not stinky—stinking." She grabbed the ice cream bowl from me. "You needs to go to bed. Sleep. Now."

I feared there were many bedrooms in this condo and I didn't know which one I was supposed to go to.

"The condo looks a little different than last time I was here. Which bedroom is mine?"

"Ack. The new fiancée, Duchess Carolina von Sauerhausen." Helga crinkled up her nose. "She loves her fanzty-pantsy designer remodels. Your bedroom is the red one of course. The red one will alvays be yourz." She slapped my ass with a towel and I jumped. "Go!"

"Thanks!" I exited the kitchen, padded barefoot down the marble hallway and paused at the first tall, wooden door. I wiggled the knob, cracked open the door and peeked inside. There was a queen bed with a big, blue canopy. Not red—not mine. I closed the door and wandered yards to the next one. Tried the handle: it opened readily. This room had a king bed with a black and gold canopy. *Not mine.*

Ten yards later I turned right for the heck of it down another hallway, poked my head inside a third doorway and broke out in a sweat. There was a ginormous, sunken hot tub in the center of the room. Metallic rails lined the steps leading down into the steaming waters. The entire room smelled like eucalyptus. Yummy.

One wall was lined with open-faced, tall, wooden cubicles filled with white, cushy towels and robes. There was an adjustable weight-lifting bench and a container of stacked dumbbells lined up next to it.

This exercise/playroom was filled with expensive toys: a 72" flat-screen TV hung high on the wall, a Ping-Pong table positioned on one end, an old-fashioned jukebox sat on a diagonal in the corner. A kitchenette was tucked in the other corner.

Except for a quick nap on British Air and passing out, I'd been up for well over twenty-four hours and desperately needed to sleep. Steam wisped from the simmering hot tub waters. It looked so warm and relaxing—it could soothe my aching muscles. I remembered the mineral waters at the Drake Hotel. This spa beckoned me, practically called my name. But I had no bathing suit.

Whatever.

I stripped off my clothes and tossed them on the floor. My underwear would suit me just fine. I leaned down, set the timer for five minutes and the waters bubbled to life. I placed one foot on the first stair that descended into the tub when I remembered Zara and Mr. Philip's lesson: *How to be Naked like a European Lady.*

I glanced around. I was completely alone. I listened— didn't hear a peep. The windows in the room were high on the walls and covered completely by blinds. And I was finally in Europe—now was as good a time as any. I stepped out of the water, unclipped my front-hook bra, pulled the straps down my shoulders, shrugged out of it and tossed it onto my clothes pile. Shimmied out of my panties and pitched them as well.

I was buck naked in the middle of a room I'd never even been in before, in a filthy rich penthouse condo, in a foreign country. I did a quick happy dance to celebrate my progress in conquering my modesty and then stepped into the tub's soothing waters. "Aah." I sighed, leaned my head back against the tiled side and flinched when that touched the painful bump on my noggin.

I flipped over onto my stomach, placed my arms on top of the hot tub's tiled lip, turned my head to the side and rested one cheek as my legs splayed out behind me. I sighed. "The perfect end to my not-so-perfect day," I said.

"Actually I'd call that the perfect 'rear-end' to my almost perfect day," Nick said.

I snapped my head up and saw him standing in front of me, still dressed in the clothes he wore on the plane, wearing a big fat grin on his face.

"Ack!" I screamed and ducked under the water.

CHAPTER 16

"Lizzie?" I heard Nick shout in the distance.

I blinked under the shallow pool and attempted to cover my private parts with both my hands. Unfortunately, I had three private part areas and only two hands. So I settled for my boobs and crotch.

"Lizzie! Lizzie! Are you drowning? Do you need me to rescue you?"

I peeked my head above the choppy waters and glared at him. "No! What are you doing here? Never mind. Go away!"

"I texted Joan Brady. She said they'd dropped you off at your dad's condo. I wanted to make sure you were okay."

"Except for the fact that you have no boundaries, I'm feeling fine, thank you. Who let you in?"

"A short, round woman. She said you were headed for bed, but I insisted that I needed to see you or I'd worry the entire night."

"Okay you saw me." I said. "Now go!"

"But I have a question for you."

"Leave!"

"But it's my turn."

I. Was. Going. To. Kill. This. Man.

"Fine!" I said. "Ask away. I like both dogs and cats equally. I vote for whomever I want. I believe in freedom of speech, marriage equality and breaking the glass ceiling. Kindness is my religion. I consider myself a feminist. I like reading mysteries, romance and thrillers. I don't like bullies or snobby people who think they're better than you or me just because they have more money or nicer clothes or went to a better school. My favorite season is autumn. I don't watch reality TV shows except for the musical stuff."

"Good to know. But that's not my question."

"Then ask it and leave, I beg you!"

He leaned down toward me, winked and then whispered. "Who looks really sexy when she's wearing only bubbles?"

When the hot tub's timer clicked off and I realized that very soon there would be no bubbles. I widened my eyes, swiveled my head and stared at the door. "Oh my God!" I sacrificed my hand that was covering my nether regions, shot gunned it out of the water and pointed. "What's that?"

Nick turned and stared. I took that moment to pull myself half out of the water, jam the timer back on and sink back in.

"Oh, it's you again," Nick said.

And just when I thought today couldn't get worse?

Cristoph strode into the room, pushed past Nick and knelt next to the Jacuzzi. "Cheryl Cavitt Carlson texted me and said that the hospital had released you." He frowned. "But you hit your head. Should you be in the Jacuzzi? Isn't that dangerous?"

"I was wondering the same thing," Nick said.

"Okay it's decided," Cristoph said. "Time for you to get out of that tub right now." He held out his hand to me.

Nick also held out his hand to me. "I'll help you. Like always."

Cristoph glared at him. "I don't even know what you're doing here, dude."

"The same thing you are, man. Just making sure Lizzie's okay."

"I'm not getting out of this tub now or any time soon. Something really important would have to happen to make me get out of this tub," I said. "You both need to leave—now."

"No, Nick needs to leave." Cristoph pulled out that damn black velvet jewelry box, popped the lid open and held it in front me. "I'd say this is important. Marry me Elizabeth?"

"I'm sleep deprived, Cristoph. I'm exhausted. I'm overwhelmed by your offer—like seriously I'm all a tingle—"

"That's just the extra strong, strategically placed water jet talking," Nick said.

"Zip it!" I shot him a dirty look and then smiled at Cristoph. "I need to sleep on your incredible question and I'll give you an answer tomorrow."

"She'll answer your question tomorrow," Nick said.

"Who died and put you in charge Nick? Oh and hah! That would never happen. You just want more time to influence and change her mind," Cristoph said. "You hit your head thousands of times in soccer tournaments, Elizabeth. I know because I watched you and cheered from the sidelines. You were always fine after those games. Always knew exactly what you wanted: vanilla ice cream and lots of it."

"You used Elizabeth's soccer tournaments to pick up the girls who were a few years older than her," Nick said.

"Like you didn't?" Cristoph asked.

I stared at the timer and watched as precious bubbly seconds ticked away.

"Once," Nick said. "How many times for you? Twenty? Thirty? Or is that number conservative? Besides, Elizabeth likes chocolate ice cream," Nick said. "The darker the better."

"Might I remind you, *I am* the Crown Prince of Fredonia," Cristoph said. "I am the heir apparent. As much as I like you, dude, I get first dibs—on everything."

"Elizabeth is not a dib!" I yelled.

They turned and stared at me confused.

"I mean—*I am not a dib.* Or maybe I am. What's a dib?" I whistled under my breath.

Carolina walked into the room and spotted the guys and me. She stopped in her tracks and fanned her face.

I waved one hand in the air. "Help?" I mouthed.

"Damaged goods," Nick said. "You still want her, Cristoph, if she's damaged goods?"

I glared at him. "No way you just called me damaged

goods?"

"Everyone here needs to call it a night," Carolina pulled it together and strode into the room. "You need to go home, gentlemen. There will be no decisions made and no important questions answered tonight."

I looked at Carolina and smiled. *Thank God someone was looking out for me.* When I heard boisterous hollering. "Get out of town, bitch!" A familiar female voice said.

"Esmeralda you know the best tapas and tequila joints in every country." Cheryl squealed as she slid through the doorway, landed on her ass and giggled uncontrollably. "Like seriously—you're gifted."

"There's been a mistake, ladies," Carolina frowned. "Even though you are Elizabeth's dear friends, this isn't an appropriate time. I invite you to visit tomorrow: for tea and scones."

"Lizzie?" Joan slurred and waved a gigantic tequila bottle in front of me. "Lizzie, I see three gorgeous men, one of you and I insist you answer Mischief's question. Are you going to marry him? Because if you don't? I will."

"No-no, Joan. I'm going to marry him," Cheryl said. "Prince Cristoph, I, Lady Cheryl Cavitt Carlson accept your ring. I will be your wife in sickness and in health, in—"

"You're already married," Joan said.

"Crap," Cheryl said. "I'll initiate divorce proceedings tomorrow. Give me the rose." She burped. "Oops, sorry. That's the enchiladas talking."

"Lizzie! He's a prince. He's gorgeous," Joan said. "He totally loves you!"

"No he doesn't," Nick said.

"I do love you, Elizabeth," Cristoph said. "I always have."

"Everyone needs to leave." Carolina clapped her hands. "Now!"

I peered around Carolina at Nick, Cristoph and the Ladies.

"For God's sake, Elizabeth, grow a backbone!" Esmeralda swiped the tequila bottle from Joan. "Don't you know what you want?"

"No. Maybe. I'm tired. Can I figure this out tomorrow?"

"Do you remember that time we attended the Running of the Bulls in Pamplona?" Esmeralda asked.

"Yes," I lied.

"Remember that brute of an animal with the huge tusks that careened through the streets while men raced in front of it and screamed like little girls?"

"How could I forget?"

"Remember the hairy, sweaty guy who was gored?"

I shuddered. "Ew."

"You said, 'Whoa, that's one big tusk and he'll be feeling that tomorrow.'"

"I bet he did," I said.

"You squeezed my hand and made me promise to remind you about the power of a big tusk?"

"You're absolutely right."

"I have it on good authority that Prince Cristoph has a big—"

"Ladies!" Carolina coughed. "Elizabeth has had an extremely long day."

"And she could be signing up to be Queen of Fredonia

135

and married to a King with a big tusk. She could have it all," Esmeralda said.

"Guards!" Carolina shouted.

Two muscular guards dressed in snappy black suits materialized at the door.

Oh God, could this get any worse?

"Yes Duchess?" one guard asked.

"Escort Prince Cristoph and Nicholas as well as the Ladies to their limos, please. Make sure no one is driving themselves home tonight."

The guards bowed.

Joan sighed. "Get up Cheryl." She grabbed her wrist. "Come on. Your husband and wee ones are waiting. We're out of here."

"Therein lies the problem. The wee ones are always weeing. And peeing and pooping," Cheryl said. "I thought becoming a mother would make me feel motherly. Not like I needed to soak in a tub of anti-bacterial soap every day."

Esmeralda grabbed Cheryl's other wrist and they dragged her out of the room.

"What about—" Cristoph said.

Carolina bowed her head. "Tomorrow." She grabbed a white bathrobe from a wall cubicle and shook it out. "Come back with your question tomorrow, Prince Cristoph."

The room went a little fuzzy, but this time I didn't black out. This time I held it together as I waved goodbye to the gorgeous men and my Ladies.

Carolina handed me a robe, turned while I exited the tub and shrugged it on. "I'm so sorry," I said.

She held up one hand. "Look. You've been gone for a while. You aren't really up to date on all that's going on around here. Everyone's excited you're back and things just got a little out of hand. I'm not sharing this with your papa by the way."

"Thank God!" I said as she led me by the hand to my very red bedroom, pulled back the cushy duvet cover and tucked me into bed. "Thank you again, Carolina. You are very kind."

"You're welcome. I only want what is best for you, your father and our beloved Fredonia. I left you some water on the nightstand. Tomorrow will be a better day, yes? Welcome home." She leaned down and kissed me on my forehead.

Her lips were cool and I couldn't help the small shudder that rippled like a wave through me.

"Interesting?" She gazed at me.

"I think you're mistaken." I shook my head. "I'm not all that interesting."

"Not you—your photos," she said. "In pictures you look like a natural blonde. But in person you're definitely more brunette." She patted my arm. "Sleep tight, Elizabeth. Don't let those bad dreams bite." She smiled and left the room.

CHAPTER 17

I spent the majority of the night tossing and turning, checking my phone for texts and e-mails as I waited for a reply from Lady and the Damp, and/or E, on how I should best handle this Cristoph engagement debacle. I suddenly felt parched and drank a little water. But Fredonia's water had a funny acidy taste. *Blech.* Note to Self/Lucy: buy bottled water as long I was here.

But the bigger question remained: *should I say yes to Cristoph's proposal?* Or should I say no? Hold out? Delay? Ack, it was too much for a real Lady to figure out, let alone an imposter from the Southside of Chicago. This part-time job was not going according to plan. I finally fell asleep in the darkest of night and awoke, God knows how many minutes or hours later, when someone shook my arm roughly.

"What?" I asked.

"The incredible handsome Mr. Philip Philips ees on ze line for yous. He says ees urgent." Helga thrust the landline phone into my face. "That I must wakes you up."

I gazed up into her beet red face and accepted the phone. "Thanks."

She pointed to the side table as she cleared the water that I'd barely sipped and replaced it with a steaming mug of coffee. "Drink."

I did. "So nice of you to finally call, Damp," I said. "I could be dead, you know. At the very least I have a sizeable lump on my head."

"Page fifty-four in the contract, paragraph three, states that we provide reasonable medical reimbursement for job-related injuries. I've been trying to get through to you for hours. Your cell isn't accepting any texts. You need to reset it to factory mode and start over."

"Factory mode? My last job was in a bar, not a factory."

"You said you could improvise."

"Of course I can improvise. But with people and situations—not electronic devices. Did you know Elizabeth once danced topless at a nightclub on the Algarve? What's an Algarve?" I paced the room. "Is that like Rush Street in Chicago? Freaking kill me now." I threw one hand up in the air.

"We bought that video footage and destroyed it. Who told you about that?"

"Esmeralda, who seems to know Elizabeth's darkest secrets. Cheryl Cavitt Carlson who is fond of tequila. And Joan Brady who rocks a sassy, red hairdo."

"Aah, yes, apparently you've met the rest of Elizabeth's Ladies-in-Waiting."

"What do you mean, 'The rest?'"

"You already know Zara."

"The tight-ass make-over queen?" My hand flew to my chest. *"She's one of my Ladies-in-Waiting?* Do you think you should have told me about the Ladies and more importantly this Prince Cristoph engagement thing before I ventured to Fredonia? And who is this Nick character?"

Mr. Philip Philips inhaled sharply. "I saw the footage of Nick on the tarmac with you and the marching band. Did anything of a… delicate nature happen between the two of you?"

"Yes, I mean no, I mean—what the hell do you care? Prince Cristoph keeps proposing to Elizabeth. What am I supposed to say? Yes, no, maybe-so? Is she going to marry him?"

I jumped out of bed and paced when I spotted camera crews and vans parked twenty plus flights below our building. At least fifteen cameras angled up toward my window. "Crap!" I dropped onto my butt, hopefully out of sight. "Does she even want to marry him?"

"Technically, yes. Elizabeth plans to marry Cristoph. She had no idea he'd propose so quickly. She thought you'd take her place for a few weeks—"

"It was supposed to be ten days tops," I said.

"Does it matter? She'll pay you more each day you're in Fredonia. Elizabeth thought you'd attend several state dinners and flirt a little. She believed that she'd be back in plenty of time to accept Cristoph's proposal and prepare a proper royal wedding."

Helga walked into the adjoining bathroom. "Running warm tub for you, Stinkzys."

"You're a peach!"

"No probs." She waved a hand at me.

I swiveled away from Helga and placed a protective hand over the phone. "I'm not dumb you know, Damp. If I accept Cristoph's proposal, the shit's going to hit Fredonia's majestic fan. Did you even see the local media coverage of The Royal Engagement Debacle? Fox-Fredonia aired a close up of my panties. They featured a half hour news special on the making of the lace. *I was humiliated!*" I grabbed the mug and slugged back the rest of the coffee.

"Actually," Mr. Philips said. "*Elizabeth* was humiliated. Because Lucille Trabbicio has never been to Fredonia, never passed out on a tarmac and not one single camera ever filmed up her pretty skirts. At least not one camera in Fredonia."

"You did not just say that!"

"Besides, Elizabeth has never held down a full-time job, let alone a part-time job."

"I. Am. Going. To kill. The three of you."

"We are holding our collective breath."

"Your tub awaits stinkzys girl," Helga said. "I have new loofah. So exciting!" She waved it high up in the air. "Very scratchy!" She disappeared into the bathroom.

"Awesome! Just give me one sec." I rolled over onto my stomach on the bed and scrunched my mouth next to the phone. "Look Damp. If I say yes to Cristoph, I'll be enduring even more media scrutiny. While I'm great at improvising and rolling with the punches? This feels like a big freaking gut sucker punch and I'm not sure I can do this on my own. *When* is Elizabeth is showing up in Fredonia? *When* are you showing up? Or at the very least—Zara?"

"A week tops. We didn't expect this turn of events, but this is also why we hired you. We trained you, did the makeover and paid the big signing bonus for this. Every detail—including this possibility—is covered in your contract."

"There was nothing in my contract that said I had to handle this alone."

"I didn't plan on undergoing disc surgery tomorrow."

I winced. "Crap, Philips. Are you going to be okay?"

"I should be able to travel in a week, ten days. Zara is with Elizabeth but has assured me that she will be winging her way to Fredonia in approximately seventy-two hours. Can you hold tight for four days, Lucille?"

"I think. But what if all hell breaks loose and I can't do this on my own? Is there anyone here who can help me?"

"The Ladies-in-Waiting," he said. "They're opinionated, a pain in the royal toucas, as well as commoners' buttocks, but they're also incredibly loyal—to Elizabeth. Ask the Ladies for assistance until we get there: I doubt that they'd let you down. But whatever you do—*don't tell them you're not Elizabeth.* Except for Zara, the Ladies are not privy to our secret business arrangement. The last thing you want is for them to turn against you."

"But they seem so nice? What's the worst that could happen?"

"Trust me on this Groucho—you don't want to know."

I soaked in the deep, lavender infused bath waters and allowed Helga to scrub me from head to toe and then dry me off with the cushiest towel I'd ever felt. While it felt really weird to let someone give me a bath, I had protested fifty times and she countered that this was part of her job fifty times. I finally caved to her demands because she was so determined.

She vigorously slapped moisturizer on me from head to toe. While I might be bruised tomorrow, my skin would be incredibly hydrated and smooth as a baby's ass. She helped me pull on one of Elizabeth's very soft robes.

I was finally clean and less stinkzys, but was still losing what little remained of my mind. I had to blow out of this beautiful penthouse prison. Yes, I'd been informed that Elizabeth never exercised. But I needed to workout, burn some steam and get a grip. If someone called me on it, I'd just say Elizabeth had fallen in love with exercising when she was in America.

I spotted her designer suitcases lined up against her bedroom wall like soldiers in formation wearing dress uniforms. I walked the few feet toward them, kneeled down onto the plush carpet and dove in. I tossed Gucci, Pucci and Dior garments into a pile onto the floor as I prowled for workout clothes. With the exception of red velvet-lined handcuffs and a matching velvet-lined leather mask, I found nothing athletically inclined. And then I realized I'd forgotten to bring my Nike cross-trainers. Crap.

I yanked open the door to her huge walk-in-closet, tiptoed inside and peeked around. I gasped at the sheer enormity of the place and crossed myself. This room was a shopaholic's dream come true, and quite possibly a shrine to the Patron Saint of Women's Fine Clothing.

I rifled through full-length designer gowns, cocktail

dresses, business suits and upscale everyday attire. My hands caressed and lingered on the designer fabrics, perfect cuts and gorgeous designs. But as much as I longed to say yes? I forced my hands away from these delectables because these were all no, no, no! I was running out of time and out of luck when I poked my nose in the very back of the closet and discovered a small stash of exercise gear. Halle-freaking-lujah!

I shrugged out of Elizabeth's robe, pulled on yoga capris, a stretchy top, a cute hoodie and even scored cross-trainers that appeared nearly brand spanking new, resting in a shoebox. They were a size 9 and I was a size 7 ½, but really who cared at this point? Well, actually me—because when I tried them on and did a few jumping jacks, I wobbled like a tipsy sailor.

I could easily trip, fall and break an arm. I yanked them off, grabbed packing paper from the box, crumpled it up, shoved them in the toes and pulled the shoes back on. A little scratchy but a much more solid fit. I stomped my feet on the ground—I could live with this.

I bolted into the bathroom and stared into the mirror. I looked like the Crypt Keeper: old, exhausted and dried-up. Oh-so-attractive. *Not*. I dabbed on eye concealer, swiped on a coat of mascara, as well as tinted lip balm. I tied my hair back in a ponytail, slipped on my sunglasses and squinted at my reflection.

Now I resembled your basic twenty-something, slightly-athletic, hung-over chick. Not too cute, not too coiffed. Someone who could fit in with the masses of young-ish, post-Saturday night bar-hopping, fitness girls in just about any big city. Much better.

But what if the paparazzi were still lurking below? How would I escape their cameras? I grabbed Elizabeth's sunglasses from the bathroom sink and slipped them on. There had to be a back way out of this building. I peeked out from my bedroom mirror and saw the news vans pulling away from the curb below. Huh? Most likely some real news had come up.

I strode down the condo's hallways, turning right, turning left, turning around, whatever—this place was like a labyrinth—until I spotted the foyer and front door. Holy mother of Toledo, freedom was in sight. I reached for the doorknob when I realized if I left the condo—I had no key to get back in.

I turned and spotted Helga shlepping a load of fresh towels in one arm flush against her chest; a large, empty wicker laundry basket dangled from her other hand. "Let me help you with that," I said. "Hey—by any chance do you have a spare key to the joint? I seem to have misplaced mine."

"No Lizbet." She froze in her tracks, frowned and shifted her substantial body weight from foot to foot, the stack of towels wavering.

"You sure?" I walked the few steps toward her. "Hand me some towels. Or that basket?" *Why wouldn't she give me a key?*

She backed away, her eyes widening. "You never offered to help me evah before. Are you sick? Is it the head-hitting thing? Do I need to call 411?"

"I'm fine," I said. "Spending time in the States changed me. In the Midwest, lots of folks offer to help other people. It's kind of like saying hello. Or—How are you doing?" I yanked half the stack of towels from her arms. "Where are we going with this?"

"Oh, Lady. I don't know." She clucked. "I thinks you should geeve dose back to me. Ees not your job."

"You'd be surprised at what my job entails. Stop complaining and lead the way."

CHAPTER 18

Helga clucked as we backtracked into the bowels of the penthouse—dropping off fresh towels into the bathrooms and retrieving the used ones, plopping them into the basket.

The sixth bathroom was by far the fanciest: gilded crown moldings, a gorgeous hand-painted mural of naked young men and women on the ceiling, marble countertops filled with crystal perfume bottles with names like Chanel and Poison and Obsession. Small brown prescription pill bottles were shoved in a corner, as well as brown glass vials filled with liquid concoctions and capped with squeeze droppers.

"Whose bathroom is this?" I asked.

"Who else? The Duchess." Helga yanked the towels off the racks, the washcloths lying on the marble countertop between the double sinks and replaced them with fresh linens.

"Duchess Carolina looks so young and beautiful," I said. "Do you think these are her secret anti-aging concoctions?" I unscrewed the top of one vial, held it to my nose and sniffed its contents.

Helga slapped my hand. "No Lizbet!"

I dropped the vial: it fell and shattered onto the marble floor. "Crap!" I kneeled and reached toward its remains as thin wisps of smoke curled up from its splinters into the air. "That's some serious skin-care product."

"Glycolic peel," Carolina said from the doorway. "Stimulates collagen re-growth in skin tissue. Rejuvenates one's complexion."

Helga burst into tears. "I am sorry Duchess!"

"There's plenty more of that or every woman over forty would be in big trouble," Carolina said. "Hand me one of those towels."

Helga did but I intercepted it. "This was totally my fault," I said. "I'll find some way to repay you." I mopped up the gooey concoction and the glass shards. "How long have you and Papa been dating?"

"Practically a year."

"Six months." Helga sniffed.

I pitched the soiled rag in the wastebasket, stood up and washed my hands. "Papa seems so happy. Remind me again how you met?"

"We were introduced by friends," Carolina said.

"You met on the Internet," Helga said. "Plenty-of-Royals-in-the-Seas.com."

"You know that's not true," Carolina said. "Papa and I shared our first date at Baron Pfefferhoofen's annual Rose

Ball. I fear Helga's simply a hopeless romantic." She smiled.

"Hopeful romantic. Beeg difference. I joined Plenty-of-Royals too," Helga said.

"Seriously?" I asked. "I didn't know you wanted to date again after your beloved husband…," *what was his name again? Rhymed with Pervert…*

"It's been ten years since my Herbert died." She dropped the toilet lid, plopped down and fanned herself.

"There are so many Internet dating sites. Helga, I don't want to sound elitist—but why Plenty-of-Royals?" Carolina asked.

"Herbert was Master Hounds Keeper of Queen Cheree Timmel's Labrador Retriever Sanctuary. He was titled—that made him practically royalty."

Carolina arched one eyebrow.

"Of course it did," I said.

"Besides, Groupon offered a month trial Plenty-of-Royals for only ten euros. How could I resist?" Helga asked.

"I did Groupon for a month of Brazilian martial arts as well as unlimited henna tattoos." I nodded. "I learned how to throw a punch and looked like a badass circus side-show freak for six weeks! Score!" I held up my hand and high-fived Helga.

Carolina's hand flew to her chest. "I beg you, don't tell your father. What happens in the States stays in the States."

Shit! I had just shared my life—not Elizabeth's. *Note to Self/Lucy: don't get too comfortable and slip up.*

"One day, by complete random accident—" Helga bit her lower lip. "I logged onto Papa Billingsley's Plenty-of-

Royals account. I saw your profile on his page, Duchess. You were so young-ish and beautiful. I knew he couldn't resist you."

"*'Young-ish?'* Oh, what does it matter how we met." Carolina threw her hands up in the air. "We've been like two crazy kids in love ever since that day. I have had more fun with your father in the last nine months than I've had in years."

I hope that meant they went out to dinner a lot, went dancing and attended art exhibits. By the time we strode down the hallway, back toward the front door, I needed to exercise so badly my skin was practically crawling. "I really need my own key to the penthouse." I said. "The locks have been changed, right?"

"Of course, darling." Carolina slid open a drawer on a side table in the foyer, pulled out a set of keys and handed them to me. "But Prince Cristoph phoned this morning—twice, might I add—the second time from the royal limo. He's on his way here to speak with you. Maybe you should wait a bit longer?"

I pulled my hair, twisting a chunk of it between my fingers. "I might have been a couch potato—I mean—fancy potatoes au gratin before—but in the States, I learned working out helps control my stress." I snapped off a few strands of hair and stared at them lying lifeless in my palm. "Cristoph can hold off on his big question until after I exercise." I shoved the keys in my pocket and raced out the door.

"Ooh," Helga said. "Still fiery. I luff dat!"

My first trip jogging around Sauerhausen's majestic

Centralaski Park I heard squeaks emanating from towering trees high overhead. I glanced up and spotted fat, perky squirrels perched on branches nibbling on acorns as they chatted with their furry friends about their scores. I ran past a picturesque pond with porky ducks that quacked loudly to the passersby, insisting they needed more crumbs.

My second time circling the park I thought about Alida, my BFF, and wondered how Uncle John was doing at Vail Assisted Living. I'd find time to call them and check in. My third time sprinting on the dirt path in this outdoor wonderland, I was sweating like a horse being worked for a big race and fantasized about Nick kissing me—which apparently wasn't the smartest thing to do as I ran into a low-to-the ground sausage dog and kicked him several feet into the bushes.

The mutt's ancient female owner scrunched up her face. "Dog hater!" She hissed.

"That's not true!" I said. "I love dogs. I've always wanted a dog!"

The pooch yelped, groaned, sighed and was then deathly quiet. I freaked out, thinking I had killed an innocent creature, raced to his motionless body, kneeled down and gave him chest compressions and mouth-to-mouth resuscitation. After thirty seconds he thumped his tail on the ground and stuck his tongue down my throat.

Frankly, it wasn't the worst kiss of my life. I pulled myself off his drooley lips, palpated his long body for broken bones, when his owner suggested I meet her and Romeo the dachshund for 'special' play time every afternoon.

My fourth time around Centralaski Park I realized I

hadn't worked out in two weeks. Which was the reason my heart was pounding like wildfire and my legs felt like noodles.

I stopped for a moment to catch my breath when I spotted two spit-shiny black Mercedes SUVs surrounded by a few beefy bodyguards wearing black suits, matching sunglasses and earpieces.

Five news crews camped out next to them, several hundred yards in front of me. A pretty, young, coiffed female reporter with ducklips was accompanied by her van with a satellite dish on the roof, a cameraman and a driver.

Ducklips gazed up and batted her eyelashes at one gorgeous blonde guy in a perfectly fitted suit.

Prince Cristoph of Fredonia held a ginormous bouquet of red roses cradled in the crook of one arm and a black velvet box in his opposite hand. He talked animatedly with her while a string quartet practiced "I Can't Help Falling in Love with You" by Elvis Presley, in the near background. His bodyguards fidgeted and paced around them in a tight circle.

I doubted they'd spotted me—*yet*—so I dodged into a thick hedge of bushes surrounded by pine trees, dropped my ass onto the dirt ground and clamped my hands firmly over my ears. "No!" I mumbled as I rocked back and forth. "I can't freaking do this again. I just came here for a little cardio, to burn some steam and feel like Lucy Marie Trabbicio. *I need to feel normal—again.*"

When a big, tall, gorgeous guy with jet-black hair pulled the tree branches apart and squeezed into my hiding place. "If it's steam you want to burn, Lizzie, well, we've always been good at that," Nick said.

I gasped, fell backward and caught myself on one elbow, my gaze directly in line with his crotch.

Dear God the man was packing. And I didn't think that was a pistol in his pocket.

"What are you doing here?" I asked.

"Didn't you get my message that Cristoph was setting up this whole freak show in Centralaski Park? What the hell are you doing here? And who is Lucy-whatever-her-name-is? Why do you want to feel like her?" He held out his hand to me and helped me to sitting. "And I'm sorry, but I'm worried about you and brought you some organic dark chocolate." He pulled an extra-large dark chocolate bar from his pants pocket and handed it to me.

"Thank you!" I peeled back the wrapper and took a bite. "This is so sweet of you."

Get real, Lucy I told myself. It wasn't that sweet. I couldn't allow Nick to blow Elizabeth's secret, ruin my mission and get me fired from my job.

"Lucy's a friend from Chicago, and she's well, relatively normal." I munched. "And she's nice, funny and she plays a mean game of… Ping Pong."

"Table tennis?" He asked.

"Whatever. Some people even think she's cute." I finished the chocolate bar.

"Ah." He raised his eyebrows. "Is she a *special friend?* Is this why you've been resisting my boyish charms?"

When it dawned on me… "I'm not—I mean Elizabeth's not—I mean Lucy's not—we're not wired that way. But might I add we have *nothing* against folks who are wired that way. And you're too old to have 'boyish charms.' You big dork."

He frowned. "No one's called me a dork since the

fourth grade."

"Then you're long overdue," I said. "How did you find me? Did you secretively implant a car-jack device on me?"

"Nah." He smiled. "I splurged for the Princess-jack device. More expensive—but obviously worth it. Kidding!"

"That sounds a bit pervy."

"According to the gossip rags—almost everything I say sounds a bit pervy." He plunked down next to me on the dirt ground. "I phoned your place and talked to Helga. She said you were out exercising somewhere nearby. Had to be the park. Again with the exercising thing Lizzie. I'm confused as to why you suddenly love to exercise?"

"Have you ever had Chicago deep-dish pizza? It's delish, but it can put a few pounds on, if you know what I mean."

He nodded. "Honestly—the pizza pounds look really good on you."

"Thanks. For now. What about in twenty years?"

"I hope I'll know you in twenty years. Know you really well and be able to comment positively on that." He grinned.

Since last I'd seen Nick, he'd showered and shaved. He was wearing jeans and a V-neck T-shirt that showed off the black curls on his chest, as well as the fact that he was buff as all get-out. He smelled like sage or cedar. Not strong enough to be a men's cologne. Most likely expensive soap. Delicious, intoxicating and—frankly—totally not fair!

My job description did not include me getting all hot and bothered over some dude who was a zillion times out of my dating league. He might not have been a Prince, but he obviously hung out in royal circles.

Note to Self-aka-Lucy: *I was not here to date.*

"I owe you an apology," he said.

"For what?"

"When I saw you on the plane, all curvy and glowy with gorgeous hair—I kind of over-reacted. I behaved like an entitled asshole. I assumed our past meant that we could just take up where we left off. I'm sorry."

"Really?" I pushed a skinny tree branch out of my ear but it boomeranged and slapped his face. "Oops, I'm sorry."

"Don't worry about it." He tugged a leafy twig out of his right nostril and sneezed. "Really. And that was a stupid move on my part. I didn't think that you'd grown and moved on during that year-plus-change that we didn't have contact. But you have done all of those things. You're a different person, Elizabeth. A better person."

Wow. I can't believe he even acknowledged that. "So does that mean you want to, you want to…'" I felt my face as well as other body parts turn warm, then hot, then tingling. I fanned my face and reminded my hand not to fan any other over-heated body parts. "…*be with me?*"

CHAPTER 19

"Of course I want to be with you." Nick lowered his voice. "But everything would have to be on the hush-hush. We'd have to keep it private. We could never speak of it in public. Or acknowledge it—even to our closest friends. But Lizzie?" He reached for and held my hand. Caressed it. Pulled it to his lips and kissed the back of it.

Shivers traveled up and down my spine and the backs of my arms grew goose bumps.

"I could live with that if you could," Nick said. "It wouldn't be easy for me, but—"

"Hold on. Wait a second." I yanked my hand away. "You're saying that you want to be with me on the QT—like we'd be lovers? Or I'd be your mistress or something?"

He nodded. "Kind of. Yeah. I guess. I've always liked you. As crazy as this sounds, my feelings have grown substantially over all this time we've spent together."

"Including the time change," I glanced at my new designer watch, "that's been under three days."

"Three days which feels like three months or quite possibly a year." He ran his fingers up and down the inside of my forearm. "I always assumed you and I were just slap and tickle. That we were simply sexually drawn to each other. Like salt and pepper. Or cheese and an omelet."

"Salt and pepper are sexual?"

"No! I just meant that they're great together."

"Oh." I frowned. "Are you saying I'm cheese?"

"No! You're the omelet. Gorgeous. Fluffy. Tasty. Irresistible."

I peered down in horror at my quivering thighs. Had two weeks without exercise turned them into… "Pudding's fluffy. Persian cats are fluffy. Marshmallows are fluffy. What about me screams fluffy?"

And it better not be my thighs.

"Calm down! Jeez, you're so feisty lately. Although I admit—that's a total turn-on. Listen—these feelings took me by surprise. You've grown from a girl into a woman in less than two years. A woman I think about, dream about and frankly—do other things about. But ultimately, I fear my dearest Lizzie, you're a woman I cannot officially be with. Because you, by contract, are promised to Cristoph."

"Hmm," I said. "You obviously know each other. The other day on the tarmac it seemed like you knew each other pretty well."

I peeked through the leaves and watched gorgeous, blonde Prince Cristoph pace back and forth in front of the TV reporter lady all the while proclaiming his undying love for Elizabeth.

"Of course we do," Nick said. "We're really close and then sometimes we're not. Wait a minute. Is this the brain trauma talking? You do remember that we're—"

"Shh!" I pressed my index finger to his lips for a moment. "I need to hear this."

"I've been friends with Elizabeth for years," Cristoph said. "She's delightful, funny, smart, gorgeous, educated. We've practically grown up together. Our friendship has turned to love. I would be the happiest man in the world if she would consent to be my bride."

"Blah, blah, blah. Just like most politics—it's all fucking bullshit," Nick said. "I on the other hand, am offering you a genuine opportunity."

"Let me get this straight," I said. "The opportunity you're offering me is to be your whore?"

"Good God no! I'm asking you to be my mistress! It's a time-honored tradition. Look at Diane de Poitiers with King Henry II from France. She was his consort for over twenty-five years."

"But Prince Cristoph wants to *marry me*. He intends to make me his wife as well as the Princess of Fredonia. I would be first in line to be the Queen."

Actually Elizabeth would be first in line. That was part of what my job here entailed. Keep Cristoph happy until Elizabeth got her lady-like toucas back here. And then mine would be tucked in a narrow, coach class seat and shipped back to my less-than-ordinary, jobless life in America.

"Cristoph wants to marry you simply to seal the deal that your parents made almost twenty years ago. It's a business arrangement for him. He doesn't have feelings for you. *I do.*" Nick leaned forward and caressed my forehead, trailed a finger across my cheek. He tugged the elastic band off my ponytail and tossed it into the bushes. My hair escaped its bun, bounced off my shoulders and cascaded onto my upper back.

My heart raced in my chest and contemplated turning traitor to the reasonable thoughts in my head. "Litterer." I pushed him away. "I could have you arrested."

"Liberator," he said. "Let's do something indecent in a public place and get arrested for that instead. Way more fun—don't you think?"

"Orange jumpsuits don't suit me. Not the color or the cut."

"You're beautiful. No one gives a rat's ass what color you wear. You've got great hair. I don't remember your hair being this great." He rubbed a few locks of it between his thumb and forefinger and pulled me to him. My face toward his face. My lips toward his lips. "What's your secret?" He whispered.

If only he knew…

"I found a new hairdresser in America. D'Alba was a phat bitch. But he gave me a great cut." Our lips seemed to be drawn toward each other until they were simply one warm shared breath apart.

Nick wrapped one arm around my waist, pulled me to him and raked his fingers through my hair. "I'm applauding that phat bitch right now." He kissed me. And he kissed me like he meant it.

And even worse? I let him.

At first his lips on my mouth were soft. Then his kiss grew firmer, his tongue more insistent as he explored my mouth and gently bit my lower lip with his teeth.

Holy spitoli this guy was the best kisser of my entire life! How had I lived twenty-one years without being kissed like this?

When out of the corner of my eye I caught a glimpse of Cristoph glancing around the dirt path that circled Centralaski Park and then gazing at his watch hopefully. The Quartet amped up the volume and intensity of their song rehearsal.

What was I doing? What the hell was I doing? A prince wanted to marry me-I-mean-Elizabeth and I was throwing that all away for a handsome, sweet smartass who was the best kisser in the entire world?

"Stop!" I pushed Nick away. "We can't do this! I can't be your fool-around girl, or your mistress. Your best friend is waiting there," I pointed, "just yards away with a freaking wedding proposal on his brain."

He sighed. "It's a dilemma."

And I thought of my uncle back in Assisted Living and realized: *I had dilemmas too. This was my job. This was my employment.* Kissing Nick was not going to pay the bills. And as much as it pained me, I made my decision.

I pushed myself off the ground, stood up and brushed the dirt and leaves off my behind and T-shirt. "I wish kissing you was simple, Nick. But it's not. Maybe in a different lifetime or a different place or a different time."

"No, Lizzie. Please don't go. I feel like I just found you." He looked up at me and frowned. "Don't do this. I have this awful feeling that if you do this we will lose each other again. But this time it won't be temporary—it will be forever. This time we'll lose our Happily-Ever-After."

"I know for a fact I'm not the person you're meant to share your Happily-Ever-After with." I placed two fingers to my lips and then pressed them to his. "You're a pain in the ass, Nick, and yet you've been wonderful. I don't get it, but I really, really appreciate it. Thanks for everything." I squeezed back tears and kissed him quickly on his cheek. "Goodbye." I stumbled out of the bushes toward the newest version of the royal three-ring circus.

Cristoph spotted me, ran a few yards in my direction and dropped down on one knee. The quartet launched into an enthusiastic version of "I Can't Help Falling in Love with You" as a real Prince asked a fake Elizabeth to marry him.

And I blinked back tears that were caused by another man, exclaimed that I was the happiest girl in the world and yes, of course, I would marry Cristoph. He slipped the bunion ring on my oh-so-significant finger on my left hand. We kissed (somewhat awkwardly) and shed a few tears. The cameras captured it all.

I glanced back at the bushes surrounding my secret hiding place, where Nick took my breath away when kissed me just moments before. But I caught no glimpse of him.

He was gone.

I discovered later in that momentous, as well as monotonous, day, that for the first hour following Cristoph and Elizabeth's official engagement—we, the newly engaged royal Fredonia couple, were simply featured on local TV news channels.

I wore the sparkly bunion, while Cristoph's arm encircled my waist and he hugged me—PG rated of course, as well as camera-appropriate distance for official royalty PDA. We posed cheek to cheek as more photographers and news trucks showed up to snap photos, take videos and grab a few interviews.

A few reporters threw out questions that included:

"Prince Cristoph! When did you know Lady Elizabeth Theresa Billingsley was the right girl for you?

He smiled. "In grade school when I stole her doll and she fought back. She's always been feisty."

Laughter peeled from the on-lookers and looky-loos that quickly massed in the park.

"Prince Cristoph! Besides Prince Harry, you've been the most eligible bachelor on the royal circuit," a male reporter asked. "Why have you decided to settle down now?"

I overheard Ducklips whisper behind her palm to her cameraman, "Zoom in on her baby-bump." I sucked in my stomach and held my breath. I would not allow them to obtain cheap shots of my not-so-flat tummy just because I had a passion for Johnny's Chicago deep-dish pizza.

"Because I was scared my right girl would grow tired of waiting for me." Cristoph flashed his mesmerizing smile and showed his perfect white teeth. "And I didn't want to lose her." He leaned in and kissed me full on my lips.

Technically this was our second kiss, but I tried to make it seem like we'd been kissing forever. Perhaps I tried a bit too hard as applause crescendoed and I fluttered my eyes open. Only to spot Nick glaring daggers at us as he straddled a Harley-Davidson motorcycle idling a hundred plus yards away.

"Lady Elizabeth—you've been out of the public eye for over a year now," Ducklips said. "You've been pursuing advanced degrees at Marymount University in the State of Illinois in the United States. Did you know this was happening? Or was it a complete surprise to you upon returning to Fredonia?"

"I've always had a sweet spot for Prince Cristoph. Seriously, who hasn't?" I looked up at him adoringly and batted my eyelashes.

The female reporters giggled.

"But recently we've been more in touch: e-mails, phone calls, texting, Skype, even old-fashioned love letters. We're crazy about each other. I can't imagine a more perfect match than Cristoph and me. And if I don't say yes and I don't try this with someone who could be my best friend…" My gaze drifted toward Nick.

"Yes, Elizabeth?" Cristoph prompted.

My attention darted back to Cristoph and I smiled like I had just won five dollars on a lotto scratcher card. "I will forever wonder if we both missed out on something magical and wonderful. Something that was meant to be. Maybe I would have passed on my Happily-Ever-After. And how many people really get a chance at that?"

"Aw." The CNN-Fredonia reporter wiped a few tears away.

"Yeah," I wiped a few tears away too. "I mean yes."

Cristoph regarded me with a curious look in his beautiful eyes. He leaned down and muttered, "Seriously? After all our family bullshit, you're seriously interested in me?"

"Did you seriously fall in love with me in grade school?" I asked.

"It was either you or your super cool backpack," he said. "Maybe both."

I smiled. "I'm willing to give this engagement a shot. But only if you are too," I whispered. "No scandals from here on out. No sleeping with chambermaids or flight attendants or flirty newscasters with too much filler in their upper lips. Or our deal's off."

"We're good." He put his arm around my waist and squeezed me close to him. "We're freaking golden." He kissed me again, and this time our smooch felt a little more genuine. But considering this was my first engagement and I was *not-really-but-kind-of* engaged to a drop-dead gorgeous Prince? I found it a bit odd that I didn't have butterflies in my stomach. Only cocoons that felt like lead balloons.

Out of the corner of my eye, I watched Nick rev the engine on his Harley and speed off. No cameras followed his exit.

Only the sausage dog and his ancient female owner trailed yards behind him. "Come back," the old lady said. "You look like a dog lover!"

"What are you staring at?" Cristoph whispered.

"Oh. Nothing. Well, just a dog. I'd really like to adopt a dog some day," I said.

"Show us the ring! Show us your engagement ring from Prince Cristoph!" Ducklips demanded.

I held my left hand demurely out in front of me to thunderous applause as the cameras popped and whirred and two helicopters circled overhead. And I wondered?

Was I bleeding drops of blood into a nest of sharks? Who would be the first to bite? Who would be the first to discover I was an imposter? Who would be the first to destroy me? When I heard the revs of a motorcycle, watched Nick ride out of the park and felt my heart clench—I suspected I already knew the answer to my last question.

CHAPTER 20

A few days later I stood in front of my enormous bathroom mirror back at Papa's condo. Lady Cheryl deftly parted my hair with her fingers, rolled and styled sections of it with a large curling iron.

Lady Joan flipped back and forth between five makeup brushes, eight tiny pots of color and three pencils as she micro-managed my makeup. "Look all the way up." She tapped the underside of my chin.

I dropped my head back and stared at the ceiling.

Joan pulled the bottom of my lower eyelid down and penciled the inner rim. "Stop blinking."

"Is this necessary? You could poke my eye out," I said.

"If you shut up that might not happen. The white pencil brings out what's left of the whites of your eyes. It makes you look refreshed. Trust me, you're in need of some refreshing."

"Thank you, all of you," I said. "But my legs are cramping. We've been doing this for almost an hour. It's not like this is for a photo-shoot. Cristoph and I have already had ten of those."

"I'm sure you'll look lovely in *Pottery Castle, People More Important-than-You Magazine* and *Royally Glamorous*." Cheryl held an assortment of earrings up to my ears, eyed them and quickly sorted them into two piles: possible yeses she placed on the marble countertop and she returned the rejects into a large three-tiered jewelry box.

"This is a far, far more important occasion than a mere photo-shoot." Joan broke into a sweat as she blended concealer under my eyes with a makeup brush. "This is your first informal meet and greet with Cristoph's family since you got engaged. Have you even slept the past couple of nights? Your under eye circles are the size of Cheryl's former dowry."

"Which was huge," Cheryl said. "In olden days it would have been the equivalent of three sacks of gold coins, a few rubies, one hundred pigs, twenty goats and a couple bones from dead men who were declared saints a thousand years prior."

Joan sighed. "We're going to have to order concealer in a tub." She dipped the makeup brush into the little pot and dabbed more under my eyes. "I hope you're signed up for Amazon Prime for Royals—they have one hour free shipping, you know."

I need to sit down, I thought.

"I need you all to help me pick out the perfect outfit," I said.

While I sit down and eat, I thought. "I need something to

nosh on. Anyone else hungry?"

"Watching my waistline," Cheryl said.

"Didn't hit the gym today," Joan said.

"Got it." I punched a button on the intercom on the wall. "Helga? Do you have time to whip me up a snackie? Something sweet. Something salty. Maybe healthy?"

"Changed my mind. On sourdough," Cheryl said.

"With fresh Fredonia sausages. I'll work out tomorrow," Joan said.

"Sourdough subs with fresh Fredonia sausages and the works. Gracias-I-mean- thank you. I'll come down to the kitchen and pick it up. No really. Are you sure? Okay fine—you're a peach!"

Cheryl lifted her thumb to her mouth, tipped her head back and mimed glugging a drink.

"And can you bring us a bottle of Korbel as well?" I asked.

"Hah!" Joan said. "You're hilarious. Your Ladies-in-Waiting will work for free but we still need the decent stuff. I'd prefer the Perrier-Jouet Belle Epoque Rose Cuvee if you don't mind."

Like I could say that?

I handed the phone to Joan. "You tell her."

"Make that the Perrier-Jouet Belle Epoque Rose Cuvee, Helga," Joan said. "The 2004. Perfect. Thank you."

We noshed on sandwiches in my bedroom and the Ladies drank champagne from crystal flutes. I turned down the bubbly—I didn't want to meet Cristoph's family for the first time (for real) even a bit tipsy.

I encouraged Cheryl and Joan to invade Elizabeth's

closet, rifle through her clothes and pick the crucial meeting-the-royal family-outfit. I sat on the floor, leaned back against my bed and downed the last of that lamb/venison Fredonia sausage. It was freaking delicious.

"The key word here is—" I said, "—*informal.* I've already met Cristoph's family so many times in the past."

I could practically feel my nose growing.

"And yes, my sleep has sucked for the past three nights."

Make that the past three weeks since I'd taken this part-time job.

"Every night Carolina brings me herbal tea before I go to bed. She's so sweet," I said. "Such a lady! What a catch for Elizabeth's Da-I mean Papa. But I still toss and turn. And every morning Helga brings me fresh coffee. But it never really wakes me up. I don't feel like myself. I think it's all the stress."

Maybe it was all the lying. Or maybe I missed Nick. I hadn't heard boo from him since that day in the park.

"What stress?" Cheryl asked. "You're engaged to a hot Prince, you'll want for nothing ever again and all you really have to do to cement the deal—post-wedding of course—is pop out an heir someday. I delivered two. Hubby is quite content with his little Ladies who adore him. Of course he travels five days out of the week and only has daughter duty on weekends. Sign me up for a boob lift, a tummy tuck, a ten-pack of facial peels and valerian root tea."

"Oh cut the crap, Cheryl," Joan said. "It's called Xanax."

"I'd like to see you handle two little ones under the age of five who already snark at each other like high school mean girls," Cheryl said. "Xanax, valerian, reikki, yoga, watching too much tennis on TV—love that Rafa—

whatever it takes to keep my sanity, I'll do it. Mommy Makeover here I come."

"I read an article in *Euro Cosmopolitan* that said getting engaged was right up there on the top twenty list of major life stresses," I said. "I come by my eye circles the old-fashioned way—too much stress."

"Or perhaps your lack of sleep is from all the clandestine sex you're finally getting." Esmeralda waltzed into my bedroom. "Great job you're doing with Elizabeth's under eye circles, Joan. You're gifted." She threw herself onto her back on my bed. "Can someone pour me a glass of champagne?" She propped herself up on her elbows and held out one hand. "Por favor?"

"What do you mean, *'clandestine sex?'*" I poured a glass of Perrier Whatever and passed it to her.

"What do you mean *'finally getting?'*" Joan asked. "Good Lord, Elizabeth's been getting more than her share for years. I'm a single barrister and I work a forty-hour week. When do I have time to meet men, let alone date?"

"You meet men all the time," Cheryl said.

"I meet men 'all the time' who are married, incarcerated or married and soon to be incarcerated. My 'getting' pool is in the shallow end," Joan said.

"Trust me, all the clandestine sex will be screeching to a stop after Elizabeth gets married and pumps out two heirs. Color me happy if we have sex once a week." Cheryl guzzled what remained in her glass and held it out. "And even then it's usually in front of the TV during a soccer match. Top me off, please."

"*Clandestine,* Joan. Secret. Not out in the open. On the QT," Esmeralda said.

"*Nothing's* happening on the QT," I said.

"You're engaged to a royal, darling," Esmeralda said. "The good citizens of Fredonia assume you're doing the horizontal hokey-pokey, and while most of them fantasize about it, everything still must remain hush-hush for etiquette's sake. Excuse me while I multi-task as we chat. I have a date tonight. Yoga keeps me limber." She downed the champagne and handed me back the glass. "Gracias."

"You're welcome. Can I get you another—"

"I'm good." She widened her legs high up in the air over her head, clasped onto her big toes with her thumbs and forefingers and stretched her thighs wide apart.

Joan winced and then squinted up at the ceiling. "Esmeralda! I see London, I see France. I see that you need underpants!"

I glared at the smart-mouthed Lady-in-Waiting, rolling all over my bed like a kitten in heat. And I wondered how much dry-cleaning a down comforter in Fredonia would cost in euros.

"You're going commando again, aren't you?" Cheryl frowned. "I thought those days were over." She sighed.

Esmeralda rocked from side to side as she displayed almost everything but her private half-Spanish parts. "I just follow Elizabeth's lead. She's always been the trend setter in our group."

"Me?" I sputtered. "I've never been big on trends. And I always wear undies."

That was kind of a lie but sounded appropriate and somewhat chaste. Besides, who would call me on it?

"Not always, Ms. Smarty-No-Pants. Remember that time on va-ca during Spring Fling in Latvia when we were nineteen?" Esmeralda winked at me. "You're the one who said, 'What happens in Latvia stays in Latvia. Which includes my red lace peek-a-boo bra and panty set.' I can only assume your passionate fiancé, Cristoph—he of the big tusk—is sneaking into your room and banging you senseless every night. That's why you're not getting enough sleep—hence the eye circles."

"Cristoph is a perfect gentleman!" I wrung my hands. "No one's banging me senseless. And if I see this quote in a tabloid, I'll have your ass, Esmeralda."

"Take a number and stand in line," she said.

"Reminisce later," Joan said. "We need to pick a dress. What do you think?" She held out four—one draped across each of her forearms and one dangling from each hand.

"I like the red one," Cheryl said. "That's Elizabeth's signature color."

"The blue one's kind of cute," I said. "It's sweet and modest and—"

"Did you turn Amish in the States?" Esmeralda squinted at me perplexed. "The Elizabeth I knew wouldn't be caught dead in anything that droll. Now that one," she pointed at another dress, "the blush-pink concoction? It's feminine without being over the top. It'll bring out your complexion—which has completely lost all the acne since last year—and it practically screams virginal, although we all know that ship sailed a long time ago."

Actually not all that long ago and only with the same Johnny's pizza delivery guy. Was it my fault Danny Flynn was smoking hot, super smart and in pre-med at the University of Chicago? I said yes to dinner dates, yes to live White Sox games, and after a whole bunch of make out sessions—yes to losing my virginity. Because I thought I was Danny's girlfriend.

171

Turns out I was Danny's girlfriend for three weeks before he met a girl from a wealthier family on his pizza route who tipped him better. Live and learn.

Joan, Cheryl, Esmeralda and I eyed the dress.

"You're right." Cheryl ran her hand over the dress's pink, silk fabric.

Joan nodded. "You've always had an eye for details."

"It's beautiful. It's the perfect meet the royal family dress." I felt my face flush. "Thank you my gorgeous and talented Ladies. I'll let you know how tonight's meet and greet goes—hopefully before it hits the press."

"You're welcome." Esmeralda rolled to sitting, cracked her neck with her hands and stood up. "But I'll know all before it trickles into my Grandmother's royal Depends, which will probably happen even before it's leaked to the press. I am, after-all, Cristoph's first cousin and part of the Timmel family. I'll be at the royal meet and greet tonight. You need anything, Elizabeth, just look my way and give the secret hand signal."

I started to panic and felt my throat tighten. "What's the secret hand signal?"

"We had plenty of them. You don't remember?" She regarded me curiously.

Joan tapped her index finger to her head. "Amnesia."

"Ah, yes." Esmeralda said. "It's what we did in Latvia after you left your undies behind. We celebrated with a few shots and agreed on our secret hand signals. You've been different since you came home to Fredonia, Elizabeth."

"She passed out and hit her head on a tarmac," Cheryl said.

"I know that. But surely she can recall our signals. Because they're burned into my memory."

"Oh *those* secret hand signals. Right," I said. "Of course. I'll never forget them."

How could I? I never learned them in the first place.

There was a knock at the door. "Who is it?" I asked.

"It's Carolina, darling. I heard your Ladies had stopped by. I have a special treat for you."

Cheryl looked at me questioningly. I nodded. She walked the few feet to the door and opened it.

CHAPTER 21

"Surprise!" Carolina carried a silver tray filled with fancy cupcakes into my bedroom. "Strawberry tart cupcakes with white chocolate icing. A time-honored Sauerhausen family recipe and a good-luck tradition," she said.

"Ooh yummy!" Joan grabbed one.

"Thank you, Duchess von Sauerhausen!" Cheryl plucked one and noshed enthusiastically.

"Carolina, this is so sweet of you." I picked up a cupcake. "Really you didn't have to." I placed it to my lips…

When Esmeralda ripped it out of my hand and tossed it across the room where it splattered against my window. "Elizabeth! You're deathly allergic to strawberries!"

"I am?" I asked. "Oh right, of course I am!" I frowned and tugged on my ears. "I could swear she said fairy tart cupcakes. I think my ears are still clogged from that horrible flight on Fredonia Air when we almost crashed."

"I didn't know," Carolina said. "Oh my good God my dear girl. I am so sorry!"

"No worries! Of course you didn't know," I said.

Neither did I.

"I'm sure my Ladies will enjoy your delicious confections Carolina. And thank you so much. You're the sweetest!" I hugged her.

A few hours later I was dressed to the nines, my hair shiny and curly, my under eye circles caked in concealer and I even wore false eyelashes for the first time. I stalked around the Billingsley Penthouse rooftop terrace with its gardens and vegetable boxes. It was almost like being outside someone's house except for the tall mesh fence designed to keep folks from falling off and splattering on the concrete twenty-five floors below. I wasn't that thrilled with heights but Carolina had told me the fence was tight, secure, could hold body weight if someone tripped and fell against it. No one would be plummeting to their death of the top of this penthouse anytime soon!

I wore the pink dress and matching accessories and pressed the cell to my ear as I paced. I probably resembled a beauty queen wannabe or a desperate contestant on *The Bachelor*.

"Do *not* tell me to calm down, Mr. Philips!" I hissed into the phone. "I'm freaking out here because I had to talk to you or Zara or the increasing elusive Elizabeth. I'm meeting the frigging Fredonia royal family for the first time, neither you or Zara are here to help me, and this was not included in my job description."

"Zara hasn't called or even texted me in almost a week. Some kind of drama with Elizabeth," he said.

"Shocker," I said. "It seems there's always drama with Elizabeth. Why did no one tell me I'm deathly allergic to strawberries? What the hell did I do on Spring Break in Latvia with Esmeralda when we were nineteen? What is our secret hand signal? Why did I leave my undies behind? Questions, dammit! Too many unanswered questions!"

My head pounded like it was being walloped by an internal jackhammer and I feared my fake eyelashes were going to pop off. "What if I screw this up? Oh crap, I'm turning into a self-centered, insensitive bitch, aren't I? I'm so sorry." I grimaced and knocked my fist against my head. "How could I forget? How is your back?"

"My back is so-so. The physical therapists are making me walk and stand on my tippy toes and heels. The hospital food is God-awful. I just really want to go home to Fredonia," he said.

"Good! I can't wait for you to get back here." I frowned. "Actually, I meant to say I'm sorry you're not feeling well and I look forward to the day you're able to return to your beautiful home. Forget about me. My problems are tiny compared to what you're going through."

"You're a sweet girl, Lucy."

"Lucy?" I asked. "Not Lucille?"

"Yeah there," he said. "Regarding meeting the Royal Family? Just be you. Except for the nail-chewing or the walking like a line-backer thing."

"Got it," I said.

"Or the thing where you—"

"Feel better Philips." I hung up.

A half hour later, a shiny, black limo picked me up in the underground parking garage. A royal bodyguard opened the car's back door for me while Papa and Carolina stood next to the valet stand and waved.

Papa pulled out his iPhone, snapped a few pictures and wiped away a tear. "Oh, honey. I haven't felt this way since you went to Senior Prom."

"Wish me luck," I ducked into the limo. "I'm nervous."

"They're just royals," Carolina said. "I'm squarely mid-list nobility—a duchess—but I know all about this stuff. They put on their lederhosen one leg at a time, just like the rest of us do. Imagine them naked should they get too pompous. That's what I do. I apologize again about the strawberry dilemma."

"No worries! Great advice, thank you! I'll see you in a bit." I practiced my princess wave on them.

"Not tonight, honey," Papa said. "I'm taking my girl out for a night on the town. We'll be back late—if we're back at all." He smiled at Carolina, completely smitten and kissed her on the lips.

If I *really was* Elizabeth I probably would have felt weird about my dad's PDA. But I wasn't and I didn't—I just thought they were elegant and beautiful in that old-fashioned movie star kind of way. And yeah, he did look like George Clooney, and she resembled one of those ageless French model/actresses. I'm sure the deadly strawberry thing was simply a mistake—Duchess Carolina von Sauerhausen was growing on me.

"Text us and let us know how it goes," Carolina said. "And I predict it's all going to go fabulously."

"If they give you any pompous shit," Papa said, "remind them that our money can save their trees and lodges and chocolate factories from the theme park developers. Only if they get the deal done on time."

"Huh?"

"Shh, David." Carolina pinched his arm. "You can remind Elizabeth about that tomorrow. Just let her have fun tonight."

"You're right," Papa said. "We'll see you tomorrow my darling daughter." He placed one hand to his lips and threw me a kiss.

I threw a kiss back to the both of them. Then tried to remember when the last time anyone called me darling daughter and either of my parents tossed a kiss in my direction.

It had been a very, very long time.

A pristine palace loomed through the front window of the royal limo. It looked like it had been lifted from a fairy tale and dropped down into a bustling metropolitan city. A thick fence, manned by guards wearing uniforms sporting Fredonia's royal colors, surrounded the mid-sized castle.

We arrived at the palace's official entrance outside the sturdy wrought iron fence, and waited as the guards called ahead and got the okay to buzz us in. The gates hummed and then opened. We drove down a narrow, straight lane toward the castle in the near distance.

Royal flags waved from poles embedded into the castle walls. There were turrets, a large tower and a few ancient cannons positioned on the fortress's roof.

The chauffeur drove me to the towering front gates and slipped the limo into park. The bodyguard hopped out the passenger side, looked around in both directions and then opened my door. From what I could see outside the tinted windows, there were no paparazzi on the premises.

"Lederhosen," I mumbled, chewed on my lower lip and suddenly feared my lipstick was gone. I was meeting the royal family. Bare lips would not do!

"Coast is clear," the bodyguard beckoned to me. "Come on."

"Hang on." I raked my hand through my new designer purse but couldn't find my Pretty-in-Pink Maybelline gloss with the sparkles. Only a stupid Chanel lipstick. I pulled the lid off and looked at the color. It totally wasn't my shade of pink and it didn't even sparkle. "Dammit!" I swiped it across my lips.

"Is everything all right, Lady Billingsley?" the guard asked.

"I'm newly engaged, meeting my fiancée's family for almost the first time and I can't find my favorite lipstick."

The guard hid a smile. "You sound like my wife when her beloved mascara was discontinued. You'll do fine." He held out his hand to me. "Let's get you inside the castle safe and sound before we get any more death threats."

"Death threats?" I took his hand as he helped me out of the limo.

"I'm sorry. I shouldn't have said anything."

"Death threats? Seriously? Who would want Eliza- me dead?"

He shook his head. "It's nothing unusual. Happens to

everyone. Probably just a prank. This is Fredonia Secret Service's job to handle. Not yours. Good luck. Have fun. You're perfectly safe." He bowed to me as the front door to the castle flew open.

Cristoph held his arms out wide. "Elizabeth! You're finally here! You look so beautiful. Come inside!" He gestured.

I wore the pretty pink dress and stood, head held high, shoulders back, stomach sucked in, with Cristoph at my side in a long, high-ceilinged hallway in the Fredonia Royal Palace. Marble busts of former kings sat on pedestals and lined the corridor. Fetching oil paintings of coiffed Fredonia queens adorned the walls.

"You look gorgeous," Cristoph said. "I used to think red suited you best. I've changed my mind. I think pink might be your new signature color." He smiled.

"Thanks." I bit one of my manicured nails.

He took my hand and eased my finger from my mouth. "No nail biting in front of my family. They'll perceive that as a sign of weakness."

I frowned. "What if they don't like me?"

"That's not going to happen. You already know them," Cristoph said. "Depending on which relative we're talking about—you simply haven't seen them in two or five or eight years." He squeezed my hand. "Besides. They'll take one look at you all grown up and curvy and gorgeous in pink and they'll fall in love with you all over again. Just the way I did."

"You think?" I bit my lip.

"I know," he said. "Getting through the paparazzi and

the magazine photo-shoots—that was the real pain in the ass. But you've charmed everybody."

I nodded.

"This is the easy part," he said. "This is cake. Just hold my hand and we'll be good." He leaned in and smooched me on the lips.

His kiss was tender. It was sweet. There was more than a hint of sexy.

I should have felt swoony. I didn't.

He pulled away, swiped his long blonde hair off his forehead and smiled. I batted my eyes and smiled back at him.

As I thought of Nick. Where was he? What was he doing? Did he leave the country on another business trip? Oh for God's sake Lucy—let the Nick thing go. You're on a job here. Concentrate. Suck it up and concentrate.

"If I didn't know better Cristoph, I'd think you're actually a good man disguised as a bad boy."

"Shh. That's my secret." He said. "You can't tell anyone: it'll destroy my wild-child image and reputation."

"But you're-I mean-*we're* getting married. You don't need the bad-boy reputation anymore," I said.

"Oh, Elizabeth," he said. "There's no fairy tale more enchanting than the one about the girl who tamed the bad boy. The press is eating it up. Your picture is everywhere. Twitter. Instagram. Blogs. Facebook. Tumblr. The press had dubbed you 'The Lady with a Heart.'"

"I don't get it? Why?"

"Because you're genuinely nice to everybody. You don't reserve your kindness for the wealthy or powerful. You're kind to a cameraman. You're nice to the tuba player. You were even sweet to Ducklips."

"You call her that too?"

"I overheard you mutter it under your breath when she mentioned your possible baby bump. You graciously told her you weren't pregnant, just a little bloated, and that you'd give her the first interview once you were. Pregnant that is. Hey." He tickled my waist and I jumped. "Maybe we should get working on that—soon."

"Right." I nodded, then shook my head. "Not 'till after the wedding, mister. Why is being nice such a rare trait? Aren't the majority of folks nice and kind unless they're provoked?"

"What happened to you in the States?" Cristoph asked. "You seem to have grown more idealistic."

When a uniformed butler in a penguin suit pushed open two tall, ornately carved wooden doors. He bowed to Cristoph, then to me, one hand held behind his back. "Your family awaits, your Highness."

"Thank you, Mr. Philips," Cristoph said.

I inhaled sharply and stared at the butler. He was indeed the spitting image of Mr. Philip Philips—but forty years younger. "Are you by any chance related to…"

"Not now." Cristoph tugged my arm and pointed to narrow stone steps that descended into the bowels of the castle.

"Good luck," the young Mr. Philips said and closed the creaking doors with two thuds as I jumped.

CHAPTER 22

Cristoph led the way, holding lightly to my hand. We descended three thin flights of stairs into a skinny, damp, dark passageway lit solely by flickering torches mounted high on the walls.

The temperature dropped nearly twenty degrees in less than a minute and I shivered. The floors were made of cobblestones, as were the walls. We walked past ancient pens with short, sagging, rotting wooden doors accented with tiny peepholes covered in thick, rusty, chain-linked mesh.

I looked up and spotted massive spider webs on the ceiling. The torches cast weird shadows and suddenly Cristoph's handsome face appeared devilish and his eyes glowed a creepy color.

Oh crap. This place reminded me of the dungeons on my favorite TV show. Note to Lucy: get a grip!

It took all my will power to resist pulling away from Cristoph's hand. "Why does this place look like a dungeon?" I asked.

"Because it is a dungeon," he said.

Holy shit, had my real identity been discovered? Was I about to be incarcerated, fed stale bread and briny water through a small hole in the door to my decrepit cell and never see the light of day again?

And after a decade down here my hair would have turned white, my spine twisted, turned and hunched. I'd never get to go the dentist for teeth cleaning and I'd become one of those snaggle-tooth hags that had bit roles on my fave TV show?

My breath grew raspy.

"What's wrong," Cristoph asked.

I bent forward, clutched my chest and hacked. "I can't breathe!"

"It's the mold," he said. "Everyone's allergic to the mold. Just tough it out for another hundred yards. Come on. You can do it. " He yanked on my hand.

Convinced this might be my death march, I followed him and composed my silent farewells in my head.

Adios my BFF, Alida. I adore you and Mateo. Don't let the asshats dictate how you run your life.

Farewell Uncle John. My life insurance policy and will leaves everything to you. It's not a lot but it will buy you a couple of years at The Vail Assisted Living. I hope someday you find peace.

Bye-bye Buddy Paulsen from MadDog: I'll always love you even though you threw me under the bus, which, by the way, I'll never forget.

Au revoir my Ladies-in-Waiting. I have no words. Actually I do: you are fabulous. I wish you all lived back in Chicago. Why did I have to fly thousands of miles away from home just to meet you? I hope when, or if, you discover I'm missing or dead that you will miss me too. That you will think a kind thought about Lucy Marie Trabbicio—I mean Lady Elizabeth Theresa Billingsley.

Last but not least, I am NOT saying goodbye to you Nick. Because I don't care enough about you to include you in my grand farewell. I don't care enough—okay—who the frick are you? Honestly, I'm not sure I want to know. But if I could leave you with parting words?

I wish I had met you, Nick, before the real Elizabeth did. I wish you knew me in kindergarten. I wish you had made love to me instead of Elizabeth in exotic locations including the Mile High Club. I wish I could have spent more time with you as, well, me. I miss you.

~~I'm crazy about you.~~

Fondly,
Lucy Marie Trabbicio.
P.S. Will you please come rescue me from this dungeon?

My heart was already pounding when a guard dressed in full medieval armor stepped out from the shadows and I jumped.

He wore a codpiece and a metal helmet with a facemask. Something about him looked familiar. "Who approaches the secret royal door?" He casually tossed an axe back and forth from meaty hand to hand.

My eyes widened and I started to cough. "No one! Oopskies, sorry to bother you. We'll just go back the way we came." I clutched my throat and I coughed some more. "I need some Claritin pronto!" I tugged on Cristoph's arm but it was like his freaking feet were glued to the floor.

"Guardsman!" Cristoph bellowed. "It is I: Prince Cristoph Edward George Timmel the Third of Fredonia."

"And who accompanies you Dauphine?"

"I'm not the Dauphine," Cristoph said. "We're in Fredonia. Not France."

"Sorry Your Highness. I recently relocated."

"Not a problem. Guardsman, this is my fiancé—"

"The Lady must speak for herself. It is royally decreed!" The guard hurled his axe over our heads.

"Eeps!" I ducked.

The weapon embedded into a wall above a dungeon cell and the skeletal remains of a human hand fell to the floor and broke into pieces.

"Yikes!" I jumped and pointed to the bony pieces.

Cristoph squeezed my arm, hoisted me to standing and hissed, "Don't show weakness!"

It took all my courage, but I looked the guard in his eyes. Well, technically where his eyes should have been behind his metal headgear with the eye slits. "Nice throw Helmet Head. But frankly, that wouldn't have even earned you a first down in a Bears' game."

He harrumphed.

I shook off Cristoph's grasp and took a step toward the tin man. "I am Lady Elizabeth Theresa Billingsley. I am betrothed to Prince Cristoph. And apparently we need to get through that door you're protecting so I can officially meet his family and gain royal approval." I shoved my hands on my hips.

He grunted.

"I spent four hours with my Ladies-in-Waiting getting ready for this shin-dig and so help me God and I swear on my mother's grave if you get one piece of my dress dirty or ripped or covered in dead people parts?" I jabbed my manicured index finger in his face. "I will hunt you down. I will rip that ridiculous helmet from your pompous head. I will snatch that codpiece from your cod and send my Ladies-in-Waiting after you. And you, Mister Guard, will regret the day you were born, let alone conceived."

"Merde!" he said.

"That's right, whatever that means," I said. "Open that damn door—now!"

The guard's hands shook as he pulled a key from a pocket. "Yes, my Lady." He stuck the key in the door, wriggled it a few times and then turned the lock.

"Way to get it done, Elizabeth." Cristoph planted a kiss on my cheek.

"You could have warned me about her ahead of time," the guard hissed.

I strolled through the entrance, head held high, gait regal. Even though my stomach was completely in knots I still practiced my royal wave on him—because I was a trooper. I had not only promised to get this job done—I was getting a fat paycheck for this.

I would be the best princess impersonator—ever.

I expected a large ornate room. I expected a majestic chamber with two thrones. I expected a posh, intimate cocktail party. I did not expect to see Cristoph's family dressed in J. Crew-like casual attire, lined up in one long row on a grassy lawn surrounded by an impossibly tall fence.

Some members of the royal family regarded me curiously. Others appeared bored—like the pimply teenage boy who tossed his basketball from one hand to the next. "Yo—what up Cristoph's fiancé'?" he asked.

Cristoph strode toward him, grabbed him by the ear and twisted it. "Her name is Lady Elizabeth Theresa Billingsley," he said. "Show some respect you little turd."

"Ow! That's Duke Liam Little Turd to you cousin big-shot," he said. "I said hello. Can I get back to playing hoops now?"

Cristoph released him. The boy jogged off. Cristoph shook his head as he walked back toward me. "Welcome to the family," he whispered into my ear. "Still up for this gig?"

I nodded.

A few nobles clapped their hands, jumped up in the air, giggled and high-fived. They collapsed on the ground in a heap as they pinched, kicked and kissed each other. They were a gaggle of five-year-old girls with decoratively painted faces wearing multi-colored tutus, ballet flats and sporting tiny tiaras.

"Eliza-bet, you are so pretty!" one girl said. "I'm Lady Jeannie. But you can call me Jeannie the Beanie."

"We are the Ladies!" a second girl giggled.

I smiled at them, held out one hand and they fist-bumped me.

"I'm Lady Tonya," a third girl with a head full of

189

brunette ringlets said. "We want to look just like you when we grow up!"

"You are beautiful Ladies but never forget how smart you are. Because smart girls rule!" Which led to more high-fiving and our chant: "Smart girls rule! Smart girls rule!"

"Do you and Cristoph kiss?" Tonya asked.

"Yes," I said. "Prince Cristoph is my fiancé, so of course we kiss."

"I kissed a boy once and he ran away," Jeannie looked at her ballet shoes and kicked the ground. "Does Cristoph run away when you kiss him?"

"No," I said. "If a boy runs away when you kiss him? He's definitely not the right boy for you."

"Excellent advice." King Frederick Wilhelm Gustave Timmel the Fourteenth stepped from the line and walked a few feet toward us.

The mini-Ladies giggled and ran off as I executed a near perfect curtsey.

"Father. I'd like to present my new fiancé—Lady Elizabeth Theresa Billingsley." Cristoph bowed. "We anxiously await your official approval of our betrothal."

I pulled my shoulders back and imagined I was watching The Golf Channel. Mr. Philips had suggested that envisioning an incredibly boring sporting event could possibly help one appear more dignified. "So lovely to meet you again, Your Royal Highness," I said.

"You seem a bit more mature than last we met," he said.

"Thank you sir." I curtseyed again and caught sight of Esmeralda dressed in a full-length luau themed dress cut low in the bodice. A flower lei draped around her neck, adorned her chest and vanished from sight down her cleavage. She sucked loudly on a straw stuck in a tall, festive umbrella drink impaled with chunks of fruit. She discretely placed two fingers to her eyes and then pointed at me.

I subtly shot her a thumbs up.

Frederick swiveled, eyed Esmeralda and grunted.

She waved at him—cheery.

"I see, Elizabeth, that you still spend time with the more risqué members of our family," he said. "Who am I to judge? I sowed my share of wild oats when I was younger as well. Someday Cristoph, my first-born son—you will govern Fredonia. Is this the woman you want to be your queen and rule by your side?" he asked.

CHAPTER 23

"Yes Father," Cristoph said. "I want Elizabeth to be my wife as well as Fredonia's Queen one day."

King Frederick nodded and waved one hand high in the air. "You have my approval." He strode back to the line. "Carry on. I must get back to work. I'm concerned about the Bergers."

Were the Bergers another noble family that would be threatened if the Billingsleys merged with the Timmels? Even more importantly— was a Berger endangering my/Elizabeth's life?

"Thank you so very much your Royal Highness," I said.

The forever-beautiful Queen Cheree Dussair Timmel stepped forward. She wore board shorts, a 'Keep Calm,

Carry on and Feel Free in Fredonia' T-shirt and her blonde hair was pulled back in a high ponytail. She rolled her eyes. "For God's sakes, Fredrick, you're always worried about the burgers, the chicken, the steaks or the sausages. Just attend to the matter at hand for a change and your BBQ will turn out fine!"

Apparently I didn't have to worry about the 'Bergers'.

Queen Cheree took my hand and looked me square in the eyes. "I remember you—Elizabeth—from years ago. You've always been a very smart girl. You've filled out since the last time I saw you." She took a step back and eyed me up and down.

I inhaled sharply and froze.

"Ahem!" Esmeralda coughed and my eyes swiveled toward her. She swirled her index finger and then pointed to the ground.

"Right," I said and curtseyed to Queen Cheree.

Who turned and regarded Cristoph. "Is she the one you want to merge bloodlines and produce Fredonia's future princes and or princesses?"

He smiled at me, put his strong arm around my waist and pulled me tight to him—flush against his hard muscular chest and his hip. He winked at me. "Yes Mother."

I blushed and couldn't help but fan my face. I heard a short whistle. I looked to the source and saw Esmeralda nonchalantly waving a dripping ice cube in front of her face and pointing to it repeatedly with the index finger on her other hand.

I reminded myself to just play it cool and stopped fanning my face.

Queen Cheree kissed me on both cheeks. "I approve." She leaned in and whispered, "We need to talk later tonight about your upcoming schedule. Planning these types of things on abrupt notice can be monstrous, darling."

"Yes," I whispered back. "Totally awful. I agree."

What types of monstrous things were we planning on abrupt notice?

"And—I have an engagement present for you dear," she said. "A special 'Welcome to the Timmel' family giftie.'"

"I know what it is!" Cristoph said.

"Don't ruin the surprise!" She wagged her finger at him, turned and walked back toward the line of royals. "I swear the men in this family always ruin the surprises."

An elderly woman, whose chin nearly rested on her chest, wearing a lopsided tiara on her coiffed white hairdo, moved toward us with the aid of her walker: one painful step at a time.

Queen Cheree paused next to her and placed a hand on her shoulder. "You need help Mama?"

"No my precious bundle of American joy," the woman said. "I already surrendered my dream of my eldest son marrying into the British Royal Family. You've helped me quite enough for one lifetime."

Queen Cheree bit her lip.

"I'm the one who needs help, Cheree." King Frederick stood next to a huge, glossy BBQ. "I forgot the tongs! Please ring young Mr. Philips immediately before something burns."

Cheree nodded. "Yes, honey." She pulled out her pocket cell and tapped the screen.

"Cristoph, my beloved grandson." The elderly woman rolled toward us.

"Yes, Nana," he said.

I curtseyed again—right as the woman parked her walker on my foot. I heard a tiny 'crack', felt a painful zing and I winced. "Ow." I remained sunk low in the fairly deep knee bend. It hurt too much to move.

"My sincerest apologies," she said. "I think I broke your foot."

"No problem." Tears filled my eyes.

"Are you all right?" Cristoph grabbed my arm.

"Peachy."

"If you're going to be in the royal Timmel family, you need to learn to speak up for yourself," Nana said.

"Fine." I winced. "Could you back up a few inches please? I'd be eternally grateful. Your Most Gracious Grandmother."

"Much better." She squinted up at me with her bright crystal blue eyes—the same color as Cristoph's. She pinched my cheek but wouldn't let go. "Pretty face. You can call me the Queen Mum. Or Your Royal Nana. Whatever you prefer."

"Thanks," I said. "Your Royal Nana."

"Happy to hear you have an opinion." She reached around and slapped my ass.

Which startled me from a frozen position back into a standing posture. "Ow!"

"She has ample hips, Cristoph. Good for babies, and ever since the Kardashian debacle, everyone likes a decent toucas. She'll photograph well. Is she any good in the sack?"

Cristoph and I hacked and covered our mouths.

Esmeralda coughed as well. "Goodness!" She exclaimed. "Seasonal allergies going around—must be that time of year."

I glanced at her as she mouthed the word 'no' and sliced her index finger across her throat.

"Cristoph doesn't know if I'm any good in the sack, Nana. But I predict he will be plenty pleased in the sack on our wedding night," I said. "Because I, Lady Elizabeth Theresa Billingsley, am an old-fashioned girl. Until he puts *the* ring on it in front of God, church, family and country, he'll only be getting the appetizers."

Esmeralda burst out clapping and the little ladies followed her lead, forming finger shaped hearts. "Yay! We heart Princess Elizabeth! We heart Princess Elizabeth!" The girls squealed, high-fived each other and collapsed on the green grass in squidgy giggles.

"Surprise!" the line of royal Timmels hollered in unison. "Welcome to the family!"

And just like that, the official Fredonia Meet and Greet the Royals turned into a backyard BBQ and party. The Timmels and extended family went back to playing basketball, soccer, chess and badminton while King Fredrick obsessed over his grill. Nana rolled her walker off my foot. A bartender whipped up drinks at a small outdoor bar. Two uniformed servants refilled drinks and passed around plates of food.

Cristoph helped me hobble into their midst where I plunked down on a cushy outdoor chaise lounge next to a table with an umbrella over it. The palace doctor was paged. His assistant X-rayed my foot on site, confirmed it wasn't broken—just a nasty contusion. He wrapped my foot with an ace bandage, instructed me to keep it elevated and gave me a cane.

Cristoph held ice packs on my foot as I ate a cheeseburger. "I'm so sorry," he said. "Nana's getting up there. Are you doing okay?"

"Yes. It's been a little weird, but I guess I'm getting used to it."

"How's the burger Elizabeth? I didn't over cook it did I?" King Frederick yelled to me from the grill as he waved away billows of smoke.

"It's perfect," I said. "Where'd you get this cheese?"

"That's organic from our goats that feed in the pastures next to our castle in the foothills of the Alps."

"I've never tasted anything like it," I said. "It's delish."

"Glad you like it," he said. "That's another thing your marriage to Cristoph will be saving."

"What's he talking about?" I asked Cristoph.

"You know I love you," he said. "But I'm sure your Papa told you about the business arrangement and the contract. Right?"

Both Nick and Papa had mentioned a business arrangement. And here it was being brought up again.

Queen Cheree strolled up accompanied by a gorgeous yellow Labrador Retriever. "I'm so sorry about the foot, darling. Do you mind if Sunny and I sit next to you?"

"Be my guest," I pet Sunny's head and smiled. The dog wagged her tail and licked my hand.

Cheree took a seat in a lawn chair next to my chaise. "Cristoph—amscray. I'm kidnapping Elizabeth—just for a bit. Go help your father with his…" she waved one hand in the air. "… grilling."

"Boring, Mom," he said but stood up.

"Buck it up, kiddo. I've done it for thirty years." She smiled at him.

Cristoph leaned in, kissed me on my cheek and whispered. "Best family introduction, ever. You nailed it Elizabeth. See you in a bit. Mom's acting sneaky. Don't let her talk you into anything you don't want to do." He ran his finger across my lower lip, and then strode off toward his dad holding court at the BBQ.

Sunny glanced around and whimpered.

"Yes, Sunny, soon. You're a good mama." Queen Cheree cooed at her and scratched her chest. "Sorry about the dungeon," she said. "It's a secret Timmel family prank thing. They did it to me too. I sprouted my first silver hairs that very night. Please don't let that stop you from joining the family."

"I won't."

"Good!" She patted my arm. "We're an odd but kind of a fun group once you get to know us better. Besides your increased blood pressure and injured foot, I swear things will improve from here on out. I can't wait to help you plan your wedding! Truth be told, I already called a few folks a couple of days ago. I hope you don't mind if I get involved. It's the first wedding in our immediate family since, well, mine, and I'm so excited! Do you think you can walk?"

"Yes," I said.

"Good." She extended her hand and helped me to standing. "I want to give you your welcome to the family gift." She handed me the cane and walked away.

"Thank you." I limped behind her. "This is the nicest

cane that anyone has ever given me."

She laughed. "That's not your gift, silly!" Sunny barked. "I don't remember you being this funny. I can call a couple of guards to carry you on a stretcher?"

"Thanks," I said and remembered the death threats. "Let the guards do the guarding and I'll stick with the limping."

We reached a small doorway in a stone wall that surrounded the enormous backyard. Queen Cheree keyed in a code and hit a button. The door slid open and Sunny bounded through. "Follow me," she said.

We entered a small yard covered with a tarp stretched overhead that screened out the majority of the weather: sun, snow and sleet.

Sunny raced to a medium-sized pen in the yard's corner, pawed at it and barked. Three blonde, fuzzy, fat puppies stretched up against its metal confines and yipped back at her.

"I'm sure you've already been informed that I'm a bit of a nut when it comes to Labrador Retrievers," Queen Cheree said.

"Everyone said you really love Labs."

"I do. I grew up with them. There are worse addictions to have." She bent down, unlatched the gate and two puppies bounded onto the lawn.

Sunny tackled one pup, pinned it with her front paw and licked her baby from head to paw.

Queen Cheree jogged a few feet, grabbed the second puppy off the ground, raised it to her face and smooched it. "Scrumptious!" she said. "I adore them! So much easier raising dogs than my own children."

I didn't remember Lady or the Damp telling me Cristoph had siblings.

But this wasn't the time or place to ask.

When I heard a whimper and my gaze was drawn to a chubby puppy still in the pen that glanced around, a bit confused. I recognized that look—I saw it every day in the mirror since I left Chicago. I hobbled toward her, plopped down on the lawn adjacent to the pen's open gate and held out my hand. "Here, baby. Come here."

The puppy eyed me curiously, planted two fat paws onto the lawn and licked my fingers.

And I smiled. "You are so cute." I picked her up, pulled her out of the cage and cradled her like a baby against my chest. She wiggled for a few moments and then relaxed.

I inhaled her puppy breath (best scent in the whole entire world) and sighed. I tickled her fuzzy belly as she squirmed again. "She is the sweetest thing ever!" I said. "She is a she—right?"

"Yes." Queen Cheree released her pup. He raced across the lawn and tackled a rope toy, sinking his teeth into it, wrestling it from side to side while growling in a wicked soprano tone.

"Now I know why you love the Labradors." I kissed the puppy's cheek. "This is the absolute best I've felt in months."

"Good," she said. "Because she's your present. You're holding Tulip von Pumpernickel. She's twelve weeks old. You can change her name if you don't like it. You can also turn down this gift, no harm, no foul. Not everyone likes or wants a dog. In fact, I don't want you adopting this dog unless you truly want her."

"I totally want her! Thank you!"

"You're welcome. And if you ever decide you don't want her? In twelve weeks or twelve years—give her back to me. And we'll be good. Fair?" Cheree asked.

"Oh my God. Beyond fair." Tulip wriggled in my arms, I lowered her to the lawn and watched her trot off. "Queen Cheree? Best. Present. Ever. Can we go shopping for puppy supplies? I'm going to need food and a dog bed and—"

She laughed. "Please call me Cheree when we're in private. All your puppy needs are being delivered to your father's condo even as we speak. Let's get down to business and plan your wedding, yes? I told Young Mr. Philips to bring out the bridal dress sketches and the fabric swatches. They're waiting for us back at the BBQ."

I hoped Elizabeth, Lady and the Damp would be cool with this. Especially Elizabeth. She'd be marching down the aisle very soon.

"Sounds perfect," I said. "I have no idea how to plan a wedding."

Cheree laughed. "Hah! You and your Ladies have been planning your weddings since grade school."

We sat at an outdoor table piled high with dress sketches of designer wedding gowns and fabric swatches while Queen Cheree flipped through and then passed them to me. "Too old-fashioned. Too tragically hip," she said. "Too over the top fairy princess."

"Agree." I tossed the rejects into a pile on the side.

"Hmm. Definite possibility." She handed me a

drawing.

I shook my head. "Too stern."

"You're right. We should convene your Ladies for a bridal conference: they can weigh in on the gowns and the flowers. I'm assuming you want them to be your bridesmaids?"

Would Elizabeth want them to be her bridesmaids?

"Of course!" I said and glanced at the mini-Ladies playing with the puppies and Sunny on the lawn. "Can Jeannie and her friends be my flower girls?"

"They'd be thrilled!" Cheree said. "Considering this is all happening in less than two weeks—holy smokes we've got our work cut out for us!"

"Two weeks?" I squeaked. "Two weeks? I thought royal weddings took months to plan?"

"Not this one darling. We're on a tight time schedule. But you know that right?"

I heard a ruckus, a loud roar from the basketball court. "Dude! Most excellent–you scored from outside the paint," teenage Liam said. "Who's the hottie? She looks familiar?"

"Squee!" Jeannie exclaimed. "He's here! He's finally here!"

"Who's the scary girl squeezing his arm?" Tonya asked.

"I luff him," a third girl exclaimed. She and the mini-Ladies sprung up from the lawn and raced off.

"Sorry I'm late for the family party," a familiar voice said with a hint of a slur.

I knew that voice. I missed that voice. I hated to admit it, but I ached for the man it belonged to. I swiveled as if in slow motion, willing the sea of royals to part so I could see if it was indeed him.

And just like I'd issued a royal edict—Nick came into view. His hair was messy, he looked a little flushed and he sported a more than five o'clock shadow. He wore a leather biker jacket and held a lager in one hand. His other arm was wrapped around the waist of raven-haired, petite, booby girl wearing too much makeup, a micro-mini and sky-high platforms.

"Ivanka and I just arrived in town from Croatia and well—" his eyes locked onto mine. "—let's just say we were delayed by some bumpy weather."

My hand flew to my chest.

Esmeralda glared at him. Then stared at me. "Oh, crap," she said.

CHAPTER 24

Cheree frowned but pulled it together. "Hi honey." She stood up and walked toward Nick. She passed Esmeralda, who strode the opposite direction toward me as she tugged her thumb and forefinger across her lips in the universal sign for 'zip it.'

"I didn't know you were bringing I-wanna." Cheree and Nick hugged.

"That's Ivanka, Your Royal Highness," Ivanka said.

Cheree waved her hand in the air. "Whatever darling."

"Cristoph has a date," Nick said. "I can have one too."

"Absolutely, honey," Cheree said. "I'm just a little surprised it's Ivanka."

"So nice to see you again, Queen Cheree." Ivanka bent her knee ever-so-slightly.

Way to show respect—not. Even I knew that curtsey was totally pathetic.

"And you, as well," Cheree said, her face frozen. "It's been a few months since we were graced with your company. I could only imagine what had become of you."

"Travels, work," Ivanka said. "I've been out of the country since Cristoph and I—"

Cheree held up one hand. "Splendid!" She said. "How nice for you."

"Glad you could put in an appearance—black sheep," King Frederick said.

"I wouldn't miss this for the world," Nick said.

"Burger, chicken or sausage?" King Frederick asked. "I remember what Ivanka wants."

Queen Cheree and Royal Nana shot each other looks, turned and frowned at him.

"The combo platter!" the King said, oblivious.

Ivanka giggled. "Oh your Royal Highness." This time she performed a perfect deep curtsey and flashed the entire party an enormous amount of cleavage. "As always—you flatter me."

Cristoph strode toward Nick. "This is a cheap shot, dude," he hissed.

"I have no idea what you're talking about." Nick shrugged and slugged back his lager.

"Oh yes you do," Cristoph said. "This is family. This is an old-school tradition. And you show up here with my ex—"

"I showed up here with your brother, Cristoph," Ivanka said. "At least Nick is a gentleman. It's so nice to see you again, too." She turned toward the King. "I'd love that combo platter, your Highness. I'm ravenous."

"She always is," Queen Cheree muttered under her breath, turned and walked back toward me, one eyelid twitching.

Liam kept bouncing his basketball.

"So nice to see you again, Lizzie." Nick guzzled his drink and slammed the bottle down on a table.

"You're… you're… you're Cristoph's brother?" I asked.

Half the crowd burst out laughing. "You're hysterical," Liam said.

"I wanted a boy and a girl," Queen Cheree said. "God saw fit to bless Frederick and me with two sons. Practically Irish twins. My princes are only ten months apart."

"Don't bring up the Irish," Royal Nana said.

Queen Cheree swiveled toward her. "I'm American with half Irish descent," she said. "After thirty years, you're going to have to accept that some day. I suggest today. Oh, and the not marrying into the BRF thing too."

"BRF?" I muttered.

"British Royal Family," Esmeralda said. "You know that."

"Of course," I said.

Royal Nana sniffed. "I'm eighty-five. I don't have to accept *anything*."

"You're a prince." I said.

Nick cocked his head and regarded me quizzically. "Is that your hypoglycemia or the head trauma talking?"

"Hey Cristoph, you're marrying a girl with a sense of humor," Liam said. "Score, dude!"

Esmeralda poked my arm and whispered, "I figured

out why you've been acting differently lately."

I flicked her hand away. "It's not the head trauma or the hypoglycemia. It's just me," I said.

Esmeralda leaned in again. "I promise I won't tell anyone."

"Too late, Lizzie," Nick said, turned his back to me and wrapped his arm around Ivanka who, balanced her combo plate on one hand.

My gaze was riveted on Nick and Barbie-I-mean-whatever her name was as they stumbled toward a picnic table. "Just kill me now," I mumbled under my breath.

"You fell in love with the wrong prince, didn't you?" Esmeralda asked.

"Absolutely not!" I stamped my foot, but that hurt and I winced.

"Instant karma," Esmeralda said.

"What do you mean?"

"You just lied," she said. "Karma tends to hit liars a little faster than other sinners."

"That's not fair." I frowned.

Esmeralda shrugged. "I didn't make the Karma rules."

"Fine. I don't know. Maybe. Okay. Kind-of. I certainly wasn't planning on it." I swallowed. "I *definitely* wasn't planning on it."

"Crap," she said.

"Total crap," I said. "What should I do now?"

"One. We should have a drink."

"Okay." I stood up and limped toward the bar.

"Elizabeth!" Esmeralda said.

"What?"

"What's gotten into you? Sit down! What do you

want?"

"I don't know." I sat back down. "You pick."

Esmeralda raised her hand in the air and summoned a waiter. "Two piña coladas, por favor. Heavy on the fruit, please, I'm watching my girlish figure. Gracias!" She smiled and turned back to me. "Number Two. Definitely make out with Cristoph in front of Nick and the tramp. Three. Go home, cuddle your new puppy and get some sleep. And then there's four."

"Sounds good," I said. "I can't feel my fingers or my toes. Is that normal?"

"Yes that's normal. It's called shock," Esmeralda said.

"Aah," I said. "I should be able to identify that feeling by now. Okay. What's four?"

"I'll call the rest of your Ladies-in-Waiting. We'll convene. Except for Zara. She texted me that she's on vaca in Wisconsin. Something about Dells and brats and beer. She could do all that here. What the hell is she doing in Wisconsin?"

"Not the Dells," I said. "How long is she going to be in Wisconsin?"

"I don't know. She doesn't know."

Great. That meant Zara wasn't riding to my rescue anytime soon.

"What do you mean by 'convene'?" I asked.

"We accept no excuses, we take no prisoners and we kick ass." Esmeralda lifted her tumbler to mine and we toasted. "Watch this." She held her glass in the air, plucked a knife off the table and turned toward the royals. "Attention! Atención! Cristoph, get your fine behind over here—pronto!"

Cristoph saluted her and strode toward us carrying his drink.

I stood up and smiled at him as he wrapped his arm around my waist. "Was Ivanka your ex-girlfriend?" I whispered.

He shifted from foot to foot. "You were in the States. We weren't even going out. A guy has needs…"

"Fellow royals! Have we forgotten our manners?" Esmeralda asked the crowd.

"Girlfriend?" I asked Cristoph through my fake smile. "Or fool-around-girl?"

"I don't know," he said. "Maybe a little of both."

"Is?" I asked. "Or was?"

"Was!" Cristoph said. "Definitely was."

Esmeralda raised her glass. "I propose a toast to the future rulers of Fredonia—Prince Cristoph and his smart, beautiful, funny and charming fiancée—Lady Elizabeth Billingsley."

The Timmels raised their glasses.

Except for Nick. He tipped back another lager while Ivanka sat so close to him I feared her fake boob would melt into his arm.

Esmeralda faced Cristoph and me. "May your love be long. May your love be true. May your love climb every mountain—"

"You stole that from *The Sound of Music*." Nick said.

"And may your love be the Happily-Ever-After—for the both of you. Cheers." Esmeralda said.

"Cheers!" The royals raised their glasses as they toasted us, and then each other.

Esmeralda clinked her knife against her glass, glanced

at me, scrunched her lips and eyes and made kissy faces.

"Cristoph!" I hissed. "Kiss me."

More knives clinked against glasses.

"Kiss her!" Jeannie squealed and the little ladies giggled.

He hugged me tight and kissed me on my cheek.

"Kiss her for real," Liam hollered.

I snuck a peek at Nick, who leaned back in his chair and wore a smug grin on his face.

"For the love of God, kiss her like a man," Royal Nana said. "Or I will blame your American mother for catering to your every whim and raising you to be a precious snowflake."

Cheree sighed and rolled her eyes.

"Kiss me like you mean it, Cristoph," I whispered. "Kiss me like the world is ending in one minute and I'm the last person you'll ever kiss. Kiss me hot, plain and simple."

"But this isn't simple. It will never be simple. It's all very complicated," he said and squeezed my hand.

"Kiss me like you mean it, or you can kiss our engagement goodbye."

I think that's the first time he really looked me in the eyes. And in a heartbeat his look turned from dutiful to smoldering. He wrapped one arm around my waist and tipped me back so I balanced on one foot.

Unfortunately it was my bad foot.

"Ow!" I said.

"Sorry!" He placed his other arm under my knees and lifted me up like I was light as a feather and held me flush against his chest in his muscular arms.

"Oh!" I wrapped my arms around his neck and my lips

were inches from his.

He locked his lips on mine and kissed me hungrily, thoroughly, and for a few seconds? He really did take my breath away.

The nobles cheered.

Esmeralda winked at me as Cristoph returned me gently to the ground. I glanced up to see Nick's reaction. But I could only see the back of him as he left the party, Ivanka trailing behind him.

I stood next to the castle's front door, Tulip lying on the ground next to me. I held her leash in my hand and regarded Cristoph.

"Something's come up Elizabeth," he said. "Do you mind if I don't drive you home tonight? The bodyguards will drop you off safe and sound."

"That's fine," I said. "I'm exhausted."

"Good! I'll see you tomorrow at the event."

"What event?"

"No one gave you the itinerary?"

I shook my head.

"I'll get one for you. Tomorrow you're scheduled to pay a visit to the orphanage, then we get our official engagement picture taken in the rose garden at the palace. After that you're to peruse flowers, dresses and have your first fittings. Cocktails with the Duke and Duchess of Cambria. And then dinner with the Earl of Plank. And onto the next day."

"There's so much to do," I said.

I silently thanked God this was Elizabeth's life and not mine.

"Life of a soon to be Princess of Fredonia," he said.

"Unfortunately, because of the land buy-out, we're on a super tight time schedule."

"Right," I said. "But no one's really explained the land buy-out to me."

"I'll add that to tomorrow's itinerary," he said. "You did simply wonderful today. No one could have done better. I'm so proud of you." He pulled me close to him, hugged me and kissed me again. Sweetly, romantically; he even included a little sexy tongue action. But I didn't feel a thing this time. Not one zing. No tingles. Dang.

Which was good, dammit! Elizabeth was going to marry Cristoph. Not me.

"I'll see you tomorrow, Cristoph. And thank you for everything." I squeezed his hand. "A girl couldn't have asked for a more special day."

CHAPTER 25

Queen Cheree was true to her word. Every piece of puppy paraphernalia had been delivered to Papa's condo. Tulip's kibble, treats and wet food were stocked in the main kitchen. Her crate was in my bedroom. Scoop bags were generously distributed in every room in the house along with paper towels, organic cleaning spray, carpet cleaner and scrub brushes. Puppy toys littered the rooms, as well as the hallways.

I'd fed Tulip, scrubbed the mound of makeup off my face and changed into three hundred count cotton boxer pjs and a lacy tank top. Now I watched my new puppy explore one of the low to the ground plantar boxes on the penthouse balcony as I limped its perimeters, my cell phone pressed against my ear.

"Elizabeth is getting married in less than two weeks, Mr. Philips. Tell me she's cool with this and will be back here like really soon."

"Yes, she's absolutely cool with this," he said. "Two weeks? They're really rushing it."

"It's because of the contracts—which you all didn't fill me in on—but I'll find out more tomorrow."

"That's been shrouded in mystery for a while, so I am as curious as you to know the details."

"I'm tired, Mr. Philips. I don't know what to do?"

"I know you're tired, Lucy. I am too. I'm hoping my physical therapist will clear me for flying in a couple of days. In the meantime, Zara—"

"Zara's not coming," I said. "She texted Esmeralda and said she was va-ca-ing in Wisconsin. Apparently she's at the Dells." I watched as Tulip squatted in a dirt planter and did her business.

"That's because she doesn't want to tell Esmeralda she's helping the real Elizabeth. Because you're doing such an excellent job impersonating her that everyone thinks *you are Elizabeth*. Kudos."

"But I'm *not* doing an excellent job, Philips." I kneeled to scoop puppy poop as Tulip bounded off to chase a toy. "Esmeralda suspects I'm more interested in Nick than Cristoph. Nick's taken up with Cristoph's ex-girlfriend-tramp-call-girl-slut—whatever." I dropped the bag of poop into an outdoor trash bin. "I suspect Cristoph's still interested in Ms. Trampy. And Queen Cheree gave me a puppy."

"The Queen gave you a puppy?" Mr. Philip Philips

squealed.

"Amazing, yes?"

"That means you're golden with the royal family," he said. "Oh, God, I can't wait to get home. Don't get me wrong—Chicago's a lovely town but—"

"I know Philips." Tulip deposited her chew toy on my foot, stared at it and wagged her tail. I leaned down and picked it up. "You miss your home." I thought of Alida, and Uncle John, and MadDog and The Chicago White Sox. "I miss my home too."

"Not to rain on your parade," Mr. Philips said, "but technically this is Elizabeth's puppy."

I frowned. "Signing off now. Important royal duties to attend to."

Like playing fetch with *my* new puppy.

I threw her toy a few feet. She raced after it, brought it back and deposited it just far enough away from my foot that I had to take one ouchy step in order to pick it up. I tossed it again. She raced, grabbed and returned it.

"Good girl, Tulip! Good girl!"

She barked. I pitched it again a little more vigorously. She bounded back. She was totally into it! Okay fine. *I was totally into it.* This was way more fun than making my way through a dungeon, having my foot run over and seeing Nick with Trampy McVampy's boob super-glued to his arm. Until I tossed the toy too high and it lodged in the fence.

Tulip raced to the barrier, parked her butt next to it and yipped.

I put one finger to my lips and limped toward her. "Shh! You don't want to wake up the household." Then realized that Papa and Carolina were probably still out on the town. I reached for the toy but couldn't touch it. Tulip barked.

"Hang on!" I shuffled a few feet, grasped a sturdy lawn chair and dragged it across the concrete until it was flush against the fence. I gingerly climbed onto it and grabbed the toy that was firmly lodged in the protective mesh. "I got it!" I glanced over my shoulder and smiled at Tulip. "Am I a good dog mother or what?"

When the mesh split faster than a run in cheap pantyhose. My arm plunged through it, my chest fell through it, and suddenly I was suspended—almost horizontal—blinking at the twinkling lights twenty-five floors below. "Help!" I screamed. "Someone help me!"

Tulip barked.

"Helga! Anyone? Help!" The mesh unwound—strand by metallic strand—until it hit my waist level. I peered at the pavement thousands of yards below and realized that, based on the way things were going, I would soon be plummeting to my death. Which would not be pretty. And I wouldn't be able to keep my very first puppy ever.

So. Not. Fair.

I hooked my ankle around the chair, sucked in all my core strength, gritted my teeth and pulled myself back inside the torn fence, saving myself from splattering like an egg on the pavement far below.

I crawled off the chair onto the floor and lay on my back on the cool concrete as my heart raced and I tried to catch my breath. Tulip jumped on top of me and licked my face.

I was safe—for now. When it dawned on me—*this*

probably wasn't an accident. Someone was most likely trying to kill me—oops I meant Elizabeth.

I plucked the phone out of my pocket and called one number. But all I heard was heavy breathing and "Oh my God!"

"Esmeralda!" I screamed. "Answer your fucking phone! Talk to me! It's Elizabeth! It's important."

"How important," she moaned, "is important? Because I'm in the middle of a situation. And it's kind of... important—too."

"You bet your fine Spanish ass it's important. Get off the phone," a guy said. "How many times have I asked you to get off the phone during sex?"

"I thought you wanted me to get off while we were having phone sex?" Esmeralda asked.

"No!" the guy grunted. "Well, maybe. But not right now."

"I think someone just tried to kill me—*important*," I said.

"Oh my God! Where are you?" Esmeralda asked. "Are you okay?"

"Yes, I think. I'm scared. Papa's condo."

"I'm calling 911!"

"Don't!" I said. "Maybe it was just a freak accident. I don't know for sure and I don't want this on the news."

"I'm calling 911!" she said.

"If you do I'll twist your ear off next time I see you..." I said. "...and feed it to my puppy."

"Fine. I'm sending reinforcements and I'm on my way. Do you need to hide? I have this strange feeling you need to hide for a couple of days."

I looked at the jagged rip in the protective mesh surrounding the penthouse terrace.

"Yes," I said. "Hiding would be awesome."

Minutes later, Esmeralda arrived with the codpiece guard in tow. They quickly collected clothes and sundries, threw them into a few suitcases, grabbed some puppy essentials and checked Tulip and me into a two-bedroom junior suite at the Four Seasons overlooking the Palace grounds. It was like the Drake but a little smaller. A Detective was also on the scene.

"You'll be safe here Lady Billingsley," the guard said.

"Thank you..." I didn't even know his name. "I'm so sorry. I've forgotten my manners. I don't remember your name."

"Larry," he said and bowed to me.

"Thanks Larry, and you don't need to bow," I said. "Besides, I'm probably just over-reacting on the death-threat thing."

"Not according to the cops and the Fredonia Secret Service who are combing your Papa's condo," the Detective said. "It appears that mesh fence was deliberately sliced and sabotaged. Who knew you liked to hang out on the penthouse terrace?"

"Papa, Carolina, Helga, Mr. Philips, the paparazzi..." I said. "Everyone? Maybe a Dish Network Installer? I'm sure I'm fine. I'm safe. Go back to your lives."

The Detective peered at Larry. "You're staying here tonight?"

"Yes," he said.

"Call me if there's any trouble." He bowed to me.

"We'll get to the bottom of this, Lady Billingsley."

"Thank you Detective," I said as he left the room.

Esmeralda glanced at Larry. "I'm staying here too."

"I adore you but I need to sleep!"

"And sleep you will," Esmeralda said. "I slipped half an Ambien in your drink back at the penthouse."

"That's why I feel woozy?"

"That and all your adrenaline wore off," Larry said.

"But where will Tulip do her business?" I asked.

Larry pointed to her leash. "I'll walk her."

"Okay, I mean yes. I don't feel so good, Esmeralda," I said.

"I know, honey." She wrapped her arm around me and helped me hobble to a bedroom. "Cristoph e-mailed me your itinerary for tomorrow. I didn't tell him about the incident. We'll cross that bridge mañana. Get some sleep. You've got the orphans at 11 A.M. and they can be a demanding bunch. You need to bring your A game. Nighty night."

The Fredonia Secret Service stepped out of their cars before I did at The Holy Cross Orphanage. The head guy named Tomas, gave me the all clear, and I exited the town car wearing the chaste blue, below-the-knee dress. Lady Cheryl had accompanied me today.

"I'm nervous," I said. "I don't know that much about kids."

"Well then thank your lucky stars I'm here with you: I know a lot. Kids cry and puke and complain. They're darling, do adorable things and you fall completely, utterly in love with them. And then they do something ornery and

mean—like telling their younger sister she was adopted."
Cheryl said. "Kids are the best. If there's one thing I
know—it's how to mother."

"That's your super power," I said.

"What are you talking about?"

"Esmeralda said my Ladies-in-Waiting have super
powers. That's yours. You're a great mom!"

"I'm not so sure my girls would agree with you,"
Cheryl said.

I greeted the orphans and talked with them. Well
actually I didn't do a lot of talking; instead, I listened.

"And then one day, Mama just died and no one could
find my father. My aunt didn't want me—she said she had
more than enough kids. So they sent me here," one little
redheaded boy said.

"That sucks," I said. "My mom died too. What's your
name?"

"Peter," he said.

I leaned down toward him. "What do you want to be
when you grow up Peter?"

"I want to be a palace guard."

"I'm friends with a palace guard," I said. "Do you
want me to introduce you? Maybe he could give you some
tips?"

"Oh mum!" Peter exclaimed. "That would be the
best!" He threw himself on me and hugged me hard.

I hugged him back and heard clicks and pops, as the
paparazzi caught the moment.

My hair was coiffed by a hair stylist much nicer then
D'Alba. A professional makeup artist did my makeup. An

assistant helped me change into a demure silk suit for Cristoph and Elizabeth's official engagement portrait photo shoot with some fancy photographer and her fluttery assistant.

After an hour of hearing:

"Please tilt your chin up ever so slightly, Lady?"

"Could you pull in your tummy a bit, Lady Billingsley?"

"Stop hunching—I mean could you please sit a bit taller, my Lady?"

"Would you stop biting your lip, Lady Billingsley?"

"And well done Prince Cristoph! It seems you just can't take a bad picture!"

I wouldn't mind if I was ever in the spotlight—ever again.

CHAPTER 26

And then there was the Trying-on-of-the-Wedding-Gowns-and-Bridesmaid-Dresses Event held in one of the smaller palace ballrooms. In attendance were a dozen servants and assistants, Queen Cheree, Duchess Carolina von Sauerhausen, two seamstresses, one photographer, two designers who'd flown in at the last minute from London and Rome, my Ladies-in-Waiting, our dogs, as well as the girlies.

Cheryl's girls, Diana and Violet, ran around the room playing hide and seek with Jeannie Beanie, the little ladies and the dogs.

The event was catered—no yummy BBQ this time. Just finger-foods, sparkling water and a little bubbly. The assistants helped me as I tried on gown after gown.

"I can't believe that someone tampered with that protective netting," Carolina said. "Your papa and I had no idea there had been an incident until we got the phone call from the police department. We were frantic with worry, but Joan texted me and said you were safe and sound and staying with Esmeralda."

"My Ladies take such great care of me," I said. "There's nothing you or Papa could have done." My eyes swiveled until I found Joan in the crowd. "Hey Joan Brady!"

"What?" she asked as an assistant helped her try on a bridesmaid dress. "I don't like this one, Elizabeth. It looks like a cupcake exploded all over me."

"No worries. We will not pick exploding cupcake dresses for the bridesmaids. I just wanted to say thanks for helping last night."

She waved her hand. "I'm good at passing along the information and smoothing things over. I'm a barrister, but I pride myself on using my lawyer powers for good—instead of being a control-freak, power hungry asshat, who tries to take advantage of people when they're going through a tough time. Unfortunately, I've met more than a few of those types."

I gave her a thumbs up. "I think your superior communication skills and ability to finesse might be your Ladies-in-Waiting Super Power!"

She laughed.

Cheryl ran after the girls, who were now pulling each other's hair. "Stop it!" she said. "Ladies do not pull other Ladies' hair. Unless you want to be professional wrestlers. And so help me God, if any of you aspire to that, I will ship all of you off to boarding school. Even if I'm not your mother."

"I don't know." Carolina wrung her gloved hands. "I'm starting to worry. Who could have tampered with those nets?"

"Don't worry about it. Let the police and Secret Service figure it out," I said. "I don't think who ever did this is after you or Papa. But if you're worried, maybe you should stay at a hotel."

"We're moving to my chateau until the wedding's over. I think you should come with us. There's plenty of room. We hired armed guards."

I glanced at Esmeralda, who shook her head, 'No'.

"I'm fine at the hotel, really. The suite's lovely. And it's so close to the castle. There are so many things to get done before the wedding. And the chateaux's about…"

Esmeralda held up four fingers on one hand and five on her other.

"… forty-five minutes away from the capitol, yes?" I asked.

"Yes," Carolina said. "But you would be safe."

"Duchess von Sauerhausen." Esmeralda curtseyed with some effort.

If I had to guess, I'd say she hadn't done that in quite a while.

"My recommendation—if you don't mind?" Esmeralda asked.

Carolina nodded.

"Relax. Enjoy. Show up for the important events. Elizabeth's Ladies-in-Waiting will take care of the details. Stop worrying."

"But what if something terrible happens to Elizabeth? I

would be distraught," Carolina said.

I was deep inside a gown and felt like I was drowning in tulle, but still managed to peek at her. I could swear she covered a small smile. How much did I really know about Papa's fiancé?

Could Duchess Carolina von Sauerhausen have been the person who sliced the netting? Did she want me/Elizabeth dead? And if she did—why?

I kept my eye on Carolina as the hours ticked by while I tried on a hundred dresses and despised eighty of them.

"Oh, I love that one," Cheryl said. "You look sexy and enchanting. I used to look that way too—back in the day."

"You still look that way today," I said. "This isn't the one for me. I'm a little too fleshy for the lace cutouts."

"I met my husband wearing a dress that looked almost exactly like that," Cheryl said. "We were at a charity gala raising funds for the tsunami victims. He strode across a crowded dance floor with fire in his eyes and asked me if I wanted to dance. He was so handsome and commanding. I said yes. He practically took my breath away. Seven years later, he only has fire in his eyes when he watches a soccer match on TV. And the only time I'm knocked over is when one of my girls tackles me."

"Do you still love him?" I asked her as an assistant unzipped the lacy dress and helped me out of it.

"Of course!" Cheryl said. "If Lucas saw me in that dress? He'd turn off the damn soccer game, forget we had kids and we'd be doing the between-the-sheets tango all over again."

When the girlies screamed and hollered. "You!" one girl said.

"No you!" the other girlie screamed.

"I'm a flower girl," Jeannie stuck her tongue out at Cheryl's daughter, Violet. "You don't get to be anything in the wedding."

"Oh yeah?" Violet asked. "My mommy's a real Lady-in-Waiting and not some stupid flower girl. She's a Blindsmaid."

"That's Bridesmaid, stupid."

"I'm not stupid," Violet said. "That's my younger sister."

"Wah!" Diana plunked on the floor and cried.

"Be right back." Cheryl ran over, hugged her little one and whispered into her ear.

"Esmeralda! Joan!" I hissed. "I've got an idea." They made their way toward me and we huddled with our arms around each other, our heads nearly touching as I whispered.

Joan smiled. "I'm happy to help you make that happen."

"Most excellent." Esmeralda pulled out her phone and hit one a key. "Larry. Lady Elizabeth has a request... no, not another death threat. Something a little different. Can you help... Excellent! I'll text you the info. Make the calls, yes?" She fanned her cleavage. "Fabulous! You are my knight in shining armor. Thank you! Mwah!"

We finally picked THE dress. It was beautiful. It wasn't really me but I think *it probably was* Elizabeth. Considering she'd be the one walking down the aisle—that's really all that mattered. I must admit, I hedged a little bit. I said I was still really drawn to the gown with the lacey cut-outs.

That was kind-of a lie. But that kind-of lie was for a really good reason…

As for picking the bridesmaid dresses—well that was a different story. Esmeralda wanted a gown cut low in the bodice to show off her cleavage. Cheryl desired a fitted gown to display her petite figure. Joan preferred something sleeveless to show-off her toned arms that she'd spent hours sculpting at the gym.

At this point I didn't really care what Zara wanted as I wasn't including her in Elizabeth's wedding. If she wanted in, she could beg Elizabeth at the last minute. Personally—I was done with Zara. Although I will forever be grateful to her for insisting I get the full Brazilian. Which, sadly, was totally temporary and once again on the itinerary.

Carolina and Queen Cheree chose their 'Mother-of the Bride and Groom' dresses. (While technically, Carolina wasn't Elizabeth's mother—apparently she was playing the part for this gig.) Both gowns were exquisite. Each cost more than two years' rent on my apartment.

Jeez, this was the most difficult day since my first day that I applied for the part-time job. All the gowns and fabrics and finery. All the negotiating over blush pink versus ecru and white and inlaid pearls and hints of lace and neckline dilemmas. Except for the thigh high, tightly pinching, pleather boots, I suddenly longed for the life of your average Southside Chicago cocktail waitress; especially one who worked at a biker bar called MadDog.

I glanced at my watch—there was a seven-hour time difference between Fredonia and Chicago. I missed Alida and Uncle John so much I practically hallucinated they were in front of me.

"I'll be right back," I said. "Must hit the Ladies Room."

"I'm coming with you," Esmeralda said.

"No, no," I said. "Some things a girl has to do in private."

"You never had to do that in private before," she said. "I need to talk to you about the thing."

"You don't know what I'm doing in private," I said.

"Well whatever it is, you've always done it in front of me before. I remember that time in Morocco…"

"Yes, yes, I know, but Morocco was the exception to the rule," I said.

"Whatever," Esmeralda said. "Look. I called—"

"Must see a man about a horse," I said. "Back in a few. Tell Cheryl to try on the gown she liked with the lace cutouts. I command you, Lady Esmeralda."

"Now you sound like the old Elizabeth," Esmeralda said.

I giggled, gave her the royal wave and left the ballroom. I paced—a little gimpy—down a few corridors until I found an empty hallway. I lowered myself gingerly to the floor, leaned against a wall, pulled my phone from my purse and dialed. She picked up.

"I don't know this number or the area code. You have three seconds to convince me you're not a telemarketer before I hang up," Alida said.

"It's me!" I hissed. "Elizabeth—I mean Lucy."

"Lucy?"

"Yes! Squee! I'm finally talking to you. How are you? How's Mateo? I miss you so much!"

"Mateo's kicking ass in Little League. I'm cool

considering Mark Whitford still runs MadDog like Stalin ruled Russia. How's the new job?" she asked. "When are you coming home? Why'd you call yourself Elizabeth? I miss you!"

"New job's good and bad," I said. "I'll probably be home in two weeks. I totally miss you too! And just between you and me—like you totally have to promise—"

"I promise," she said.

"Pinky swear?" I squirmed excitedly. "You can't tell a soul."

"Totally pinky swear. Who would I tell?"

I giggled and whispered. "I'm pretending to be Elizabeth because it's part of my job."

When I heard the harsh clip clop of shoes down the marble hallway, approaching me.

"That's kind of freaky-weird," Alida said. "Who's Elizabeth and why are you pretending to be her?"

I looked up and froze as Nick approached me, a determined look on his handsome, stone cold sober face.

"Mwah! Love you! Must run!" I hung up.

We were toe to toe. His toes were obviously bigger than mine and he was much taller than me, especially considering he was standing and I was sitting.

"I had to hear—from a palace guard who's shtooping Esmeralda by the way—that you were almost killed last night?" Nick held out his hand.

"The guard's name is Larry." I took his hand and he helped me to my feet.

"I know his name. We play blackjack once a month. After all we've been through Lizzie—why didn't you call me?" Nick asked.

"I wanted to," I said. "But when I saw you at the BBQ you seemed, well, occupied."

"Ivanka's a diversion," he said.

"Just like I was for all those years?"

"It's different between us now."

"It's different between us *now* because I'm engaged to your brother and you all are competitive. Must get back to the gown festivities." I limped in the direction of the ballroom."

He followed me. "That's not why it's different. Okay. Fine. Maybe that's five percent why it's different."

I swiveled and glared at him. "What's the other ninety-five percent?"

"Always the questions and answers with the new you. I don't know. It's the way you smell. You always used to smell like perfume. Now you smell—well, simple. Like how the air smells after a spring rain. Fresh. New. Like… hope."

"That's probably just my spring rain scented soap." I resumed walking.

"It's that funny way you bite your lip when you're nervous."

"I don't bite my lip when I'm nervous," I said and bit my lip. "I bite my lip when… when I'm thinking about something—like getting back to trying on wedding gowns and picking out flowers for the big day."

He put his hands on my shoulders, squeezed them and stopped me in my tracks. "Look at me," he said.

I turned and gazed up at him. His eyes were so blue, his lips so full, his gaze so intense as he stared down at me. "Tell me I mean nothing to you," he said and pulled me to him. "Tell me you don't care about me anymore. Tell me you're over me once and for all and I will leave you alone. I need to hear you say it."

I bit my lip so hard I tasted blood.

"I'll be the best man at your wedding. I'll toast your first bridal kiss at the reception. I'll be the best uncle ever to your children. Just tell me, Lizzie. You've got to say it out loud. Or I'm not sure I can let this go. I'm not sure I can let *you* go."

"I, I, I…"

Esmeralda poked her head around the corner and frowned. Then smiled sweetly. "Nick! How nice to run into you. I was just going to ring you. I can't believe how perfect this timing is!" She clapped her hands. "Elizabeth—Queen Cheree and Giuseppe Felipe, the famous designer, are anxiously waiting your final decision about the inlaid pearls for your bodice. Over-night weddings don't plan themselves you know! Chop-chop!"

I shimmied out from under Nick's hands and loped back down the corridor, passing Esmeralda.

"I'm not letting this go," he said.

"You have to," I said.

"What were you thinking?" Esmeralda hissed.

"I'm thinking you're going to spin this into what we talked about," I whispered and took a few more steps.

"I'm thinking you've got some 'splaining to do—*Lucy.*"

I stopped in my tracks. Like seriously—I froze. Because on all those reruns of *The Lucille Ball Show*? Whenever Lucy's husband Ricky got irritated with her—he'd say the same thing. Which meant that—

Esmeralda knew. She absolutely knew. Oh crap. My cover was blown.

CHAPTER 27

Esmeralda, Larry and I watched reruns of *I Love Lucy* with Cheryl's kids, Violet and Diana, in their gigantic living room while we munched on popcorn prepared by their ancient, rickety live-in housekeeper.

"Mom and Dad are really going to be gone, together, one whole night?" Violet asked as she reclined on the floor snug in her sleeping bag next to Tulip.

"You cool with that?" I asked.

"Dad leaves all the time, but Mom's always here," Diana said.

"You know how you girls have play dates with your friends?" I asked.

"Yes," they said.

"Your mom and dad needed a play date," Esmeralda said.

"They'll be back tomorrow. Hey look!" I pointed to the screen. "What is Lucy doing now?"

The girls giggled and Larry guffawed as Lucy stomped on grapes in a big outdoor tub, Lucy crammed chocolates into her mouth at the factory, and Lucy pretended to be Superman for her son's party. Interspersed between the on-screen hilarity, Esmeralda and I whispered in hushed tones as we confided—and we got real.

"I knew there was something off with you," she said. "Elizabeth was never this thoughtful."

"I'm sure she's thoughtful in her own way," I said. "Why did Zara spill the beans?"

"I called and told her about your possible murder attempt. I thought she should know. She's your, I mean-Elizabeth's, best friend, after all. She broke down and confided the gist of the situation. They hired and trained you to impersonate Elizabeth for a couple of weeks until she concluded her 'pressing business' in the States."

"Yup," I said. "That pretty much nails it. Was Zara the least bit upset that someone tried to kill me?"

"Zara's always been a little icy," Esmeralda said. "Similar to Elizabeth. In spite of all these years and our adventures, I still can't quite get a read on them. Kudos, by the way, on being the best princess impersonator ever. I hope Elizabeth's paying you a royal arm and a leg."

"The pay's decent," I said. "My Uncle John's in Assisted Living. The money I earn from this job will be spent keeping him there."

"Good. Or I'll kick Elizabeth's entitled ass when she gets back here," Esmeralda said. "I like you. You're a little… apasionada."

I smiled. "I like you too. Are you pissed at me that I fooled you?"

"For a second. Until I figured out you'd fallen for Nick. And I realized your life right now is even suckier than I imagined, because he doesn't know you're not Lizzie and you have to turn him down even though you really do care for him. Because—"

"Because I'm an imposter from America. And if Nick ever found out, he'd never speak to me again."

"I don't know," she said. "He's got an arrogant streak, but he doesn't seem to be that kind of guy. Have you all done it?"

"No! Well he has with Elizabeth. Apparently everywhere. Are you going to out me?" I asked.

"Nah. This is all too interesting to spill the beans. I might write a tell-all some day. I've always wanted to write a book. This would make a good one."

"Question. No one's explained the whole urgency of this wedding in regards to the land buyout. Do you know what's going on?" I asked.

She dragged her itinerary from her purse. "Tomorrow, 1 p.m. Confirmed meeting with King Frederick Timmel, Lord David Billingsley, Princes Cristoph and Nicholas Timmel, Lady Elizabeth Billingsley and her Ladies-in-Waiting, at the Chateaux Chocolat' in Friedricksburg, Fredonia. Attire: Casual. Please allow ninety minutes of driving time and bring a warm jacket as the temperature can drop precipitously in the mountain foothills. Tour of the chocolate factory. Private late lunch meeting thereafter, catered by Laura DeVries from Cupcakes-A-Go-Go Café. Ooh," Esmeralda said. "Lunch will be fabulous. That

DeVries chef is the bomb."

"I can live with a tour of a chocolate factory. Do you think Cheryl and her husband are having fun on their play date?"

"We made reservations at Sauerhausen's premiere Supper Club that has a live band and an amazing dance floor. She's wearing the loaner dress with the lace cut-outs. They will be plied with fine wine, a five star meal and then enjoy the musical stylings of the Florence Belk Band. After an evening of total pleasure and no children, they'll retire to your suite at the Four Seasons. And strangely enough, they only have movies on their TV—no sports channels are available. Front desk has been alerted that the problem is not fixable."

"You mean the front desk has been paid off."

"Alerted, paid off, same thing as long as it gets the job done."

"What about the hotel bar?"

"In a strange coincidence, the bartender has been tipped to ix-nay the soccer-nay."

"What about the tennis-nay?"

"All gone. Operation *Light My Fire* has commenced."

"I like how you work, Lady Esmeralda Ilona Castile Hapsburg the Fourth."

"You're making me up my game, Lucy..."

"Just Lucy for now," I said.

"You know I'll figure out your last name."

"I dare you," I said as we both giggled.

Early the next morning I received word from the police that the Penthouse had been thoroughly searched, scanned, finger prints lifted and was given the 'All Clear.' The Fredonia Secret Service even granted Elizabeth's family and me permission to return.

Back in Elizabeth's closet, Tulip wrestled a high-heeled pump on the floor. "You'd better stop that," I wriggled into jeans. "She'll kill you if you eat one of her precious Stewart Weitzman's." I slid into a pair of extra fleecy Uggs, a long-sleeved T-shirt covered by a thick, cotton sweater and grabbed a light down jacket should the weather get chilly.

As much as I wanted to bring Tulip with me on my trip, let's face it—chocolate was deadly poisonous for dogs. She was a puppy, had her nose in everything and I just knew she'd find some chocolate leftovers somewhere. But who would walk her while I was gone?

I took Tulip for a quick spin in Centralaski Park, came home and made her a breakfast of organic puppy kibble mixed with wild duck, wet with gravy. I smiled as she gulped down her food like she'd never eaten before and would never eat again.

When Helga popped into the kitchen and filled up a large bucket with cleaner and water. "You're spoiling zat dog," she said. "You're turning her into a leetle princess."

"She deserves to be spoiled! Isn't she darling? Helga—could I pay you extra to take care of Tulip today? We've got this meeting at some chocolate factory and I'm not comfortable bringing her with me. Chocolate's deadly poisonous for dogs."

"Dogs are so much work," Helga scrubbed the kitchen floor. "Just like children. You love them and love them, but in the end they always want more. They always want to be a princess. What's a mother to do?"

"Yes," I said. "I don't know about children because I've never had any, but I hear you. If you can't or don't want to take care of Tulip—that's fine. I'll find someone else…"

"No, no." Helga sighed. "I'll do it."

"Thank you!" I said. "Just take her for a couple of short walks. Don't let her off her leash. Play with her for a couple of minutes. Don't let her eat too many treats. I'll pay you extra. I really appreciate it."

"Everyone always appreciates it."

"I really do. Thanks!" Maybe I was being a bit paranoid, but something seemed off with Helga.

The Ladies picked me up in Cheryl's SUV, outfitted with massive snow tires. We were all dressed pretty much the same. Larry the guard drove as Cheryl sat in the front passenger seat, swiveled toward us in the back and filled us in on her date night with her husband.

"And then, oh my God, it was crazy. There were no sports channels available on cable in our suite. Not one single sports channel. It was like a miracle! And my husband looked into my eyes, said, 'You're still the hottest lady I've ever met,' and one thing led to the next and…"

"How many times, Cheryl?" Esmeralda asked.

"Oh." She smiled. "A Lady doesn't tell."

"I'm betting three," Joan said.

"I'll venture there was fourth encounter the next morning in the shower," Esmeralda said.

Cheryl giggled. "I'm instituting a mommy and daddy play date once a month."

Esmeralda, Joan and I smiled at each other and fist-bumped.

"Operation *Light my Fire*'s a success," Esmeralda said.

"Power to the Ladies," Joan said.

"And kudos to Luc-I mean- Elizabeth for the superb idea!" Esmeralda said.

I frowned and then smiled. "Thank you. I couldn't have done it without you!"

We exited the freeway and made our way up increasingly winding roads that eventually thinned down to two lanes. We passed farms and pastures with goats and cows in the field. Some places looked prosperous, others poor, as we ascended into the foothills of the Alps. The grass was green but there were small patches of melting snow. We finally arrived at a smallish hamlet with an arched sign that read "Welcome to Friedricksburg: The home of Chateaux Chocolat'".

Good thing I'd packed a parka. When the Ladies and I stepped out of the SUV the temperature had dropped at least forty degrees. The town looked like a fairy tale village in a movie. There were cobblestone streets and mom and pop storefronts painted in candy colors with decorated signs advertising what was for sale in each shop.

"I can't believe King Frederick was born here," Joan said. "You'd think Royal Nana would have had him in a hospital in a bigger city like Sauerhausen."

"He was a month premature," Cheryl said. "The family was staying at their lake chateaux several miles from here."

"No wonder he wants to keep this town preserved," I said. "It's darling. I can even smell the chocolate in the air."

Several nuns wearing wimples walked a pack of Labrador Retrievers past us.

"What's up with all the Labs?" I asked.

"Queen Cheree plunked down a small fortune and restored the town's dilapidated five-hundred-year-old church," Esmeralda said. "She turned the Saint Francis of Assisi Chapel grounds into a sanctuary for Labrador Retrievers."

"Oh, I'd love to see it."

"No time," Esmeralda pointed to her watch. "We're supposed to meet up with your fiancé and family at the chocolate factory."

I'd never been given a tour of a chocolate factory before and I wasn't going to let this opportunity slip through my fingers. The Ladies, King Frederick, Nick, Cristoph, various advisors, guards and I were in the tasting room. Per usual, Nick ignored me.

Cristoph smiled at me and held out a small chocolate in front of my lips. "Try this." He said. "Darkest chocolate imaginable with a hint of espresso."

I bit into it and almost swooned. "Holy moly! That's amazing!"

"It dawned on me you haven't even seen my new digs since you got back into town and we got engaged. I took the liberty of cancelling the dinner with Duchess Amy Moore tomorrow night because I want to spend that time with you, Elizabeth. No crowds, no photographers. Just you and me. What say you?"

What say I? Could I be more nervous? Would this be the royal sack attempt?

"I couldn't be more thrilled, Cristoph. What a fabulous idea. Formal or informal?"

"I think we should be informal," he said. "Let's just be ourselves, warts and all, and see how this goes. Yes?"

"Sounds perfect," I said. "Can I bring anything?"

"Just yourself, darling."

After a three course meal in a private room at Cupcakes-a-Go-Go Café, we were finally dusting off the crumbs from our fingers and getting down to business. The secret contract that demanded this urgent wedding.

"So you're saying that Cristoph and I need to marry by next week so my Papa, Lord David Billingsley, will enter into a joint partnership with the Royal Timmel family of Fredonia," I said. "He will pay off the deed on this land in order to keep all the acquisitions... royal. And save them from being parceled out to the highest bidder—to some asshat investor like Mark Whitford. Who wants to turn this beautiful town of Friedricksburg into a giant theme park."

"Yes," King Frederick said. "You've got a head for business on you, young Lady. Another reason I'm thrilled you are marrying my eldest son Cristoph."

"I told you Elizabeth was the one for me," Prince Cristoph said.

"It seems my darling daughter has returned from the States not only more beautiful, but financially savvy." Papa said.

"How do you know Mark Whitford from the States, Lizzie?" Nick asked.

"I don't. I do, however, read the *Wall Street Journal.*"

Hah hah! I read it before I picked up Tulip's dog poop with it

243

when I ran out of scoop bags.

"It could be Whitford or any scum like him." I sighed. "But this explains the pressing need for the haste of the marriage contract between The Fredonia royal family and family of Lord Billingsley. It's almost like a shotgun marriage—but for different reasons."

"Lizzie," Nick said. "As the financial advisor for the Timmel Royal Family, you need to marry Prince Cristoph in five days for the money to pass hands from your father, Lord David Billingsley, to the current lender on this loan. Do you or your family anticipate any impediment happening that could delay this marriage, as well as the financial contraction, that will save the Fredonia royal lands?"

I attempted to look into his blue eyes but he would not meet my gaze. I coughed, but he would not acknowledge my pathetic attempt at clandestine communication. Fine. I turned and stared at Papa. "What do you think Papa? Because you hold the purse strings and basically this is up to you."

"It was your mother's most cherished wish that someday you would marry into the royal family and become a Princess," he said. "I will do everything in my power to honor your mother's memory." He faced Nick. "Yes, Nicholas. Yes, the money will be transferred the moment my daughter says, 'I do.'

CHAPTER 28

Cristoph didn't live with his parents at the royal castle. He actually lived across the park from Elizabeth's Papa in a three-story brownstone. A guard, dressed in khakis and a long-sleeve T-shirt with a jean jacket, sat on the step in front of Cristoph's front door and read on his e-reader.

Esmeralda and Larry had driven me over a little before eight p.m. I was dressed casual in jeans, a long-sleeve, lacy T-shirt and a light jacket. "Well, here we are," I said. "Gorgeous brownstone. This looks like something in Hyde Park in Chicago."

"Do you miss Chicago, Lady Billingsley?" Larry asked.

Would a fork miss a knife? Would Christmas miss angels?

I waved my hand. "Kind of, I guess. I'm mostly just happy to be home."

"Larry, go ask that guard what kind of protocol they

have to make sure Elizabeth's safe here." Esmeralda said.

"Absolutely, my Spanish flower." He smiled and hopped out of the driver's seat.

She threw a kiss to him. "Gracias mi mejor Conquistador." She turned and glared at me. "Okay. There's no way you can sleep with Cristoph, Lucy."

"What made you think I'm going to sleep with Cristoph?"

"One. He's drop-dead gorgeous. Two. I saw the way he was feeding you chocolates at Chateaux Chocolat' yesterday. He was undressing you with his eyes."

"I think you're projecting your own love life onto mine. Because mine is quite pathetic."

She shook her head. "Nope. Cristoph hasn't earned the nickname 'The Playboy Prince' for nothing," she said. "He's going to try and seal the deal tonight. I can just feel it. I'm slightly psychic when it comes to love, you know. The pinch of Gypsy blood that runs through my veins is speaking to me via the tingle in my private girlie parts."

"Perhaps the pinch of your silk thong underwear is speaking to your private girlie parts," I said, peeved.

"Don't get defensive with me, Lucy. I'm just looking out for the greater picture here."

"And what is the greater picture?"

"Frankly at this point—I don't know? But what I do know is Cristoph's going to make a move tonight, and when he does? Promise me you'll keep your phone on you at all times. Text me before it's too late. I've alerted the other Ladies. We'll be waiting nearby and concoct some fabulous excuse to whisk you away."

Larry popped his head in the car. "Prince Cristoph just

has the one guard—but they're stationed around the clock. He does, however, have an extensive security system and Sauerhausen's entire police force will be here in seconds if alerted. Elizabeth will be in good hands."

"Splendid!" I said and stepped out of the car.

Esmeralda sighed. "And that's what worries me."

Cristoph's three level townhouse was simply gorgeous. He gave me the tour. Brick walls lined the majority of the space. The first level was furnished with built-in floor-to-ceiling bookcases filled with books and knick knacks. Signed lithographs hung on the walls. A bar was tucked into a corner of the room. There was a blackjack table and a billiard table. Three flat screen TVs were mounted high on the wall. French doors opened onto a large walled-in patio accented with tasteful outdoor furniture and a firepit.

"Can I get you a drink, Elizabeth?" Cristoph asked.

"Sure," I said. "How about a Pellegrino?"

"I thought we'd live it up." He popped the cork on a chilled bottle of champagne. "I've saved this Dom Perignon for a special occasion. Tonight's the night." He poured two glasses and handed me one. "A toast," he said. "To the most beautiful, smart fiancé a guy could ever hope for."

We toasted and sipped.

"Nice," I said. "I never used to drink champagne before. I think I'm developing a taste for it."

"That's funny," he said. "I remember that you always liked the bubbly."

"Perhaps you were thinking of my fondness for mineral water." I took another sip.

"No. You always enjoyed several glasses of expensive

247

champagne." He reached for and took my free hand. "Let's continue the tour, shall we?"

We climbed a tall staircase to the second floor. It had a more than decent kitchen and a gorgeous living room with a huge fireplace, dark, distressed, lustrous wooden floors and large windows that looked out on Centralaski Park. It was nighttime and the city lights twinkled like stars.

"This view is awesome, but aren't you worried that people can see inside?" I asked.

"I had the windows replaced with mirrored, bullet proof glass before I asked you to marry me. I didn't want you feeling unsafe, or have your privacy be violated. No one can look in here, Elizabeth. No paparazzi can snap a single picture. I want you to feel completely comfortable inside your new home."

"That's sweet of you," I said.

Elizabeth's new home—not mine.

"You're welcome," he said and held out the champagne bottle. "Top you off?

"Sure. Thank you."

He filled my flute with more primo bubbly. "Your townhouse is beautiful," I said.

"Come see the third floor."

"I think I've seen enough."

"No," he said. "I don't think you have."

The top floor was the bedroom floor. There were three guest bedrooms, baths and the master suite. "So, what do you think? Will you be comfortable moving in after we get married and honeymoon?" Cristoph asked.

"We're honeymooning?" I said.

"Of course," he said "St. Bart's. My friends have a private estate. We're scheduled to leave the day after the wedding. White sands, warm water and balmy weather. I took the liberty of buying you a little pre-wedding gift." He took a few steps to his bureau, picked up a wrapped package and held it out to me.

It was a relatively small box adorned with a festive white bow on top.

"That's so sweet of you, Cristoph." I opened it. "Really, you didn't have to get me anything."

I pulled the lid off the box, unfolded the soft, white paper and revealed bikinis. A lot of really teeny tiny bikinis. Most were floral. A few were solid, one was a leopard print. When it dawned on me that while there were many bikini bottoms—there was only one top. "Wow," I said. "I hope I fit into them. They're really little." I held one out in front of me. It was the size of a handkerchief. *If your cat used a handkerchief.* "There seems to be some confusion—most likely with your personal shopper or whoever helped pick these out."

"I picked them out personally, Elizabeth. Right after Father gave us his blessing."

Well that was unusual. Most guys hated shopping. I had to give him points for that.

"You are so sweet," I said. "There's just one teensy problem—there are twelve bikini bottoms and only one top."

He pulled me to him, stared down into my eyes and grinned. "Isn't it fabulous! You won't need them darling. Simply sunscreen. Where we're staying the beaches are topless! I have one more surprise for you. Hang on!" He raced off into his bathroom. "No peeking!"

"Then you should shut the door. Otherwise I'll be incredibly tempted."

He laughed and slammed the door shut.

Note to self/Lucy: this is Elizabeth's problem—not yours.

I strolled around his gigantic bedroom suite. The furniture was rugged and masculine. I ran my hand across a wooden bureau; I didn't think this was from Ikea. French doors opened onto a terrace. The view was to-die-for.

I moved to his bed. It was king-sized, again with thick, rugged, hewn wooden posts. There were a few framed photos on his nightstand. I sat down gingerly on the bed and leaned in to take a look. His mom and dad were in one picture. He wore a cap and gown and beamed as he hugged his Nana; had to be his college graduation. There was a photo of him on the soccer field kicking a goal as his mates screamed in joy and jumped up in the air around him.

Tucked behind all the pictures, almost as it had been shoved into hiding, was a picture of him kissing some girl's cheek. I leaned in to get a better view when my bad foot, that I thought was completely healed, twisted and I winced. It started throbbing. I hope I hadn't strained it again. I kicked off my shoe, lay back on Cristoph's bed for a moment, lifted my leg into the air and grunted as I massaged my foot.

Which was the exact moment he came out of the bathroom. "Darling!" He said. "I was hoping we'd fool around a bit tonight, but you seem to have started without me!"

"Huh?" I glanced up at him and then I think my eyes

did flip-flops. He was naked except for board shorts that matched one of my floral bikini bottoms. Holy crap, he was the spitting image of a Greek God—tanned and chiseled. His body was filled with lean, ripped muscles. Fortunately, or unfortunately for me, the bulge in his board shorts grew to overwhelming proportions in mere seconds as he strode toward the bed and leaped on top of me.

"Elizabeth!" He said. And then stopped talking as he kissed me thoroughly, his teeth nibbling my lower lip, his tongue darting inside my mouth. One hand bunched my hair, while the other caressed my face, my shoulders and pulled my top up.

Let's get something straight. It's not like I meant to kiss him back, but mother of God, holy hell, when a hot prince is kissing you—it's not like you have a lot of time to decide to have a discussion with your body about the most prudent course of action.

"Oh good God, Elizabeth, after all these years—it's you and me together at last. I can't tell you how excited I am."

I could tell him how excited he was by the heat as well as the pressure from his massive erection grinding into my pelvis. I remembered when Esmeralda shared the rumors that Cristoph was known for his "Big Tusk." This was the moment I surmised the rumor was true.

If I was back in Chicago and Cristoph was the Johnny's Pizzeria Delivery Guy, I would seriously be tempted to give this a go. Like—he was model gorgeous, thoughtful, sweet, hot and would probably set the sheets on fire. However, we weren't in Chicago, I was crazy about his brother and I was also under strict orders not to allow

Cristoph to get me in the sack. But just like during a Green Bay Packer vs. The Chicago Bears playoff game, this was a very strong sack attempt.

"Ah, yes, my sweets," I said as he trailed kisses down my now naked belly, headed south toward my, I-must-admit, somewhat excited private girlie parts. "But really, shouldn't we wait for our wedding night, when this will be so much more special?"

"I think it's pretty damn special right now." He unzipped my pants with his teeth as I started to breathe a little heavy.

"Oh sweetie-kins, I'm absolutely parched. Do you think you could get me a little more of that yummy champagne before we continue on?" I asked.

"Are you sure? Maybe you'd like that champagne afterward?" He kissed my stomach, his mouth moist and warm on my skin.

You can't do this, Lucy. Think about Nick. Think about Nick.
I moaned.
Ack! No! Do NOT think about Nick!

"No, like seriously, Cristoph, best fiancé ever. I need it now. And a Pellegrino please. And some chocolate. I fear I'm getting lightheaded just like that day on the tarmac." I waved one hand in front of my face dramatically and tried to appear weak.

He rolled off me. "God, Elizabeth. You're killing me. But there's no way I could take seeing you pass out again." He shuffled away awkwardly.

I grabbed my cell from my purse and frantically texted Esmeralda: "911! BIG TUSK!" I pulled my shirt back down below my bra. Pulled my pants back up over my panties, zipped them, attempted to stand up, got caught and twisted in the sheets and I flopped with a loud thud onto the expensive oriental carpet. "Crap!" I said.

"What was that, darling?"

"Fat," I said. "I have to fit in that beautiful gown in just a few days when I marry you. So nothing too calorie rich for me, Cristoph. I don't want to get fat."

"Oh, Elizabeth." Cristoph entered the room, carrying a tray filled with chocolate bars, another bottle of champagne and a Pellegrino. "Where are you? Are we playing hide and seek?" He put the tray down on the bureau. "Marco?"

When there was a knock on the door. "Prince Cristoph! It is I, Royal Guard Fingerlachen reporting."

"I told you not to interrupt me Fingerlachen!" Cristoph said.

"I know your grace. But Lady Elizabeth's Ladies-in-Waiting are here and need to see her for an emergency bridal situation."

"Tell them to go away. Lady Elizabeth and I are indisposed until the morning," Cristoph said.

"They say they won't take no for an answer, Prince—"

There were loud kicking sounds as the wooden door broke from its hinges and fell into the room. "Ack!" I screamed.

The Ladies Joan Brady, Cheryl Cavitt Carlson and Esmeralda Ilona Castile Hapsburg the Fourth strode into the room.

"Chocolate!" Cheryl said and helped herself. "Yum!"

"I've never seen you in your undies before, Cristoph," Joan said. "You could totally do one of those David

Beckham undie ads."

"You all must leave now!" Cristoph declared.

"No cousin. You're forgetting the bride's most important night before her wedding. Her Bachelorette Party, dude." She grabbed my arm. "Get up," she hissed.

"I'm trying," I said as we both untwisted the sheets wrapped like knotted shoelaces around my ankles. "Oh Cristoph, I'm so sorry," I said. "We were having such a delightful time."

"I can't believe this is happening," he said, sat back on his bed and dropped his forehead into his hands.

The Ladies escorted me out of the room as I turned and waved goodbye to him. "You're the best, Cristoph!" I threw him a kiss. "I'll be back soon. I just know it!"

Chapter 29

The disco ball glittered over the dance floor as strobe lights flashed on and off. A female DJ with multi-colored pink, blue and purple dreads sat in a booth high above the floor and spun a combination of hits from the 70s on upward.

Club Centralaski was packed with partiers. It was loud. It was decadent. Its customers wore everything from couture to jeans and T-shirts. No one seemed to care as everyone danced with everyone else and the vast majority seemed to be having a good time.

"Have we time travelled to the 70s?" I hollered over the music.

"No," Joan said. "Someplace much more fun."

"I know you all mean well, but I'm not sure I'm up for a wild party tonight. I'm getting married in two days, and frankly, I'm pooped," I said. "I think I'll call it an early night and get some rest."

"Chill out, *Lady Billingsley*." Esmeralda said. "You'll be a princess in no time and will have plenty of time to extend your pinkie finger at tea parties."

The Ladies had secured a four-top table adjacent to the dance floor. It was piled high with glasses and plates of munchies. A sweaty bottle of champagne rested in a silver bucket next to where Esmeralda and Joan sat. Cheryl was already enjoying her free night out as she danced to the rock-and-roll stylings of "Sweet Home Alabama" with a buff, half-naked man, dressed only in jeans, boots and a cowboy hat.

I glanced around at the crowd. For the most part everyone looked normal—except for us. We wore stretch bands on our heads featuring reflective tinted visors that covered our entire faces. Esmeralda's visor was orange, Cheryl's was blue, Joan's was green—most likely to accent her red hair—and mine was obviously pink.

"Why do we have to wear these stupid visors?" I awkwardly sipped my champagne from a straw.

"Because, my darling princess to be," Esmeralda said and sucked down her margarita with a straw, "even though this is your last-minute Bachelorette Party, we still can't allow anyone to identify you, snap pictures and sell them to the press. It wouldn't be good for your new, proper image."

Cheryl made her way off the stage, fanned her cleavage and plunked down in her chair. "Phew! That guy knew how to dance, man. My hips haven't moved like that since I gave birth. I tipped him ten euros. Do you think that's enough?"

"Why in the hell are you tipping a guy who asked you to dance?" I asked. "And why did you all bring me to a place where we have to wear disguises?"

"Because how many times do you get married, Elizabeth?" Joan asked. "Once, twice. Maybe three times tops?"

"If you're super fortunate, four," Esmeralda said.

"This is your first Bachelorette Party," Cheryl said, pulled back her visor and chugged a lager. "And even though it's totally last minute and small—we, your Ladies, needed to do it right. And so tonight, we wear visors." She snapped hers back down.

"It totally worked for that chick who was dating the ancient, billionaire American sports team owner during that disgusting scandal," Joan said. "That chick was papped all over Los Angeles with her visor on."

The DJ took the mic. "Welcome Ladies and Gentleman to Club Centralaski and Throwback Thursday's special fun night. We've got a great show for you. Let's start the festivities with Lord Byron of Naughty-ham Palace performing to "Wild Thing" by the Troggs."

All the lights in the place were cut except for the strobes. A hush fell over the crowd. A few women screamed.

"Oh my God!" I said, as the first chords of "Wild Thing" played rough and ragged from the speakers. "This is like my favorite song ever! What kind of performance do you think this Lord is going to do? Is he a musician? A magician?"

A handsome, buff guy sauntered onto the stage wearing a tuxedo and carrying a small chair. He bowed to the audience. Stood back up, shrugged off his coat and hung it on the back of the seat. There were a few cheers.

He stretched his shoulders wide and took off his tie. Tossed it into the audience. The woman who caught it screamed. He winked at her. Dropped to the dance floor, did a couple of push-ups. Popped back up, stared at the crowd as he smiled and ripped off his shirt. He swung it around his head a few times, his chest smooth, his six-pack abs rock hard and defined. "So you want it—Ladies?" he asked as "Wild Thing" kept playing.

"Oh yes, your Lord," a girl said. "We want it bad!"

He tossed her his shirt, clasped his hands behind his head, flexed his chest muscles, did a few pelvic thrusts and grinds. Then brought his hands back down and slowly unzipped his trousers.

"This is no magic act. You all brought me to a strip club!" I said.

"You haven't seen the magic yet," Joan said.

"Chill out, Billingsley," Esmeralda said. "Have another cocktail."

"I fear there are more cocks around here than tails," I said.

When the male stripper turned around, shook his butt and smiled over his shoulder at the screaming crowd. And then somehow, magically, shimmied off his trousers and hung them on the back of the chair.

"Hah!" Cheryl said. "Lord Naughty-ham clearly proved you wrong on that one."

"It's two days before my wedding. Strippers? What if someone discovers I'm here, snaps a picture and it ends up on a gossip rag?"

"Hence the visors. Come on, Elizabeth! Lighten up. Have some fun." Joan giggled and stuffed a couple of euros down the front of Lord Naughty-ham's G-string as he waggled his package in front of her.

When thankfully my phone buzzed. I pulled it from my clutch, swiped my finger across the screen and read the new text:

Dear Elizabet,

I am so sorry to interrupt your super fun night with your Ladies, but it is so very very important that I speak with you immediately. Somethinzs wrong with Royal Nana. Please meet me back at my place ASAT. You are a peach!

Love,
Prince Cristoph Edward George of Fredonia

While I was a little shocked that basic spelling skills had eluded Prince Cristoph, this text did give me the perfect excuse to leave my Bachelorette Party.

"Oh hey, Ladies! So sorry, but there's something going on with Royal Nana and I've got to go. But stay! You're having fun. I'm sure it's nothing serious. I'll text you if there's cause for worry."

"But I just paid Lord Naughty-ham forty euros to give you a lap-dance!" Joan pouted.

"Then be a good and loyal soldier for our beloved country, Lady Joan Brady, and take that bullet for me. I order you." I waved my hand at her like it was a royal scepter.

She giggled, clutched her stomach and tipped over onto Cheryl's lap.

"No-no Joan!" Cheryl pushed her upright. "You need to sit up straight. I'm not the one giving you the lap-dance... he is." She pointed to Lord Naughty-ham.

"Crap," Esmeralda said. "I'd ask Larry to drive you, but his palace guard union requires that he only work eight to ten hour shifts. He already left. I thought we'd share a cab ride home."

"I'm fine." I stood up from the table. "I can call a cab. Stay. Have fun. I love you all." I threw them a kiss.

I think the drive from Cristoph's townhouse to the Club Centralaski took all of five minutes. So I decided to skip the cab line and walked the streets of Sauerhausen back toward his place.

The capital was pretty quiet this time of night. It felt great to stride down city streets. I hadn't exercised in days. I was dying to break into a run, but feared that might grab someone's attention. So I stuck with my quick pace. Eventually I spotted a trashcan and ditched my pink visor.

The temperature dropped quickly during nighttime in Fredonia. I shivered, and wished I'd brought a coat. Just a few minutes later I arrived at Cristoph's townhouse.

A fine mist hovered in the air as I knocked on his front door. But there was no answer. I hit the doorbell three times. I wouldn't have bothered if we were talking wedding plans. But the text specifically said something important was up with Royal Nana. And even though she was feisty, overly opinionated and nearly broke my foot, I cared about her.

Finally, Royal Guard Fingerlachen unbolted the door, peeked out and rubbed his eyes. "Lady Billingsley?" he asked. "What are you doing here?"

"Prince Cristoph texted me. He needs to see me immediately." I said and elbowed my way inside.

Fingerlachen looked upstairs somewhat nervously. "Oh, I don't know Lady. I do believe Prince Cristoph is sleeping."

"No offense Fingerlachen, but if he was asleep, why did he text me?" I held out my phone in front of his face. "It's about Royal Nana. I am not going to sit on my toucas and do nothing if something is happening with Royal Nana." I raced up the stairs and ran through the living room.

"Seriously, Lady Billingsley." Fingerlachen followed me. "I can pretty much guarantee Cristoph is sawing wood right now."

"I need to know if she's all right." I bounded up the next flight of stairs, two steps at a time, to the bedroom floor.

"I don't think you want to wake him," Fingerlachen said.

I strode down the hallway leading to the master suite as I heard a few bangs and some moans. Perhaps he was watching late-night porn. I threw the door open to his room. "I came as soon as I got your text. What's up with Royal Nana? Please tell me she's okay?"

And that's when I caught Cristoph and his big tusk banging Ivanka, the scantily-clad brunette bimbo that Nick had brought to his family's engagement party. Ivanka— who Cristoph insisted he *used* to be involved with, but

261

apparently was *still involved with.*

"You've got to be kidding me? You're screwing a bimbo when there's something wrong with your grandmother? Are you heartless?"

"What are you talking about? My grandmother's fine!"

"Are you an asshole? Are you, are you…"

"It's nothing!" Cristoph said. "It's just a farewell roll in the hay." He rolled off her and pulled a sheet over them.

"That's not what you told me," Ivanka pouted.

I twisted my bunion ring from my finger. "I know what you are," I said. "You're fucking single—that's what you are." I pitched the ring at him. It bounced off his chest and Ivanka leaped high in the air and caught it.

"No!" Cristoph said.

"Happy?" I said. "I hope you are all very happy together."

"Elizabeth, no," Cristoph said. "No. This was a one time mistake. It won't happen again. I would never risk our marriage for Ivanka."

But Ivanka had already put the engagement ring on her fourth finger and was holding it up in the air and admiring it. "You promised me, Cristoph. You said if it didn't work out with Elizabeth, I would be your girl. I could be the next Princess of Fredonia."

"Enjoy your fancy ring and your fancy engagement ceremonies. I'm out of here." I ran out of the room, raced down two flights of stairs and out the door.

CHAPTER 30

I raced at breakneck speed down miles of city blocks. I ran not only to help get this whole scene out of my head but also to burn through terrible feelings. Why did I even care? I wasn't in love with Cristoph. This was simply a job. But in some way, I still felt violated. I felt fooled. I felt embarrassed for both myself as well as Elizabeth.

If a sane person in normal circumstances heard my story, they'd say I didn't have a leg to stand on.

Because I was crazy about Cristoph's brother—Nick.

So I ran as fast as I could, my head down. By the time I reached Papa's condominium, my endorphins had kicked in and I felt a smidge better. I greeted the doorman, took the elevator up to the Billingsley family penthouse, stuck my key in the door and entered. To be greeted by—silence.

"Hello!" I said. "Is anyone home?"

No one answered. I remembered that Papa and Carolina were at some soirée with stuffy investment banker types and wouldn't be home until very late.

I walked down hallways to my bedroom. "Tulip? Tulip did you miss me? I love you so much." I knelt down next to her puppy pen, but the door was ajar and it was empty.

Where was my puppy?

I heard a few excited barks and a couple of muffled yips in the distance. Where was she? Had she eaten tonight? Was she hungry? Did she need to go outside and relieve herself? I'd been paying Helga a few euros to look after her when I was tied up with all the engagement festivities and couldn't be home to take care of her. I assumed she was taking good care of Tulip.

I wandered into the kitchen. Tulip's empty food bowls rested on the marble floor. I paced down hallways following the sound of her muffled cries until I reached the living room. I spotted Helga on the Penthouse patio holding onto Tulip with a short leash.

"Thank God!" I stepped outside. "I was starting to worry about her. She's eaten tonight, right?"

"Your little princess is fine, Lizbet." Helga scooped up Tulip in her arms. "You worry about her just like a mama worries about her daughter."

"Yes, I do." I held out my arms. "You can give her to me now, Helga. Thanks so much for taking good care of her while I was gone. Are we square on how much I owe you? I can write you a check tonight, or I might have some extra cash in my wallet."

But Helga held Tulip tight to her under one beefy arm and extracted a large chocolate bar from her pocket with her other hand and ripped the wrapper open. "No, Lizbet. We are not square. Youz leave a couple years ago and I think you are gone for goods. Then you come back and you are nicer than you used to be. Which makes this difficult for me." She held the huge chocolate bar a foot away from Tulip's face; my puppy squirming as she tried to grab it.

"Helga! What are you doing?" I lunged toward her but she took two steps back. "Chocolate is deadly poisonous for dogs. I already told you this. Eat your damn chocolate bar, but keep it away from Tulip. And hand her to me, immediately!"

"No can do, Lizbet," Helga said. "Because I too have a daughter I love. I have a daughter who dreams of marrying a Prince some day. And I told my Ivanka many times, 'No, my sweetie girl. You are not royalty. You cannot marry a prince some day. You can find a nice man who is a commoner. Or perhaps a lesser titled royal.'"

My hand flew to my chest. "Ivanka who shtoops—I-mean—used to date Prince Cristoph is *your daughter*?"

"Why do you think I joined Plenty-of-Royals-in-the-Seas.com? I lied about looking for me. Yes, I loved my Herbert and am sorry he passed away. But I am happy being widow. Who wants to spend time caring for an old, cranky man? I was searching Internet to find Ivanka a suitable husband. Not Playboy Prince Cristoph. He comes and he goes like the tide."

"She can have him," I said.

"But only if you are not here, Lizbet, because I know these Royals. They speak with spooned tongues. They say anything to get what they want. And then they go back on their promises. But maybe if you are gone, maybe Ivanka has chance with Cristoph. Maybe Ivanka's dream can come true after all."

"Oh my God!" I exclaimed. "You're the one who sabotaged the netting! You tried to kill me! I can't believe you'd give me the best loofah bath of my life and still try to murder me. That's cold, man."

"I am a good mother. Just like you are. Puppy hasn't eaten tonight. Puppy is very hungry. Puppy will gobble this chocolate in seconds." Helga waved the chocolate bar in front of Tulip's face.

"Stop it!" I stepped toward Helga and tried to smack her, but she backed up again. Now she was situated closer to the door that led to the Penthouse living room and I was back against the edge of the terrace. Thank God the protective netting had been replaced. I casually poked my fingers against it for a quick test only to feel my hand punch through it—again. "Frick!"

"That's right, Lizbet. Think of your dear, sweet Tulip. Because I fear it is your life or hers," Helga said.

"No one's going to buy that there were two 'accidents' with sabotaged netting on this Penthouse terrace," I said.

"I thought of that." She juggled the candy bar and Tulip, reached in her pocket for a crumpled up piece of paper and tossed it on the ground in front of me.

I picked it up, un-crumpled it and read it out loud: "I, Lady Lizbet Billingsley, have been feeling somevat despondent of late. I fear my figure is failing me. I fear I'm soon to be over the hillz. I fear I eat too much chocolate and drink too much champagne. Don't cry for me, Fredonia. Farewellz. Yourz truly, Lady Billingsley."

"Your suizide letter." She tossed me a pen. "Sign it or

the puppy gets the chocolate."

Oh jeez. I really didn't want Tulip to be poisoned and die. I also really didn't want to bite it—especially not on a part-time job. How much time would it take to get Tulip to an Emergency Vet? I'd have to take out Helga. She had about forty pounds on me, appeared strong like bull and seemed determined.

When I saw a familiar figure sneaking through the living room. Nick made eye contact with me, placed his index finger to his mouth and quietly made his way toward the terrace door.

I backed toward the broken netting. "I'll HELP you Helga," I shouted, "if you HELP me! I WILL NOT JUMP until you put down the puppy and throw the chocolate bar in that trash can," I pointed, "right there." Which was located directly behind Helga. Just in case Nick couldn't see her from behind the curtain.

"No need to be so dramatics, Lizbet." Helga's eyes narrowed. "First, sign ze paper."

My hand shook as I signed the paper, glanced up and saw Nick peeking out from behind a curtain next to the door. I crumpled the paper back up and stuck it in my pocket.

"Toss the chocolate bar and I'll throw you my suicide note," I said.

"No can do, Lizbet. I'll toss the chocolate bar when you jump off the roof."

Nick snuck up behind her as I edged the remaining steps toward the netting. I glanced down. It was a long, long way down to the pavement below and I feared I would not land in a Lady-like pose. Elizabeth and Zara would probably be irritated.

I widened my eyes in fake shock and pointed in the opposite direction from Nick. "Oh look! Is that Ivanka?"

Helga swiveled. Nick grabbed her from behind in a bear hug. Tulip dropped to the ground and landed on her feet as the chocolate bar skidded across the patio. My puppy chased after it.

Helga elbowed Nick in the stomach. "Oof!" he said. My attention was torn between their fight and Tulip racing for the oh-so-delicious poison.

"No!" I screamed and leapt on top of the chocolate bar, landing on the ground. I shoved the bar down my shirt as Tulip jumped on top of me and licked my face.

"Lizzie!" Nick said as his attention turned to me. "Lizzie, are you okay?"

Helga seized her opportunity and bit his arm. He hollered and released her. She raced through the door into the living room and disappeared from sight.

Again the Fredonia police and Fredonia Secret Service interviewed me, as well as Nick and the condominium building's security guard. Duchess Carolina and Papa came home from their event to a house filled with men in uniform.

"Is your arm okay?" I asked Nick in the kitchen as the interviews were winding down and I watched Tulip eat safe food in her bowl.

"She apparently has short, squat teeth that didn't break the skin."

"Good" I said. "You saved me, Nick. Thank you. But why did you come here?"

"Cristoph called and told me what happened. He knew Ivanka was up to no good. She even bragged about some kind of retribution before she stormed off with your engagement ring. He knew you wouldn't talk to him and still wanted me to check on you."

"Why you and not my Ladies?" I asked.

"Oh he tried calling them first. All he heard was giggling, a few drunken slurs, loud music and 'Take it off Lord Naughty-ham. Take it all off!' He surmised they were still celebrating your Bachelorette Party."

"Does he know what happened here?"

"I called him. Look, Lizzie. We need to get you to a hotel or someplace safe, someplace with guards—maybe the castle."

I looked up at Nick. "No hotel. No castle. No guards. *Just you.*"

He shook his head. "But what about Tulip?"

"Carolina!" I hollered.

She poked her head in the kitchen. "Yes?"

"Can you watch Tulip for what's left of tonight?"

She eyed me and then Nick. "Of course, my love. Your Papa and I will take her to the Four Seasons. We're not staying here tonight. You're not either."

"I know. Thank you!"

She kissed me on the cheek and whispered. "You're a jewel, Elizabeth. I'm so glad we are getting to know each other. And by the way? Go for it. And you know what I mean by that." She snapped a leash on Tulip's collar and led her off. "Come on my little grand-puppy!"

"Let's go, Nick," I said.

"But what about Cristoph?" he asked.

I held my left hand in front of him. "What do you see on this hand?" I asked.

"Nothing," he said.

"That's right," I said. "And that's not changing tonight."

After my parents died in a motorcycle accident I swore I would never ride on one of those bikes again. And yet here I was in the darkest of night, my first time on the back of a motorcycle, holding tight to a gorgeous man, my arms wrapped around his waist. We sped along mountainous roads that curved around mist-covered lakes.

Every so often Nick would glance over his shoulder. "How are you doing?"

"I'm good." I shivered, hugged him tighter and leaned my mouth toward his ear. "My turn. Where are you taking me?"

"Someplace safe," he said over the roar of the engine.

We idled at a fenced in, thickly wooded property armed with one guard at the entry, who saluted Nick and opened the gates for us.

Now we lounged on pillows in front of a roaring fireplace in the Timmel Chateau's living room. The upscale lodge was located in the foothills above Friedricksburgh and overlooked beautiful Lake Susannah. Nick made us hot chocolate, called in a favor and found a local chef who delivered home-made pizza with organic Fredonia sausages in the middle of the night. Pizza and hot chocolate might sound like an odd combination—but in front of a fireplace after nearly being killed for the second time, it was comfort food and it was perfect.

And then it got even better. I looked out the three-story, floor-to-ceiling windows that faced the Lake and startled. "It's snowing!"

"How is it that you don't remember it snows in Fredonia in the summer?" Nick asked.

I shrugged, got up, found the door to the patio and stepped outside onto the deck. Nick followed me. I looked up at the sky: light gray clouds bumped up against each other in the sky as fat, wet snowflakes fell in a flurry onto the lake and all around us.

"It's magical." I held out my hands as the snowflakes landed on my palms, my hair, my eyelashes. I laughed and tilted my head back and closed my eyes. "It's perfect, here, Nick. It's perfect here with you. It almost reminds me of the better version of being with you in the airplane when I thought we were going to crash."

"Oh, Lizzie." He wrapped his arms around my waist and pulled me close to him. I opened my eyes and stared into his brilliant blue ones.

"I fear you have a snowflake on your forehead that is threatening to melt."

"Then you must do something about that immediately," I said.

"Close your eyes."

I did.

He kissed my forehead. He kissed both of my eyelids. He kissed my face. His hands moved down my neck, skimmed my breasts and landed at my waist. I shivered.

"I think we should go inside, Nick," I said.

"I thought you'd never ask," He scooped me up in his

arms   and   carried   me   back   inside   the   chateau.

CHAPTER 31

"I give you an A on your lady-carrying skills," I said after he deposited me gently on my back on a large feather bed. "My turn to ask a question. What else are you good at?"

He laughed, unbuttoned his shirt and tossed it.

"Nice!" I said as I admired his chest with just the right amount of black hair and his six pack abs that disappeared into his jeans. "Perhaps I missed your performance at the strip club the other night? What a bummer."

He leaned over me. "You. I don't remember that you were always talking. Will you let me answer your question?" he asked.

"Yes," I said.

"This is what I'm good at."

"Well then fine, have at it," I gave him my royal wave.

He peeled my top from my stomach, up over my chest and head until it was wrapped around my arms stretched overhead. He leaned on top of me and held both my wrists. "Wow." He eyed me from head to toe and smiled. "Has it been that long since we've seen each other half naked? You look so different."

He released my wrists and I flung off my top. He leaned in and kissed me on my mouth, my collarbones, making his way down my cleavage. "You still smell like mountain rain and hope." He unhooked my bra.

I shimmied out of it, tossed it across the room, but managed to cover my breasts with one arm.

"Are those *your* stripper moves?" He asked. "Teasing me a bit, are you love?"

"No. But I do have one more question for you."

"What, Lizzie?"

"Just for now, don't call me Lizzie. Make love to me like you've never made love to me before. Like we are two strangers who first met in First Class on a transatlantic flight. Would you do that for me, Nick?"

He stopped smiling and gazed into my eyes, his look intense. He peeled my arm away from my breasts. My breath quickened and I lost myself in my own personal fantasy, as the most gorgeous guy in the world made me feel like I was the only girl in his.

I sat across from Nick on the chateau's terrace overlooking Lake Susannah as we ate French toast and drank dark coffee at two p.m. in the afternoon. I gazed up into his crystal blue eyes, marveled at his high cheekbones and admired his strong arms that held me. Even better than that—I respected that he always seemed to show up when I needed help. He was a kind man. And holy spitoli was he good in bed. While I will always have a fondness for pizza, I was forever over pizza delivery boys.

But he still didn't know my truth. "Cristoph's texted me a million times saying how sorry he is. What if I change my mind and marry him tomorrow. Would you still be his best man?" I asked.

"Reluctantly."

"Why?"

"He's my brother. I owe him some kind of loyalty."

"Which is why we're here and we've done what we've done—five times?"

He sighed. "I think if you accept Cristoph's apology, there's a carriage with white horses waiting to escort you to the cathedral. I think there's a wedding dress that's been sized to your recently, curvier figure. I think that there are millions of people tuning in all over the world to catch a glimpse of you as well as the festivities."

"That's all fine," I said. "But I want to hear what *you feel.*"

"I will always be your best friend. The guy you can turn to. No matter what the problem, or the dilemma, I will always be there for you."

"Aah," I said. "So you think my wedding to your brother tomorrow is a done deal."

"Yeah, I do."

"Did you just say, 'Yeah?'" I asked.

He nodded. "Yeah, I just said yeah. The new Elizabeth is rubbing off on me."

"What if I told you a secret that might change the way

you think about me? A secret that could change everything?"

"I wish you could share a secret that would change everything, Lizzie. But I don't think you can. And because of that. *Because of that?* I need to share one more thing with you, Lady Elizabeth Theresa Billingsley."

"What? What? I asked.

"You might look almost the same from sixteen months ago? But let's cut to the chase, shall we? Expose the truth."

I inhaled sharply. "What truth?"

"Something happened to you when you were in The States. You're funnier and you're kinder. You're sexier and a little sassier. I've always enjoyed the old Lizzie, but I'm completely smitten, utterly whipped and hopelessly in love with the new and improved Lizzie."

"Oh," I said as my eyes widened. Maybe this was the time to tell him. This was the moment. "Perhaps I should share something with you—"

"Hear me out," he said. "I crushed on and tormented you when you were in junior high. I pursued you when you grew up and became hot. But, Lizzie?"

"What?" I asked. *Even though I wasn't Lizzie.*

"This is the first time I really fell in love with you. When I'm eighty-five fucking years old, I will still love you. When I'm named godfather to your firstborn that you have conceived, carried and popped out with my no-good brother Cristoph? I will still love you. I might date other women, marry another woman—but in my heart of hearts?"

"What?" *My own heart beat so loudly I wasn't sure I could hear him.*

"In a way, you will always be my first love. And I have come to the tragic realization, too late, that you will be my last love."

"What do you mean?"

"This marriage between you and Cristoph cements our families' futures. It saves Friedricksburg, my father's heart and the Timmel family from financial disaster. It promotes good will to all Fredonians. I can't allow my personal feelings to screw that up. *I won't allow it.*"

"Let me get this straight. You love me. *But you're not willing to fight for me?*"

"Yes. Because if I don't fight for Fredonia first? I'm a shitty brother, a crappy son, a rotten prince and not the man that any self-respecting woman should fall in love with."

"So nothing will change your decision?" I asked.

"Nothing," he said.

"But—I love you," I said.

"And I love you back." He stood up, walked a few steps, drew me to him and kissed me. He kissed me hard. He kissed me soft. He ran his fingers through my hair, slid his hands down my neck onto my back where he traced circles. He placed both hands on my waist and pulled me to him; my chest against his, my pelvis flush against his.

"Oh," I said. He was so hard and I remembered how incredible he felt inside me. My face grew hot, I blushed and prayed he wouldn't notice. What was I doing?

What was I freaking doing? Was I the biggest moron in the world?

I pulled away from him and back stepped. "Give me one reason I shouldn't marry Cristoph? Just please give me one really good reason?"

He shook his head. "I can't. I'll see you tomorrow in front of the priest. I'll be the guy in the tux standing next to the luckiest guy in the entire fucking world—my brother. My wish for you, my beloved, is that you get your Happily-Ever-After that you, of all people, deserve."

Queen Cheree had plunked down a small fortune and restored the dilapidated five-hundred-year-old church on the grounds of her beloved Labrador Retriever sanctuary in Friedricksbugh. The Royal Fredonia Saint Francis of Assisi Chapel was small, pristine and remarkable in that it featured paintings and busts of St. Francis surrounded by the animals he helped, loved and purportedly rescued. Oddly—in this chapel's artistic renditions—St. Francis was always surrounded by Labs.

I bowed my head as I perched on the red-velvet kneeler in the first pew in front of the small altar, my hands clasped tightly together in a prayer. "Dear God and St. Francis. Just hear me out, okay? I mean—yes. I'm totally spun around and lost right now. I took this part-time job because I really needed the money. And you know me, I always work extra hard at all my jobs. Point in case? Girl Scouts—the 5th grade—I sold more cookies than any other Scout. The sign-twirling gig outside Hop Li's Chinese Restaurant when I was sixteen? I was voted best twirler on the Southside. I still have the framed certificate on my wall. I thought this job would be short. I didn't expect to hurt people's feelings, trick or lie to them. But now—I really don't know what to do. Please just give me a sign. I promise I will listen."

As if on cue, someone with light hesitant steps entered

the chapel. I prayed it wasn't a member of the paparazzi, or Ivanka, hell-bent on revenging her mother. I peeked over my shoulder.

Mr. Philip Philips eased into a pew, gingerly sat down, hunched forward and stared up at me with his all-knowing, blue eyes.

"*Now* you're here? Oh my God, you're finally here!" I jumped up and down for a few moments and then raced the few yards to hug him. "The Damp is in the house!"

He extended one arm stiffly in front of him and shook his head. "No hugging. Sorry. Doctor's orders."

"Mr. Philips!" I frowned. "Don't you think after everything I've been through that you're a little late?"

"Actually I might be just in time."

"Oh!" I huffed and stalked back to my pew, but stopped, swiveled and pushed my hands on my hips. "This is a church and it's supposed to be holy ground. A bastion of privacy for tortured souls." I shook my index finger at him. "You need to leave me alone, Mr. Philips. Just like you and Zara and Elizabeth have done all these weeks. I don't need your help. I'll figure out on my own what comes next."

"Hear me out."

"I've heard you out a hundred times. I've gone over and above for Elizabeth and Zara and Fredonia. I've done everything everyone wanted me to do and more. I'm tired. I'm exhausted. I'm a stinking fraud. And that realization haunts me. At least I'm alive. If Helga had her way—I'd be dead. Do you have a policy for *that* in your job contract? Leave. Do not darken my door no matter where my door is."

279

"But Lucille—you're not a fraud. Elizabeth hired you to impersonate her for a week, ten days tops. And now it's been over a month. You've done an amazing job."

When Esmeralda trotted into the chapel holding Tulip's leash as my puppy yanked her toward me. "I figured this is where I'd find you, Lucy." She let go of the tether and Tulip bounded down the small aisle toward me. I kneeled down and scratched her ears. She planted her paws on my knees and licked my face.

"Esmeralda knows?" Mr. Philips asked.

I nodded. "She's known for a while now. Zara told her. *Where is Elizabeth?* She's supposed to walk down the aisle in less than twenty-four hours. Don't you think we're dragging this thing down to the wire?"

"Don't kill the messenger." He sighed and shook his head. "Elizabeth's not coming back."

"*What?*" I screeched.

"Crap!" Esmeralda said, plopped into a pew, reclined on her back and fanned her face. "I need a cocktail."

"Elizabeth fell in love with a hunky American commoner when she was attending graduate school in the States," Mr. Philips said. "She hired you because she wanted, no she *needed,* a little more time to determine if her feelings for the heir to the Appleton, Wisconsin, John Deere dealership were real."

Tulip licked my hand. I looked up at the altar and the large mural of St. Francis. A black, a yellow and a brown Labrador nibbled dog treats from his outstretched hands. "This is not what I meant by a sign," I hissed to St. Francis and stood back up.

"That's just great, Philips. Did she know someone

would try and kill her? Did she knowingly put me in harm's way?" Tulip wandered around the chapel, stopping to sniff every couple of yards.

He shook his head. "The way Elizabeth's grown up, there's always been someone who wanted to kill her."

"I can vouch for that," Esmeralda said as she furiously texted.

"I admit she waited too long to tell you she was never returning to Fredonia," Mr. Philips said. "For the record? She didn't tell me either. Or I would have told you before now."

"You think? Elizabeth didn't know that a prince wanted to cement their family ties, that his brother still had the hots for her? She didn't realize Queen Cheree would give me a puppy and Helga would try to kill me? She didn't suspect any of that?"

"She also didn't know for sure if she'd be able to carry her baby full-term when she hired you."

"What?" I asked. "She's pregnant?" I face-palmed my forehead into my hand. "Of course! That's why she kept running out of the room during our training sessions."

He nodded. "In all fairness..." he winced and dug his fist into his lower back, "...I don't believe Elizabeth decided she was never returning to Fredonia until after she had her ultrasound and the babies appeared healthy." He pulled a pill from his pocket, popped it into his mouth and swallowed it. "She's having twins, by the way."

I snapped my fingers at him. "If that's a Xanax, you totally need to share."

"It's a Tic-Tac."

"Dammit! Good for Elizabeth. I hope she and John

Deere and their twins will be very happy. I can only imagine the shit storm that will descend upon us once the media discovers I'm not her. That I'm actually Lucille Marie Trabbicio from Chicago's Southside. Prince Cristoph's," I made finger quotes in the air, "*'fiancé.'* That the girl who's been kissing babies' heads, hugging Fredonian orphans and being interviewed for *Euro Elle Magazine* is but a lowly, former cocktail waitress. And even worse in their eyes? *A commoner from The States.* Just fuck me now."

"Lucille!" Mr. Philips said. "Mind your language!"

"Don't you Lucille me!" I paced in front of the altar. "I've busted my ass on this job and I can't even list it on my future résumé due to the confidentiality agreement that I signed. I'm screwed. You're obviously here to transport me out of the country—like some top-secret CIA rendition mission, before this whole thing blows up into a media frenzy."

"You mean the FIA," Esmeralda said and continued texting.

"Yes," Mr. Philips said. "And no."

I screeched to a stop in front of him and jammed my hands on top of my hips. "What do you mean, 'No'?"

"You could stay," he said.

Chapter 32

"That's not even a remote possibility."

When the large front door squeaked open and Ladies Joan Brady and Cheryl Cavitt Carlson maneuvered inside, each holding one handle of a medium-sized cooler between them.

"It's about time you got here," Esmeralda said.

"Your text specifically said drive two more kilometers and turn left on the lane at the crossroads next to the hovel in front of the bleating goats in the pasture," Cheryl dropped her end of the cooler onto the stone floor with a thud.

"We couldn't find the bleating goats." Joan lowered her end of the cooler and popped the lid off. "Besides, don't goats make a 'maaa' sound? We drove four kilometers out of our way where we finally stopped at a pig farm." She tugged a large thermos from the cooler and shook it vigorously.

"I even got out of the car to ask the farmer where the hovel with the goats was located back in the direction that we'd driven." Cheryl pulled out a goblet, flipped open the thermos's spigot and filled it to the rim.

"Thank God you're finally here," Esmeralda said. "I'm parched and we've got some major decision making to do."

"Here Lucy. This one's for you." Cheryl handed me the glass while Joan filled another one and passed it to Esmeralda. "You drinking these days, Philips?"

"Just a thimbleful, my Lady."

I stared aghast at Cheryl and Joan. *"You know?"* I asked.

"Of course we know," Joan said and filled four more goblets.

"Lucille Marie Trabbicio from Chicago. I raise my glass to you—my new BFF," Cheryl held her goblet in the high in the air. "The real Elizabeth was always a little too self-centered. Not you."

"The real Elizabeth would never have gone out of her way to hook me up with the hot, smart, male stripper who's working his way through med school," Joan said. "To Lucy! Best princess impersonator ever!"

"Here's to Lucy! Long may she reign!" Esmeralda lifted her glass and the ladies and Mr. Philips toasted me.

I burst out crying. "I love you all so much and I can't do this. I have to go home." Tulip raced to me. I picked her up and hugged her.

"I don't think you do, Lucille," Mr. Philips said.

"But I'm not Elizabeth. And I never will be. Of course I have to leave."

"Hear us out," Esmeralda said.

"Every place you've visited in this country, Lucy, you

made friends," Joan said.

"Every baby you burped, every orphan you hugged, each senior citizen with dementia whose hand you held and listened to their stories, over and over. You gained fans, but more importantly you won hearts," Esmeralda said.

"The people of Fredonia love you. They're practically frothing at the mouth for you to be their new royal princess," Cheryl held out the thermos. "Can I top anyone off?"

Esmeralda held out her goblet.

"Please," Mr. Philips said.

"Ditto," Joan said.

"Just a smidge." I held out my glass as Cheryl made the rounds. "Because the citizens of Fredonia *are dying* for an American commoner from the south side of Chicago to be their Princess." I took a drink. "They want Lucille Marie Trabbicio who says yeah instead of yes, could give a rat's ass about soccer but knows American football stats and lies like a rug to someday be their Queen."

"They don't care if their Princess swears on occasion or follows American football. Because they recognize your kindness. And your kindness is, well, it's you—Lucille. Elizabeth has her own unique qualities," Mr. Philips said. "But the people of Fredonia will never love her the way they love you."

"That's the bad back pain killers talking," I said.

He sighed and shook his head. "I found a local chiropractor and I'm back to popping Advil and Tic-Tacs. I seriously think you should stay here in Fredonia."

"That's crazy! Someone will find out. They'll track down my fingerprints or find a connection to my past. The media will out me. It will be a freaking disaster."

"*So what if they do?* It won't matter," Esmeralda said. "There will be a ginormous news kerfuffle and then some vapid reporter will show you bottle-feeding abandoned kittens, followed by a news clip with your new royal baby at his or her christening. And after a week or two, all will be right with the world."

"But how can that be?" My hand flew to my heart. "Cristoph is a great guy. I seriously like him. He's an amazing catch: gorgeous, funny and who wouldn't want to be with him? Except for his ridiculous, playboy thing." I wiped a few tears away. "But while I like him, I don't love him and I'll never love him. Because…"

I thought of Nick on the plane as I dug my fingernails into his arm, as he held me while I trembled in fear. I remembered the first time we kissed in the park. I remembered making love with him in a feather bed in a chateau overlooking a mountain lake.

"You could grow to love Cristoph." Mr. Philips said. "Many people marry for friendship or political purposes. Over the course of years they grow to love each other. It's not out of the question."

I shook my head. "It's not possible, Mr. Philips. I'm in love with someone else."

"But you have a solid friendship with Cristoph," Joan said. "You could be the perfect Fredonia royal couple. You'll both have lovers on the side—that's a given."

"Perhaps your lover would be Nick," Cheryl said.

I shook my head. "No way he would go for that."

"I've seen the way he looks at you," Esmeralda said. "It's not just lust."

"I don't think he'd share me with another man. Especially not Cristoph."

"You'd just have to keep everything hush-hush. That is the royal way." Mr. Philips pushed himself to standing, got stuck in an awkward position half way up and broke into a sweat.

I stood in front of him and held out my hands. "Come on, Damp. I'll help you up."

He smiled for a heartbeat, then winced. He took my hands and I hoisted him to standing. "Thank you," he said. "Don't leave Fredonia, Lucille. Stay here, marry Prince Cristoph and have the best life in the world with a million people who already adore you."

"Who adores you back in Chicago?" Cheryl asked.

"Alida and Mateo. A few guys at MadDog. Mrs. Rosalie Santiago from Vail Assisted Living. My Uncle John—who I promised I'd never leave."

"Your Uncle John will be quietly relocated from Vail to The Retired Royalty Chateau in Sauerhausen," Esmeralda said.

"He'll live a life of luxury, convenience and have the best doctors at his disposal. You'll be able to visit him whenever you like," Joan said.

I blinked. "But... But?"

"Exactly." Mr. Philips walked awkwardly down the short aisle toward the chapel's entrance. He grimaced as he pushed the massive wooden doors open. A gust of chilly, autumn air burst into the chapel, accompanied by a few jewel-colored leaves.

"You're leaving?" I asked.

"You could have the best life in the entire world, here

Lucille. But ultimately—it's your decision to make."

I rubbed my temples. "I'm confused."

"I would be too if I were you," Mr. Philips said. "On the other hand, if I were your parents? If God or St. Francis granted me one last wish before their motorcycle accident? I'd wish for you, my only daughter, a life of love and a life of ease. A life filled with less struggle and more possibilities. Because, Lucille, out of all the young women I have met in my life, you deserve a Happily-Ever-After. And I truly hope you find it."

The Ladies and I started crying. Joan passed around a packet of tissues as they dabbed their eyes. Esmeralda blew her nose loudly. "Allergies," she said.

I ran to Mr. Philips, Tulip prancing behind me on my heels. "I need to tell you thank you," I said. "Thank you for taking a chance on me."

He nodded and smiled. "I hope I see you tomorrow at the Royal Cathedral wearing a long white dress with a veil resting gently over your beautiful face," Mr. Philips said. Then he leaned in, hugged me for a moment, looked me square in the eyes and kissed me once—tenderly—on each cheek. "You are our knight-ress in shining armor, Lucille, after all. *You*—are our fucking one." He turned and walked out of the church.

"Stay Lucy," Cheryl said. "We love you. You'll be a great Princess and a wonderful Queen some day. Please don't go."

I glanced around at my Ladies' faces: sincere, beautiful and hopeful.

Tulip yipped at me and pawed my leg.

Oh crap. What was a chick from the Southside of Chicago

supposed to do?

Well, this chick drove back to her 'family's Penthouse', stayed up late with her Ladies-in-Waiting, ordered Chinese, played with her puppy and drank too much champagne as we watched reruns of *I Love Lucy*.

"Lady, lady, lady, lady," the irritating female customer at MadDog hissed.

"Yeth," My tongue seemed to be glued to the top of my mouth, it felt like it was filled with cotton. "Got it. One Rum and Coke. Two shots of Cuervo. And a refill on the pretzel mix bowl, pronto. Give me a second, okay?"

Make that more like a couple of hours because something was definitely off. My eyelids were super-glued shut. I ran my tongue across my lips; they were swollen like they'd been stung by bees. And my tongue felt like an over-sized slab in my mouth like something you'd buy in an Italian deli.

When—holy smokes—the origin of my predicament dawned on me—I vaguely remembered over-imbibing in fancy champagne last night. I hope I didn't sleep with that Johnny's Pizza Delivery Guy again.

"I don't need more pretzels. I need you to wake up." The woman customer shook my shoulders. *When did the job description for being a waitress transition from slightly subservient to a victim of violence?*

"Good decision on the pretzels," I said. "They put some kind of preservative in those things that makes them last ten years. Blech. Terrible for the human body. But I do believe those pretzel manufacturers could make a fortune if they discovered a way to market that ingredient as an anti-aging cream."

"Wake up and smell the coffee."

"I have a name you know. It's…" I blinked my eyes open and squinted: a glorious sunrise bloomed on the horizon outside my bedroom window, high over the pristine streets of Sauerhausen. "…Lady Elizabeth Billingsley," I said. "I'd like another wake-up call in like an hour, please? Thank you so very much." I pulled my sleepy-time mask back over my eyes, clamped my hands over my ears and rolled over in my gigantic, pillow topped, queen-sized bed.

"Elizabeth!" Esmeralda hollered. "You're not the only one who had an early morning wake up call. Cut the crap and get your precious behind out of bed—now!"

I pulled off the mask, rolled over again, and squinted at her.

"Better," she said.

"Finally," Cheryl said.

Joan held a steaming mug of coffee in front of my face. "It's the double dark Ethiopian brew. I brought an extra large thermos and set it up on a side table. I think we all need to be a little over-caffeinated today."

I sat up in bed, took the mug and sipped. "Yikes. Strong. Delish." I racked my brain for what was on today's agenda. "So what's on today's itinerary? Walking my puppy. Sucking up to some dour Count or Countess. Another photo shoot? A meet and greet with the lovely citizens of Fredonia? Where's Tulip?"

"Larry's taking her for a run in Centralaski Park," Esmeralda said. "We want her to be as worn out as possible.

"That's nice of him. We want her worn out—why? Oh crap, I'm getting married today, aren't I?"

Cheryl hummed the bridal march as she smiled and waved a platter of croissants in front of me. "Freshly baked for the Princess to be."

Esmeralda picked up a remote from a nightstand, aimed it at the flatscreen TV high on the wall and clicked.

The screen flashed to ducklips, the female news reporter, dressed in a floor-length, sparkly gown. She ran a few fingers over her immovable hair, swiped her tongue over her upper lip and caressed the mic like it was a lover. "Gwendolyne Joffries reporting for Fredonia Cable News. Welcome, one and all, to today's Fredonia royal wedding festivities. We at FCN have round-the-clock reporting, covering the gowns to the bridesmaids. The bride's family's reactions to the inside scoop on the Royal Family. And even a few surprises… Stay tuned for the pageantry, the fun, the gossip… and the scandals!"

"I'm so happy for you that butterflies are dancing on my head," Esmeralda said. "And that irritates the shit out of me, so let's get this show on the road."

A thunderous round of applause swept my bedroom.

I sprayed coffee out my mouth, tossed the mug and dove back under the covers. "Who the crap is in my bedroom besides you Ladies?"

"Your entire bridal entourage, sweetie," Cheryl said.

"Come on Luc—I mean—Elizabeth," Joan said. "This will be so much fun!"

I peeked out and saw a makeup artist, my wedding gown designer, Giuseppe Felipe and his two attendants, Duchess Carolina von Sauerhausen, two guards, a makeup artist, three hair stylists, a photographer, and five general assistants. Everyone curtseyed as if on cue.

Carolina burst into tears.

Giuseppe held out a huge linen garment bag high in the air. "It is perfection," he said.

I sat up in bed.

His assistant unzipped it, revealing my wedding dress. A chorus of 'Ooh!' and 'Aah!' bounced around the room.

When Elizabeth's Papa cracked open the door and peered at the crowd. "I need a moment alone with my daughter," he said.

There was a cacophony of 'Yes sir,' as the designer and attendants scurried out of the room.

Esmeralda, Joan and Cheryl regarded me, eyebrows raised.

"It's okay." I nodded.

They bustled away. "Do you still have Prince Harry's Private Reserve?" Joan asked.

"Funny you should ask," Cheryl pulled a flask from her purse.

Carolina went to Papa and took his hand. "David? Are you okay?"

He nodded but couldn't hold her look. "I will be, sweetheart. Thank you. I'll see you in just a few moments."

She patted his arm, smiled at me and left the room.

CHAPTER 33

Elizabeth's Papa sat on the edge of my bed and stared at me.

"Do you want a cup of coffee Papa? Or a croissant?"

"No, sweetie. I just want you to be happy."

I pulled the covers up to just under my chin. "Papa?"

He peered at me and his eyes misted over. "I remember when you were born, Elizabeth. I held you in one hand and I thought: this is my daughter. She will be smart and she will be savvy. She's already beautiful. I will wipe every snotty nose with an extra cushy tissue. I will make sure she gets a great education. And no matter what, I will always love her."

"You did a great job, Papa," I said. "Thank you for being a great father. I'm so lucky to have you in my life."

He shook his head. "I should have done better by you.

You were only ten-years-old when your mama passed. I shut down. I was scared and angry. I wanted to find you a new mother—but I haven't been so great at doing that."

"Papa—no." I dropped the covers from my face, and took his hand in mine.

"I knew when you hit those precarious teen years, that you'd fall in love a hundred times. I promised myself to wipe away your heartaches as well as your tears. And I knew that one day I'd have to let my beloved daughter go. Because one of those times you fell in love—it would stick."

"You did a great job," I said and thought of Nick. "I think it did stick."

"Did I? Your wedding is a business. Planned, arranged—and like Marie Antoinette on Bastille Day— soon to be executed."

"Promise me I won't be guillotined after I get married today and we'll be good." I smiled.

He smiled back. "Do you love Cristoph, Elizabeth? Does he make you happy?" Because as much as your dear mother wanted this for you, as much as we stand to gain from this royal alliance? I'll pull the plug if you want me to. I'll call off this wedding if you don't want to be with him."

A few tears leaked from my eyes. Elizabeth's Papa loved her enough that he was giving her a way out. *Elizabeth's Papa loved her just perfect.* I wished my parents were here. I wished they hadn't died in a motorcycle accident. I wished I were marrying Nick today. But maybe the love of my life wasn't a person—maybe it was actually this life— *Elizabeth's life.*

Elizabeth didn't want her life in Fredonia. She gave it away. And except for a handful of folks back in Chicago—

no one really wanted me. If I stayed here, what would be the harm? I could still be around my Ladies, Cristoph, Elizabeth's Papa, Queen Cheree, Royal Nana, Tulip, Mr. Philip Philips, and maybe even... Nick.

"What say you, Elizabeth?" Papa stroked my hand.

Did I want to give everybody and everything I'd grown to love in this part-time job up just for principle? Just so I could be right? Just so I could be broke, unloved and alone? *And I made my decision.*

I intertwined my fingers between his. "I say that you are the best daddy a girl could hope for." I squeezed his hand and cradled it next to my cheek. "I'm getting married today. You're walking me down the aisle, yes?"

"Yes, my darling daughter." He pulled me close and hugged me. "Yes I am."

Lady Elizabeth Theresa Billingsley was getting married today. And considering I was her imposter I guess that meant I was getting married today. I hadn't planned on this when I took this part-time job.

Note to self: check the fine print on work-related contracts.

I stood in the vestibule of Fredonia's Royal Cathedral and peeked out from behind one of the ginormous wooden doors, both opened to allow wedding guests to enter. Stained glass windows were lined up high on the cathedral's stone walls like soldiers on alert. An organist played a medley of the wedding classics: Bach. Beethoven. Mozart. Pachelbel.

Ushers in tuxedos escorted formally attired guests into row upon row of wooden pews. I spotted a magnificent mix of odd hats, extravagant gowns and impeccable tuxedos. There were bouquets of roses hanging by white, silk ribbons on the side of every pew.

My bridesmaids, the Ladies Cheryl, Joan, Esmeralda and my flower girls fluttered around me like hummingbirds hopped up on sugar, prettiness and adrenaline. They too looked like brides—except their dresses were pastel-colored versions of mine and less extravagant in the poofy department.

Church bells pealed high above our heads. I gazed in an ancient mirror: I held a gorgeous bouquet of trailing roses, but I still resembled an overly frosted vanilla cupcake on steroids. For the record? When you don't have a strong opinion about your own wedding dress—too many folks will be happy to choose it for you.

And you will most likely not be thrilled with the results.

There were yards and yards of white fabric. Tulle, sparkles, in-laid pearls, glitter, a veil, a headpiece, and thankfully—low heels. The only thing I had insisted on were low heels because I couldn't walk in high ones. "I look like a meringue pie exploded."

"Elizabeth, stop that." Cheryl twirled next to me in her smaller lemony version of my dress. "You look adorbs! Thank you for getting married. As much as I love my munchkins, I'm kid-free for two whole days!"

"Squee!" Joan hiked her boobs up and played with the spikes on her pretty, shiny, short-cropped red hair. "Did you see that guy toward the front of the cathedral seated on the groom's side? I do believe that's Theodore, the Grand Duke of Latvia. I spotted him on the field at a polo match a year ago and I've been dying to meet him. He's so hot!"

"What happened to the handsome, medical doctor-in-training stripper?"

"A girl needs more than one man on her plate. Don't you watch *The Bachelorette?*"

Folks craned their heads and smiled as they tried to catch a glimpse of me—the bride—the future Princess of Fredonia. Or as I liked to call me?

The no good, lying Princess Impersonator.

In the front of the Royal Church of Fredonia's sacristy the Archbishop of Sauerhausen walked onto center-stage.

Mr. Philips was seated in the third row from the front on the bride's side of the cathedral. He swiveled back toward me and I swear he winked. I gave him a clandestine thumbs-up. But then my hands started to shake. Had I eaten today? Had I not eaten today? Oh good God, I couldn't remember. Crap.

But—I could do this. I could marry Cristoph, Prince of Fredonia, and have this amazing life.

My Uncle John would be taken care of. We would never have to worry about money or support or love—well, perhaps we'd eventually be dealing with the gossip-mongers. But I could handle that.

Two of Cristoph's groomsmen, attired in immaculate tuxes, strode into the front of the church. I then watched as the most handsome smart-ass in the world walked to the front of the church.

Nick.

Fucking Prince Nicholas of Fredonia was dressed in a tux and looked absolutely stunning and delicious. He stared at the floor and rocked back and forth on his heels.

"Nick looks so handsome!" Joan said.

"He'll be the hottest bachelor in Europe as soon as Cristoph's off the market," Cheryl said.

I frowned. *They were right. All the tarts in tiaras would be after my Nick.*

The Trumpet Voluntary played—the same version that was performed during Princess Diana's royal wedding march.

My Ladies' eyes turned to me.

"It's time," Cheryl said and sniffled.

"Hang on. I need to adjust your veil." Joan leaned in and fluffed the veil that draped over my face and adjusted my tiara.

"You look beautiful," Esmeralda wiped a tear away.

I peeked out at the crowd. Photographers huddled in every corner imaginable.

Cristoph walked into the front of the church. His eyes met mine and he smiled. My eyes glazed over, time slowed down and I froze as Nick continued to stare at his feet.

I felt like a deer caught in the headlights. A fake, a phony, an imposter. A girl from Southside Chicago caught up in a big fat womping lie of a part-time job who was about to become the Princess of Fredonia.

Papa approached me, dressed to the nines, in a handsome tuxedo. "I'm here to walk my favorite daughter down the aisle." He hugged me and smiled.

He looked so debonair in his black tuxedo with his silver hair. "But I'm your only daughter," I said, "Daddy."

And for a moment—he was. And I wondered how—with or without child—how could Elizabeth leave him behind?

"My Princess." He clicked his heels and bowed as we both wiped a few tears away. "Time waits for no one. Your carriage awaits." He held out his arm to me.

My hand shook as I took his arm.

"Papa," I said. "I'm not sure I ever told you how much

I love you. And you need to know that your daughter really does love you," I said. "So very, very much."

"If you make me cry again, I'll disown you." He wiped away a tear.

As did I. "If you make me ruin my makeup, I'll have you thrown into the royal dungeons. I can do that after today—I think. Walk me down the aisle, Papa."

"If you or anyone else in this church has an objection to holy matrimony between Lady Elizabeth Theresa Billingsley and Prince Cristoph Edward George Timmel the Third? Speak now or forever hold your peace," the Archbishop in his flowing robes said.

Cristoph looked down at me, smiled and whispered, "We've got this, Elizabeth. We are the new face of Fredonia."

I glanced at my Ladies-in-Waiting: they smiled and gave me a thumbs up. With the exception of Lady Joan, who stared over her shoulder, completely smitten, at Theodore of Latvia.

I swiveled and peered at Mr. Philips. But his head was collapsed in his hands and he wouldn't meet my look.

Nick coughed.

I turned and stared at him. "What?" I hissed.

"Elizabeth?" Cristoph whispered.

Nick's hacks escalated from a rumble to full throttle. The nattily attired wedding guests' dilated eyes started to veer from focusing on me—to fixating on him.

I felt like I was back on the airplane flight from London to Fredonia as we dropped like a bag of stones toward the jagged mountain peeks below. I broke into a sweat, clutched one perfectly manicured hand to my pearl-embedded silken clad chest and wheezed as the cathedral appeared to wobble a little side to side.

"Elizabeth, what's wrong?" Cristoph whispered. "Tell me what's wrong, love. Is it your hypoglycemia?"

Flashbulbs popped from every corner of the cathedral. The wedding guests murmured amongst themselves. The room felt like it was closing in on me. "Nick," I hissed, but he wouldn't meet my eye. The room started spinning.

Tulip barked, broke free from her handler and raced toward me. In a haze I scooped her up, buried my face in her face and inhaled her puppy breath.

"This is highly unorthodox," the Archbishop said. "I clearly stated that I'd only allowed the dogs if they were confined."

Queen Cheree jumped up from the front pew as Sunny stood next to her. "You only allowed my Labrador Retrievers because I paid the cathedral an extra three thousand euros. Do *not* denigrate my dogs."

Nick coughed.

"I repeat! If anyone present here has an objection to holy matrimony between Lady Elizabeth Theresa Billingsley and Prince Cristoph Edward George Timmel the Third? Speak now or forever hold your peace," the Archbishop said.

"No one has an objection!" Cristoph said.

Tulip barked.

"Could you get on with it?" Nick asked.

"There are no objections!" Mr. Philips yelled from the third pew.

I peered at Nick, who hyperventilated as he gazed back

at his shoes. We were both on the verge of having panic attacks. And it dawned on me that as much as I loved my part-time job and the people of Fredonia, I couldn't live a lie for the rest of my life.

Time was precious. The people you love might not be with you forever. And maybe sometimes, in spite of all the odds, in spite of everything, you just needed to stick up for your heart. Stick up for your life. Stick up for your dreams.

And I made a better decision.

CHAPTER 34

I placed Tulip gently on the ground, turned toward Cristoph, wrapped my arms around him and hugged him tight. The crowd gasped.

I whispered into his ear. "I adore you. You deserve to marry a girl who is better for you than me. I sincerely apologize for what is about to happen."

"What's about to happen?"

"This." I lifted my veil, kissed him on the cheek, pulled away from him and peered up at the Archbishop. "Um, excuse me your holiness?"

"Yes Lady Billingsley," he said.

"I'm speaking now because I can't forever hold my peace."

He shook his head. "What say you Lady?"

"It pains me something fierce to say this—but I know a

reason that I cannot marry Prince Cristoph."

"Merde!" A wedding guest hissed.

"Sacrilege!" Another one said.

"Honey? Are you okay?" Papa asked.

"Shit," Mr. Philips said.

Hisses and gasps rose from the crowd as flashbulbs popped and cameras whirred. I heard a thud and I think someone passed out.

"Are you *absolutely sure* you want to do this?" Esmeralda asked.

"Yes," I whispered.

"Okay," she said softly. "The Ladies have your back."

"Speak up, Lady Billingsley," the Archbishop said. "Speak your truth, now. In front of God, the Royal Family and all present here today. What is the reason you should not be united in holy matrimony with Prince Cristoph?"

"You see—therein lies the dilemma." I gazed out into the crowd of folks in the cathedral who were deathly quiet as they leaned forward, practically on their tippy toes, waiting for my answer.

A few guests wearing big hats fanned themselves. Royal Nana snored in the first pew.

Nick stared at me and shook his head, 'No'.

My hand flew into my chest. Because I knew he wasn't expecting what I was about to say next.

"I can't marry Prince Cristoph because—I'm not Lady Elizabeth Theresa Billingsley."

"Oh my sweet darling," Queen Cheree said. "Who else would you be? You're simply sleep-deprived and stressed out from that awful woman's terrible machinations."

Royal Nana woke with a start. "Cocoa," she said.

"Make me hot cocoa with the mini-marshmallows Elizabeth. It's so yummy the way you make it."

"Of course," I turned to my Ladies. "Will one of you please make hot cocoa for Royal Nana? I'm in the middle of something."

Joan's hand popped up. "Consider it done." She pulled her cell out of her cleavage and texted.

"Elizabeth." Cristoph eyed his brother Nick and then regarded me. "What's going on?"

"What's going on is that I'm not Elizabeth."

"Hah!" He said. "No. Seriously."

"Seriously. I'm not Elizabeth. My name is Lucy." Out of the corner of my eyes I spotted the cameras creeping closer to the front of the church.

He shook his head. "But, but... then where's Elizabeth?"

"Somewhere—" Mr. Philips caught my eye as he ran his fingers across his lips in the universal sign for 'zip it'. I nodded at him. "I'm not exactly sure," I said. "But I don't think she's in Fredonia." I back-stepped down the few stairs, but my feet tangled in my gown and I teetered on the last one.

Cheryl hiked up her dress, jumped down the stairs, grabbed my arm and stopped me from falling.

"But why?" Cristoph asked. "I don't get it. I'm offering you—I mean her—my allegiance, my throne, my heart. Why?"

I shook my arm free from Cheryl's grasp and I started crying. "I can't speak for Elizabeth's reasons, Cristoph. She hired me to impersonate her for just ten days. And then ten days turned into over a month. And in that short time, I've grown so fond of you. I've fallen in love with all of you really. And I'm so sorry. Because I never ever wanted or planned to hurt anybody."

"God dammit!" Nick exclaimed.

"Don't you swear in church young man," the Archbishop exclaimed. "I mean Your Royal Highness."

I looked up and Nick stared at me like he was seeing me for the first time. His eyes were wide open, and his gaze calculated: as if it all started to make sense.

The Archbishop of Sauerhausen's face had turned beet red and I feared his head was going to pop off his robed body like the top of a Pez dispenser. "So, Elizabeth, or Lucy, or whatever your name is—*you do not take* Prince Cristoph Edward George Timmel the Third of Fredonia to be your lawfully wedded husband, to have and to hold from this day forward, for better or for worse, for richer, for poorer, in sickness and in health, to love and to cherish, from this day forward until death do you part?"

"That's right," I said. "*I do not.* However, except for the husband part, I do solemnly vow I will do all those things with Tulip. Queen Cheree—can I keep the puppy?"

She leaned back in her pew, sighed and nodded. "So be it."

"Thank you everyone! Have a splendid day! I think the food at the reception will still be fabulous!" I turned, picked up the end of Tulip's leash from the ground and hiked up my dress with my other hand. We raced back down the aisle as flashbulbs exploded like the grand finale of a fireworks show on the Fourth of July.

I wore over-sized, reflective Aviator sunglasses, a Denver Bronco's ball cap and a Tampa Bay Buccaneers jersey to thoroughly disguise my identity. I had promised Jane Dawson an interview—but I hadn't promised that I'd divulge my *real* identity to her millions of viewers.

We sat across from each other in a hotel suite in Tampa (hence the Buccaneers attire), where she had a much more important story lined up after our interview. Her crew of makeup, camera and lighting people was positioned around us.

Jane faced the camera. "With us tonight is the young woman who stunned not only the entire country of Fredonia, but, frankly, the entire world, when she literally ran out of her royal wedding to Prince Cristoph Edward George Timmel the Third on her actual wedding day. But as she said—it really wasn't *her* wedding day. Because this young woman wasn't really Lady Elizabeth Theresa Billingsley—she was an imposter."

Jane swiveled toward me. "You have asked that your real name not be revealed on camera."

"That's right Ms. Dawson." I sat regal, posture-perfect, on a settee overlooking the bay. "Thank you for honoring my wishes."

She nodded. "The public press has deemed you Almost Fake Fredonia Princess with a Heart—or," she swiveled back to the camera, "for those of you following us on Twitter—#AFFPHeart."

"That's right." I winced.

"I met you on a transatlantic flight from Chicago to London in early July of this year," she said.

"Yes," I said.

"You sat next to me. You seemed like a lovely young woman. I suspected I knew you, but couldn't quite place your name."

"That's correct," I said.

"When I nearly died from choking, Prince Nicholas Frederick Timmel of Fredonia performed the Heimlich maneuver that saved my life. You gave up your seat for me, tucked pillows behind my head and covered me in blankets."

"Yes," I said.

"You were kind, but the truth of the matter is that you were a royal imposter. You were pretending to be Lady Elizabeth Theresa Billingsley."

I sighed. "Yes."

"On that fateful flight you also pretended to know Prince Nicholas."

"Yes."

"But in reality you did not know him?" Jane asked.

"No. Well, actually I met him after he boarded the plane. When he… flirted with me."

"Because he thought you actually were Lady Elizabeth Billingsley?" Jane asked.

I hung my head. "Yes."

"Can you elaborate on this please?"

"Unfortunately—no. I signed confidentiality agreements. I could still be sued."

"Can you tell us who employed you?"

I looked up and whistled.

Jane nodded. "I understand. But you can confirm this. Here you were—an American commoner, a former cocktail waitress, impersonating Lady Billingsley in

Fredonia's royal court. You rose from obscurity to become the center of the world's attention after Prince Cristoph Edward George Timmel the Third asked you to marry him, and you said yes?"

I nodded—albeit sheepishly.

"The world's eyes were on you," Jane said. "For example—when you visited The Holy Cross Orphanage."

I'd place bets Jane's show now cut to footage of Peter, the boy from the orphanage, hugging me.

"I had a feeling about you," Jane said. "That you were someone special, you were newsworthy and you promised to give me your story if there was a story to be given."

"Absolutely, Ms. Dawson. But I think you pretty much know everything."

"Not everything," she said. "I heard rumors that you fell in love with the Prince of Fredonia but not the one you were falsely engaged to. You fell in love with Nicholas, not Cristoph. Is that why you didn't walk down the aisle? Is that why you bolted from the cathedral in that disastrous albeit spectacular manner on that special day?"

My sunglasses couldn't hide the tears that slid down my cheeks. I wiped them away with my fingers. "Have you ever fallen in love with the wrong guy, Ms. Dawson?"

Her eyebrows arched as she handed me a tissue. "Why yes, I have."

"How did it feel?" I asked.

"It felt magical when it happened. It felt like my world crashed down around me when I realized I couldn't be with him." Jane brushed a tear away from her eye.

I picked up the tissue box and held it out toward her. "I am not confirming nor am I denying your question," I said.

Jane delicately blew her nose and then gazed into the camera. "For those of you watching tonight? Please use #AFFPHeart to let us know how you feel about Almost Fake Fredonia Princess with a Heart's situation. Should she have left Fredonia earlier? Should she have stayed? Who do you think hired her?" Jane swiveled back toward me. "Do you have regrets?"

"Oh God, yes." I said. "I never thought for a second that I could harm people if I took this job. But I did. And that haunts me."

"Anyone you want to apologize to? They're probably watching. You can say it to them through our cameras."

"Prince Cristoph. You're so handsome and such a gentleman. I'm so sorry if I hurt you. I really didn't mean to. Queen Cheree. You are such a class act and I could never be as wonderful and kind as you are: you set the bar too high. I sincerely apologize. And I'm taking excellent care of my puppy. I can never thank you enough. Royal Nana. Except for nearly breaking my toe, I still wish you were my Nana in real life. And perhaps my biggest apology goes out to the people of Fredonia. You have a beautiful country. You were so very kind to me. I'm so sorry if I let you down. Except for the two people who tried to kill me, seriously, you are all very close to my heart."

"Helga Humperdink and her daughter Ivanka managed to flee the country and are now on Interpol's most-wanted list. Do you still fear for your life?"

"No," I said.

"Good."

"What about Prince Nicholas of Fredonia?"

"What about him?" I asked.

"Is there anything you want to say to him? Any parting words?"

I thought about it for a moment. "Yes and No. *Yes?* I'll miss him forever. *No?* How do you say goodbye to someone who never actually met *the real you?*"

Jane nodded. "So what will you do now?"

"I'll walk my puppy. I'll thank God every night that I was able to meet the kind people of Fredonia and live in their country for over an unforgettable month. I'll remember the good times. I'll try and let my heart scab over from the bad ones. I'll really miss Elizabeth's Ladies-In-Waiting. They're like the sisters I never had, but always wanted. I'll get back to living my life." I said. *"And I'll get a new job."*

"Good luck with that! And thank you for sharing as much as you could regarding your epic journey," Jane said.

"Thank you, Ms. Dawson." And we hugged.

"Cut camera!" she yelled. "I'm so sorry, honey. You call me if there's anything I can do. Promise me that."

"Promise. Thanks." I sniffled.

CHAPTER 35

I lay in my bed with Tulip next to me for two weeks as I cried, ate dark chocolate ice cream (not as fabulous as the ice cream in Fredonia) and watched reruns of *I Love Lucy*. I could no longer view my favorite medieval show—it reminded me too much of Nick and Fredonia and my Ladies. I read *The Wall Street Journal* for real, but didn't see any mention of Friedricksburg being sold off to developers.

I hadn't heard from Nick, or Cristoph. Mr. Philips left me a couple of messages that I didn't return. The Ladies texted me incessantly until I responded that *they were killing me* and I just wasn't ready to talk about it. Their texts stopped abruptly.

About three weeks after my most epic journey I ventured back into the land of the living. I jogged with Tulip around my local park. I secured her six-foot lead to the outdoor weight machines, stuffed a liver treat in her chew toy and let her have at it as I pumped iron. My exercising dealt with my grief. Attempting to dig out the liver treats seemed to make her happy. It was a win-win.

I played Ping-Pong and hung out with Uncle John at Vail Assisted Living. Alida, Mateo and I watched some *real* football: Chicago Bears vs. The Green Bay Packers on a big-screen at a sports-themed restaurant.

In late September, Chicago's Indian summer changed overnight from scorching hot to crisp fall. The leaves turned from green to different shades of oranges and reds and browns. Lawns yellowed. My neighborhood grew quieter. Not as many partiers opened their windows in the autumn as the summer. Even the cockroaches calmed down and made room for the spiders. Fine by me. Seems like there was a time and a season for everyone and everything.

Every day Tulip seemed to grow like one of those wild flowers that stuck out of a patch of melting snow in Fredonia's Alps. First her legs got long and her gait grew even goofier. For a while her butt was higher than her chest. Two weeks later her chest caught up to her behind and her spine straightened. Her golden hair changed texture from fluffy to sleek and short. Her face started to fill out. She loved me too much and I loved her back the same way.

I thanked my lucky stars every night that Queen Cheree had let me keep her.

I missed the fall semester at Columbia Technical Academy. I couldn't handle going back to school yet, but I contacted Columbia's administration, semi-explained my circumstances and deferred my classes to the winter semester that started in January the following year.

One day in October it dawned on me I really did need to get back to life. Which meant I needed to hunker down and *find a job.* I applied via a website and was hired by Cheswick's of Boston to be an online chat service representative. I fielded questions about clothing and accessories: color, cut, orders and other customer concerns. Unfortunately, I quit after being 'screamed at' online for an hour in a furious chat session with a woman who insisted she had ordered a suit in autumn brisk orange but received said outfit in spring tangerine dew.

I scanned more listings on Daveslist. Lucky for me— the Wieners on Sticks mall kiosk still needed bouncing hot dog salespersons. I applied for the position, got it, and totally pulled it off; until one blustery autumn night after a Monday-Night-Football Bears game, when I received an e-mail from someone I didn't know.

Yo Wiener on Sticks Girl:
Lovd the vidio. I got the ex-large wiener and the stik, babe.
E me back. I pwomis you won't be disaponted.

There was a link to a really uncomfortable, slightly demented YouTube video that featured me and my female co-workers in slow motion, interspersed between a montage of wieners and sausages. More than suggestive Twitter comments from weirdos flew across the screen: #WienersonSticks Watch Lucy's #boobs fly next to that gigantic #Kielbasa!

Um, no. Just flat-out no. Life was just too short for this.

I quit Wieners on Sticks immediately and spent my first

night jobless—yet again—with my new, favorite time travel TV show, my glass of three buck Chuck cabernet and the best dog ever—Tulip. She napped with her head on my lap. Her paws twitched while tiny yelps escaped her mouth.

I scratched her ears and realized I was less alone than before I impersonated Lady Elizabeth Billingsley and fell in love with Nick. Before he broke my heart and before I embarrassed an entire country. I stroked Tulip's head and her back. Maybe I really had gained something beyond craziness and more important than simply money from that part-time job?

But day after relentless day I continued to yearn for Nick. Why? *Get a grip Lucy: you can never ever be with Nick. He's a prince for God's sake.*

In an odd twist of events, in November, I found myself full circle, back at MadDog, working with Alida and Buddy Paulsen. The only way this happened was that a nameless investor had bought out Mark Whitford's share. Whitford left, taking his pinkie ring and privileged party boys with him.

The new investors shut down the place for a week to remodel. And it wasn't just a deep clean and a coat of paint on the walls. There were some major renovations since I was last here: a small wooden dance floor was built in the middle of the bar. An 'old-fashioned' looking jukebox was tucked on a diagonal in a corner nearby. Harley Davidson paraphernalia still hung on the walls but was broken up with lithographs of hot guys and pretty girls riding motorcycles. I stared at one of the pictures. There were mountains in the distance and it made me think of Nick and our wild ride. Yes—*I mean yeah*—the art worked for me.

Once again, we wore our MadDog T-shirts, jeans and low-heeled biker boots as we cocktailed to a crowd of folks that were, for the most part, likeable—the majority of the customers, old and new, played nice in the sand box.

One night, the first week after Thanksgiving, snowflakes descended from the skies and fell outside the bar's windows as fall skidded into winter. The bar was packed—most likely because tonight was MadDog's first ever 'Ladies Night'.

"Two Jack and Cokes, two Stolis on the rocks, a fake lemonade for Artie and some stale pretzels, please, Lucy," Mr. Fitzpatrick asked.

"Are there any other kind?" I asked. "Coming right up." I stacked the empty glasses on my tray and hoisted it to my shoulder.

"I don't know," Artie said. "Things are looking a little fancier around here since the remodel. Look at that jukebox. The music's changed up a bit since the new owners took over. I wanted to hear "Born to be Wild" and emptied my pockets looking for quarters. But when I walked up to that machine, dang if it accepted my debit card as well as my coins. Maybe the new management will serve organic pretzels. Or even—gluten-free."

"And maybe we'll all get a pony for Christmas. It's a bar, Artie. We serve drinks, not Happily-Ever-Afters. Or pixie dust. Dreams don't come true. It *won't* happen for you. Accept that and you'll enjoy your pretzels the old fashioned way—stale." I strode away from their table.

"It'll be Christmas before you know it, George Bailey—I mean—Lucy Trabbicio." Mr. Fitzpatrick said.

"What do you want for Christmas, Lucy?"

"My two front teeth," I said. "Because I no longer believe in *It's a Wonderful Life* or *Zuzu's petals.*"

"Aw, come on! You gotta ask for more than that," Artie said.

"Fine. I'll hold out hope for you on the organic pretzel thing." I smiled at them, then turned and schlepped my tray to the long, mahogany bar.

I unloaded the empty glasses onto the rubber mat. "I need two Jack and Cokes, two Stolis on the rocks and one fake lemonade. Hey Buddy—how did you find the bucks to buy out Mark Whitford and lose his crowd of dickwipes?"

"Yes on the drinks, but hell no on the buy-out, Luce." He mixed and poured cocktails from behind the bar. "I didn't have the cash. Some swanky corporation did the deed."

I looked up at the banner of the dance floor emblazoned with the words, "Ladies' Night Out every Thursday at MadDog. Because—Hell yeah!"

I smiled. "I'm liking the job the new majority share investors did updating the joint. A dance floor? A jukebox with better tunes? Score! And Ladies' Night? What does that include?"

"Two for one specials on drinks for the ladies from five to seven p.m. A little entertainment. Some swag. Festivities."

"Festivities?" Alida hustled up to the bar and unloaded her tray of dirty glasses. "A pitcher of margaritas, that new champagne that's on the menu and a pitcher of pineapple daiquiris. Real pineapple is requested. Not that fruity make-believe crap. Do we even have real pineapple? Like what kind of festivities?"

Buddy shrugged. "Up to the new majority share owners. I don't know the details. They informed me a couple of hours ahead of time. Said it was on the itinerary and it's all just supposed to just magically unfold. Tonight's the first night. Let's see how magical it is." He loaded up my tray with drinks.

"Have you actually met the new owners?" I lifted the tray and hoisted it onto my shoulder.

"Nope. The attorneys walked me through the paperwork. Step by excruciating freaking step. Which reminds me." He stepped out from behind the bar, walked to the jukebox and slid a credit card through the slot.

"Buddy!" Alida squealed. "You have a lower body!"

"Yes, smartass," he said. "Want to do something with it?" He punched a few keys in the music box's keypad. "I was instructed by MadDog's new co-owners to play this song at," he looked at the huge clock on the wall that hung over the front door, "now."

He stepped onto the dance floor and waved his arms in the air. "Quiet! Quiet please!"

The crowd hushed.

"As you know, we here at MadDog have loved our customers like crazy for nearly the past four decades. But we've been through some changes in the past year. And change isn't always easy. So—thanks for sticking with us. We're under new management—again. I'm proud to announce that tonight is our first Ladies' Night. So if you have any requests, make them known. All liquor is two for one for the ladies! And that includes the good stuff. Thank you. My name is Buddy Paulsen. Co-owner of Mad-dog."

He bowed.

"Get off the fucking stage, Buddy," Mr. Fitzpatrick yelled. "Attention hog."

"It's not a stage, Easy Rider, it's a dance floor," Buddy said as he made his way back behind the bar.

"Ladies' Night" by Kool & the Gang blasted from the bar's speakers. A few people actually got up from their tables and danced.

"Seriously?" I asked.

"It's a popular song from the 70s." Buddy shrugged and poured beers. "You of all people like that music."

My gaze was drawn to a four-top table of folks in the far corner of the bar. They wore matching pink ball caps, dark sunglasses and black leather bomber jackets. They hunched over their drinks as they talked amongst themselves. There was a bottle of champagne resting in a stand-alone cooler next to the table.

"Psst! Alida!" I said.

"What?"

"That's your table, right?" I nodded at the four-top.

"Yeah," she said.

"Something's slightly off with them. Who wears sunglasses at nighttime in a bar? And the matching hats. From the looks of them I'd say they're in a sorority—which means they're probably underage and we could totally get in trouble and be shut down. And not to be selfish, but I really don't want to be looking for another job again any time soon." I squinted. "Except, from here, one of them looks like an older man. Or a very challenged-in-the-looks-department older woman."

"Yeah, one of them is definitely an older guy." She

loaded up her tray filled with glasses, pitchers and a sweaty bottle of champagne.

I stared at the bottle of bubbly and my eyes widened. "That champagne's not on our menu. *That's...*"

"2004 Perrier-Jouet Belle Epoque Rose Cuvee," Alida said. "And surprisingly, yes, it's now on our menu. How fucking weird is that? So far I'm liking MadDog's new owners." She hustled in their direction.

"Wait!" I exclaimed as I broke out into a sweat. "Can we switch? Like, seriously, I have a reason for asking. I'll take their drinks and you take mine to my guys in the corner."

Alida shook her head. "Sorry, mi amiga. I'm under strict orders to be their only cocktail waitress tonight. That might sound weird, but they offered me a huge tip. I need to pay for Mateo's Christmas presents. You cool with that?"

"Yes. Yes. Go!"

There's no way it could be. It simply wasn't possible. Note to Lucy: get real!

I meandered back to my guys' table and unloaded their drinks and a big basket of pretzels. "Sorry, Artie. I fear the pretzels are still stale."

When all the lights went out in the entire bar, only to be replaced with twinkly lights from hundreds of strands of Italian light bulbs that lit up the room like it was a Christmas parade.

I heard Alida burst out laughing from the other side of the bar. The jukebox launched into "Single Ladies (Put a Ring on It)" by Beyoncé and the next thing I knew the pink hat gang was on the floor dancing.

I saw a few bump and grind dance moves that

reminded me of my Bachelorette Party at Club Centralaski. The tall older dude wearing the pink hat kept his head down and made his way gingerly to the mic.

I wobbled for a second as my free hand flew to my chest. "Oh holy crap!"

Mr. Fitzpatrick pulled out an empty chair from the table. "You need to sit down for a second, Lucy. You look like you just saw a ghost."

"Thanks, but no. I'm fine, really. I'm just fine." I stayed standing.

"On behalf of the new co-owners of MadDog," the man said into the mic, "we'd like to welcome you to the first Ladies' Night. We'd like to dedicate this event to one of our favorite ladies—Lucy Marie Trabbicio." Mr. Philip Philips looked up, smiled and pointed to me. "That's her, right there."

"Ack!" I screamed as Cheryl Cavitt Carlson and Joan Brady made their way across the bar, grabbed my arms and escorted me to the dance floor. "What the hell are you doing here?" I asked. "How did you find me?"

"We bought the place," Cheryl said.

"We have our ways," Joan said. "Jeez, Lucy—I'm a barrister. I have a million connections."

Two more pink hats pulled something bulky into the middle of the dance floor and whipped off a cover —it was a petite, gilded throne with a pink, velvet seat.

"Sit down, Lucy," Duchess Carolina von Sauerhausen said.

"But, but…" I said. "I'm working."

"Your shift's over for the evening." Esmeralda pushed me back onto the chair. "We have a different part-time job for you tonight." She looked around. "Who has the scepter? Did we forget the scepter?"

"It's in my satchel under the table," Mr. Philips said.

"Ew, Philips, you carry a man purse," Esmeralda said.

"I'm European!" He said.

Cheryl strolled to their table, leaned down and rifled through it. "Got it." She held the small, golden scepter in the air and walked back.

The crowd was hushed except for Alida who shoved her hands over her mouth, but couldn't stop giggling.

"Go ahead, Mr. Philips," Esmeralda said.

He pulled a piece of paper from his pocket, unfolded it, held it up in the air and read it into the mic, "We, the citizens of Fredonia—"

"There are five of you here," I said. "That does not constitute an entire country."

"Shut up, Lucy," Esmeralda said.

"We organized a Changes.org petition. We received over one million signatures from Fredonia citizens," Joan said.

Mr. Philips harrumphed. "We the citizens of Fredonia on this date do solemnly declare that Lucy Marie Trabbicio of the hamlet of Chicago in the country of the United States forthwith be called Lady Lucy Marie Trabbicio, aka, Lady with a Royal Fredonia Heart."

Esmeralda, Cheryl, Joan, Carolina joined hands on the scepter and—

"Hang on!" Joan said and let go of it. She grabbed a tiara that dangled from the arm of the throne and placed it gently on my head. "Perfect," she said. "Okay, now." She placed her hand back on the other hands. "On three. Two.

One." They anointed me.

And I burst into tears.

The entire MadDog crowd leapt to their feet as they applauded and stamped their feet. There were even a few wolf whistles. All my ladies, including Alida, hugged me. Someone handed me a glass of champagne.

"Oh my God!" I said. "I can't believe you did all this for me."

Someone changed the music to my favorite song, "Wild Thing" by the Troggs.

"You even remembered my favorite song!" I wiped a few tears away.

"That's not all we remembered, honey," Esmeralda said.

The door to MadDog opened with a bang. And perhaps I was hallucinating, or perhaps I was drunk on adrenaline, or perhaps the gods smiled upon me and saw fit to shower me with pixie dust—because I saw Prince Nicholas of Fredonia walking toward me.

His hair was still black, his eyes still blue. He wore jeans, scuffed boots, a black leather biker jacket and a big, fat smile on his gorgeous face.

"Oh my God!" I said. "Oh my God!" I nearly dropped my champagne glass, shoved it at Cheryl and white-knuckled the throne's arms.

"I missed you, Lucy," he said and unzipped his jacket. "My turn to ask a question. Why didn't you tell me?"

"I missed you too, Nick. I tried to tell you. My turn to ask a question. What are you doing here?"

He pulled a black velvet box from his coat jacket, and got down on one knee. "Because I'm here to ask you a very big question, Lucy. Is it my turn, yet?"

I fanned my face. "Yes," I squeaked.

He smiled, popped open the lid on the box and revealed the most gorgeous engagement ring I'd ever seen in my life. "I love you. Will you marry me, Lucy Marie Trabbicio?"

"Yes!" I said.

He slid the ring onto my finger. He placed his hands on either side of my face and kissed me long and slow and sweet. Then whispered into my ear, "It's always been you, Lucy. *It always will be you.*"

More champagne bottles were popped open. Toasts were made. And this time I got engaged to the right prince.

And I learned that maybe, if you hold out hope despite disappointments, if you open your eyes to the magic around you, maybe Happily-Ever-Afters can really happen. Maybe fairy tales do come true.

THE END

ACKNOWLEDGMENTS

Thanks to Regina Wamba at Mae I Design for rocking this book cover! Thanks Chase Heiland for editing and Michael Canales for all your help with graphics and my website, etc.

Thanks to my Audible narrator partner on *Part-time Princess* – Lesley Ann Fogle – you rock! A shout out to my other narrator partners: Aurora de Blas, Kelly Self and Elizabeth Semida.

Thanks to my readers and supporters Allie Sinclair, Amy Moore, An'gel Molpus, Bob Bernstein, Carole Sauer, Carrie Hartney, D.C. Cheree Plank, Cheryl Cavitt Carlson, Cheryl Moore, Cheyenne Mason, Colleen Hartney, D.C., Dave Thome, Debra Sanderson, Ed Schneider, J.M. Kelly, Jeanie Whitmire Jackson, Joan Brady, Joe Wilson, Kristin Warren, Laurie Kransky, Karen Rontowski, Melanie Abed, Melissa Black Ford, Monica Mason, Rita Kempley, Rosemary Boncella, Shelly Fredman, Terri Billingsley Dunn, Tonya Wrobleski for being such awesome cheerleaders. (And I know I'm forgetting folks and I apologize.) Thanks to Bethel and Downers Grove North alumni for actually remembering who I am and embracing the fact I turned out to be a nerdy writer.

Thanks Sassy Girls FB Book Club and the talented members of LARA - the L.A. Chapter of Romance Writers or America for all your support.

A shout out to my Entertainment Manager Jeffrey Thal at Ensemble Entertainment who encourages me while he shops my works for film and TV. You're awesome!

Thanks to my family. Thanks to writer and reader and blogger friends and my writer's group POV.

And a huge special thanks to all you readers who encourage me to write more stories. I appreciate all your help. You rock!

Xo,

Pamela DuMond

About the Author

Pamela DuMond is the writer who discovered Erin Brockovich's life story, thought it would make a great movie and pitched it to 'Hollywood'.

She's addicted to the TV shows *The Voice, Reign,* and *Outlander.* The movies *Love Actually* and *The Bourne* trilogy (with Matt Damon -- not that other actor guy,) make her cry every time she watches them. (Like -- a thousand.) She likes her cabernet hearty, her chocolate dark and she lives for a good giggle.

When she's not writing Pamela's also a chiropractor and cat wrangler. She loves reading, the beach, working out, movies, TV, animals, her family and friends. She lives in Venice, California with her fur-babies.

You can find her website and contact her at http://www.pameladumond.com .

On a side note—the author's great, great, great, great to the nth degree grandfather came to America from France in the year 1657. His name was Lord Jean Petreus Dumont. So feel free to call her Lady DuMond if you wish. Carry on.

By Royal Decree:

There will be more Ladies-in-Waiting stories for you in the near future!

Thanks for reading!

Made in the USA
San Bernardino, CA
24 March 2017